Praise for Abdulrazak Gurnah's

DESERTION

"Affecting. . . . A meditation on African history, estrangement, and loss."
—*The New Yorker*

"A novel with the wonderfully intriguing promise, from the very beginning, of being not only a roving command of time and place but of charged sensibilities. A promise more than fulfilled. . . . The emotional range of relationships that come about between colonisers and the people of the mapped countries has never been better evoked than in this work."
—Nadine Gordimer, author of *The Conservationist*

"A lyrical, intensely felt work. . . . Gurnah writes beautifully and perceptively, adopting different tones for each of his characters, and lacing their stories with bits of wit and humor."
—*The Nation*

"Searing. . . . Will make you miss a meal or two until you get to its dramatic conclusion."
—*Essence*

"As beautifully written and pleasurable as anything I've read. . . . Gurnah's portrait of the society's complexities is the work of a maestro." —Mike Phillips, *The Guardian* (London)

"Lyrical. . . . Watching a talented writer such as Gurnah lead us through such intense, rich conflicts is powerfully moving."
—*Richmond Times-Dispatch*

Micropolitics of daily life

Abdulrazak Gurnah

DESERTION

Abdulrazak Gurnah was born in Zanzibar in 1948 and teaches at the University of Kent. He is the author of six novels, including *Paradise*, which was shortlisted for the Booker Prize and the Whitbread Award, and *By the Sea*, a *Los Angeles Times* Book Prize finalist.

BY THE SAME AUTHOR

Memory of Departure
Pilgrims Way
Dottie
Paradise
Admiring Silence
By the Sea

DESERTION

DESERTION

Abdulrazak Gurnah

Anchor Books
A Division of Random House, Inc.
New York

FIRST ANCHOR BOOKS EDITION, JULY 2006

Copyright © 2005 by Abdulrazak Gurnah

A Cataloging-in-Publication record has been established for the
Pantheon edition of *Desertion* by the Library of Congress.

Anchor ISBN-10: 1-4000-9540-9
Anchor ISBN-13: 978-1-4000-9540-7

www.anchorbooks.com

Printed in the United States of America
10 9 8 7 6 5 4 3 2 1

PART I

1 Hassanali

THERE WAS A STORY of his first sighting. In fact, there was more than one, but elements of the stories merged into one with time and telling. In all of them he appeared at dawn, like a figure out of myth. In one story, he was an upright shadow moving so slowly that in that peculiar underwater light his approach was almost imperceptible, inching forward like destiny. In another, he was not moving at all, not a tremor or a quiver, just looming there on the edge of the town, grey eyes glittering, waiting for someone to appear, for someone whose unavoidable luck it was to find him. Then, when someone did, he slid forward towards him, to fulfil outcomes no one had predicted. Someone else claimed to have heard him before he was seen, to have heard his beseeching, longing howl in the darkest hour of the night, like that of an animal out of legend. What was undisputed – although there was no real dispute between these stories as they all added to the strangeness of his appearance – was that it was Hassanali the shopseller who found him, or was found by him.

There is luck in all things, as there was in this first arrival, but luck is not the same as chance, and even the most unexpected events fulfil a design. That is, there were consequences in the future that made it seem less than accidental that it was Hassanali who found the man. At that time, Hassanali was *always* the first person about in the morning in this locality. He was up before dawn to open the doors and the windows of the mosque.

Then he stood on the steps to call the people to prayer, pitching his voice to all corners of the clearing in front of him. Salla, salla. Sometimes the breeze carried similar calls from nearby mosques, other cryers chiding the people to wake. As-salatu khayra minan-nawm. Prayer is better than sleep. Hassanali probably imagined the sinners turning over irritably at being disturbed, and probably felt indignant and self-righteous satisfaction. When he finished calling, he swept the dust and the grit from the mosque steps with a feathery casuarina broom whose silent efficiency gave him deep pleasure.

This task of opening the mosque, cleaning the steps, making the call to prayer, was one he had appointed himself to for his own reasons. Someone had to do it, someone had to get up first, open the mosque and make the adhan for the dawn prayers, and someone always did, for his own reasons. When that person was ill or grew tired of the charge, there was always another person to take over. The man who preceded him was called Sharif Mdogo, and had come down with fever so badly in the kaskazi two years ago that he was still bedridden. It was a little surprising that Hassanali had volunteered himself to take over as the dawn cryer, though, not least to Hassanali himself. He was not zealous about the mosque, and it required zeal to rise at every dawn and bully people out of sleep. Sharif Mdogo was like that, the kind of man who liked to barge into complacency and give it a good shake. In addition, Hassanali was a worrying man by nature, or perhaps experience had made him that way, had made him anxious and cautious. These semi-nocturnal chores tortured his nerves and disturbed his nights, and he feared the darkness and the shadows and the scuttlings of the deserted lanes. But then these were also the reasons he offered himself for the task, as a submission and a penance. He started doing the duty two years before the dawn of this sighting, when his wife Malika first arrived. It was a plea that his marriage should prosper, and a prayer for his sister's grief to end.

The mosque was only a short stroll across the clearing from his shop, but when he started making the dawn call to prayer,

4

he felt obliged to do as his predecessor Sharif Mdogo had done. He entered nearby lanes, more or less shouting into bedroom windows as he walked past, bellowing at the sleepers. He worked out a route which avoided the chasms and caves where the worst of the shadowy mischief lurked, but he was still prone to seeing spectral visions hurrying away into the darkest parts of the streets as he approached, fleeing the prayers and holy words he uttered as he exhorted the slumbering faithful. These visions were so real – a monster claw glimpsed at the turning of a lane, discontented spirits softly panting somewhere behind him, images of gross underground creatures which glowed and faded before he caught proper sight of them – that often he performed his tasks in a sweat despite the dawn chill. One morning, during another anxious, sweat-drenched round, when the dark lanes pressed in on him like the walls of a narrowing tunnel, he felt a rush of air on his arm as the shadow of a dark wing caught the corner of his eye. He ran, and after that decided to end the torment. He retreated to the mosque steps to make his call, a short walk across the clearing. He added the chore of sweeping the steps to make amends, even though the imam told him that calling from the steps was all that was required, and that Sharif Mdogo had been zealous in his duties.

Hassanali was crossing the clearing on this dawn when he saw a shadow across the open ground begin to move towards him. He blinked and swallowed in terror, nothing unpredictable. The world was teeming with the dead, and this grey time was their lair. His voice croaked, his holy words dried up, his body left him. The shadow approached him slowly, and in the fast-approaching dawn, Hassanali thought he could see its eyes glittering with a hard, stony light. This was a moment he had already lived in his imagination, and he knew that as soon as he turned his back, the ghoul would devour him. If he had been in the mosque he would have felt safe, because that is a sanctuary which no evil can enter, but he was still a long way from there and he had not yet opened the doors. In the end, overcome with panic, he shut his eyes, babbled repeated pleas for God's forgiveness, and allowed his knees to give way under him. He submitted himself to what was to come.

When he opened his eyes again, slowly, peering out as if he was lifting a sheet under which he had been hiding from a nightmare, it was to see the shadow slumped on the ground a few feet from him, half on its side and with one knee bent. Now in the brightening light he could see that it was not a spectre or a shadow or a ghoul, but an ashen-complexioned man whose grey eyes were open in exhaustion only feet away from his. 'Subhanallah, who are you? Are you human or spirit?' Hassanali asked, to be on the safe side. The man sighed and groaned all at once, and so announced himself as human without a doubt.

That was how he was when he arrived, exhausted, lost, his body worn out and his face and arms covered with cuts and bites. Hassanali, on his knees in the dust, felt for the man's breath, and when he felt it warm and strong on his palm, he smiled to himself as if he had managed something clever. The man's eyes were open, but when Hassanali waved his hand in front of them, they did not blink. Hassanali would have preferred that they did. He rose carefully, incredulous about the drama he was now part of, then stood for a moment above the bundle groaning at his feet before hurrying to call for help. By this time it was dawn. The exact moment of greatest felicity for the dawn prayer was swiftly passing – it was only very brief – and Hassanali had not performed the duties expected of him. He feared that the regular early morning worshippers would be annoyed with him when they woke up later and discovered that they had drowsed through the morning's blessing. Most of these worshippers were elderly men who needed to keep their accounts healthy and up-to-date in case of a sudden summons. But he should have remembered that they also no longer slept that well, fretted the whole night long and could not wait for the dawn and the call to prayer to release them. So even as Hassanali set off to seek help, worrying about having failed in his duty as the muadhin, some were stepping out of their houses to find out why there had not been a call that morning. Perhaps some even worried if

Hassanali was well, or if something had passed him by in the night. There were witnesses, then, to the man's first appearance, people who gathered round his wide-eyed body and saw it slumped like a shadow in the open ground in front of the mosque.

Hassanali returned with two young men he had found huddled half-asleep against the café doors. They worked there and were waiting for it to open, clinging to the last moments of rest before the day's antics began, but they rushed to help when Hassanali shook them awake. Everyone liked to help in the old days. When they arrived at the scene, urgent behind Hassanali's increasingly self-important strides, it was to find three elderly men standing a few paces from the body, watching it with fastidious interest: Hamza, Ali Kipara and Jumaane. These were the stalwarts of the dawn prayers, who stood directly behind the imam in the congregation, and who were the coffee-seller's first customers every morning. They were men well past their best years, wise men who expected their lives' endeavours to be considered unblemished, and who kept their eyes open and on the world that passed them by. They did not usually stir for anybody but themselves, and thought their age allowed them to act in this way. So they were not really three elderly men because everyone knew who they were, but by the measure of their time and place they were old, and their infirmities were part of their dignity, and their unbending display was perhaps an attempt at fulfilling what was required of them. For whatever reason, they now stood there, feigning indifference and making casual remarks while the young men and Hassanali rushed about. Hassanali opened the mosque and the young men fetched the rope bed, the one used for washing the dead. Hassanali winced but did not say anything. The young men lifted the moaning body on to the rope bed and prepared to carry it away.

All of a sudden, there was a brief tussle between Hassanali and Hamza about where the sick man should be taken. Hamza was an imposing man despite his age, with a lined, gnarled, grey-stubbled face and glaring eyes. He had been a rich simsim merchant in years gone by, but was now simply rich. His sons made money for him in a butchery business in Mombasa. He was sensitive about the awe due to him, and liked to be deferred to on any matter of the slightest importance. He liked to be treated as the informal jamadar thereabouts. In their prime, Ali Kipara had been a basket-weaver and Jumaane had been a house-painter, so both knew their place with the jamadar and occupied it when called upon to do so. Hamza began to walk away, tetchy and impatient, calling on the helpers to follow him. It was obvious that the moral duty to the exhausted man lay with Hassanali who had found him, and who therefore was obliged to offer care and hospitality to him. Hamza knew this as well as anyone else, but perhaps Hamza did what he did to remind everyone that he was a wealthy man to whom such acts of mercy were an obligation.

In any case, everyone politely ignored Hamza, even his fellow sages, and the man was duly carried on the rope bed to Hassanali's shop. The door to the adjoining yard, which was also the entrance into the house, was too narrow for the bed with the body on it, so the two young men lifted the body and carried it into the yard, then placed it on a mat under the thatched awning attached to the house.

The three elderly worshippers squeezed into the yard as well, casting swift glances around. There was not very much to see but none of them had been inside Hassanali's yard before and could not suspend curiosity even at this dramatic time. It was a large yard, running the full length of the house. There were plants in pots, two curtained windows facing out of the house, one either side of the inner door, a paved platform for washing clothes, a cluster of seredani for cooking and at one end of the yard the washroom and the room for necessities – an ordinary yard. They might have noted the recently whitewashed walls and the lushness of the pot-plants, among them a red rose, a lavender in bloom and a bristling aloe.

The crowd of six stood unspeaking around the body for a minute, as if surprised about the way everything had turned out. Then, after a moment, there were several opinions about what should be done next, spoken one after another, like pledges to an obligation. We should call Mamake Zaituni the healer. And someone should fetch the Legbreaker. I believe someone should go and tell the imam at once, in case he needs to say special prayers against contagion or worse. That was Hamza, as always going for the grand gesture. Hassanali nodded unprotestingly to the suggestions and ushered the small crowd out. They went reluctantly but they had no choice. It was only the drama of the groaning man that permitted their presence in the privacy of his home in the first place, so Hassanali only had to spread his arms and wave them gently for everyone to turn towards the yard door.

'Thank you, thank you all. Will you please ask Mamake Zaituni to come?' he asked, putting himself even further in his neighbours' debt.

'Without a doubt,' Hamza the merchant said in his self-important voice, waving his stick at one of the young men. 'Go, go, you, there is someone's life here.'

There were parting suggestions. Don't touch him until Mamake Zaituni comes. I won't touch him. Don't move him until the Legbreaker arrives. I won't move him. If you need any help . . . I'll call. Hassanali shut the yard door without bolting it – he did not want to seem too inhospitable – and returned to the traveller on the mat under the awning. He was suddenly wary, anxious about being alone with the man, as if he had allowed himself too near a wild beast. Who could he be? What kind of man went wandering alone in the wilderness? He remembered now he had said that to the man as he lay on the ground: *Who are you?* The noise of their arrival was sure to have woken up his wife and his sister, who were probably already standing behind the window curtains, waiting to come out and see what was going on. All of a sudden he was afraid that he had done something stupid in bringing the sick stranger home. The thought set off a shiver of anxiety across his sternum.

He looked on the man with a marvelling smile. What was a stranger, wounded in the wilderness, doing on the mat in their yard? It might as well have been a flying horse or a talking dove. Such things did not happen to them. He remembered his terror when he had first seen his shadow and taken it for a hideous ghoul. Many things frightened him, a grown man. Sometimes his life loomed so large on him that he saw shadows everywhere. It could have been an ugly malicious anything at that uncertain time between light and dark, between the real and the undead world, but perhaps he should not have thrown himself on the ground in the way that he did. If it had been a spectre it would have smiled before pulverising his soul. Hassanali's smile was as much for his soft-fleshed timid self as it was for the man at his feet. For this was no spectre, and no more ugly than the next person. His face was drained and covered with straggly, untrimmed, greying hair. His eyes were still open, bleary and unseeing, although even as he looked he thought he saw them blink. His breathing was shallow, softly panting, and behind it was a hardly audible groan. His arms were scratched and pierced by thorns. The calico smock he wore over trousers and sandals was grey with dust and use. It was torn and mended, streaked and stained, acquired in his wanderings perhaps rather than brought from wherever he started out from. No one would start a journey with such rags. The sandals were tied with strips of cloth, and around his middle, worn like a belt, were the remains of a brown shirt. Another strip of the same material made a headband across his brow. Hassanali smiled at the melodrama of his costume, exactly like that of an adventurer lost in a desert, or like a fighter. The thought made his stomach lighten. Had he brought a bandit to their house, a marauder who would kill them all? But no, the man was half-dead, perhaps himself a victim of bandits.

'Who is it?' his sister Rehana asked behind him.

'He's wounded,' he said, looking round. He realised he was still smiling, a little excited.

She was standing by the door, her left arm holding the curtain aside. She had only just woken up, he could see that from the dazed and heavy look in her eyes, from the roughness in her voice. She took three steps forward and looked at the man searchingly. His eyes were open, glowing like grey pebbles in brine. Gloaming. Then he saw them unmistakably blink. His broken lips were open in the middle of a groan. Rehana retreated quickly and Hassanali could only imagine what mad hope had filled her heart for that brief time.

'What have you brought us, our esteemed master?' she asked behind him, speaking in her mocking voice. Hassanali involuntarily winced. A day that started in that voice was often long and humiliating. He shut his eyes tightly for a second to prepare himself.

'He's wounded,' he said again, turning towards her.

Her mouth was turned down sourly, her chin clenched. He felt his body stiffening with distaste. He saw her chin lift fractionally, taking offence, and realised that his irritation must have shown. But he had also seen the hurt in her eyes despite her anger, so he released his face and allowed his expression to subside. Perhaps she was angry because she had been disturbed. She liked to sleep in the morning. But really, there was a man in a heap at her feet, perhaps dying, and all she could think of was her sleep. Just then, his wife Malika squeezed out from behind Rehana's right shoulder and made a gasp of sympathetic horror at the sight of the man, her hand flying to her open mouth. It brought the feeling of a smile on his face, her kindness.

'Wait, you!' Rehana said, stopping Malika as she was about to step forward. 'Don't rush over there. Who is this man? Where did you find him? What's wrong with him?'

'I don't know,' Hassanali said softly, in the placating voice he used with Rehana when she was irritated, and which sometimes irritated her more. He didn't know how else to speak to her when she was displeased, especially when he could not answer her questions. Even when he did have an answer for her, her scorn made him doubt and dissemble. His faltering now, at this moment, showed even to him that he had been credulous once again. 'He came from out there. He's wounded.'

'From out where? Which direction? Wounded by what? What is he sick with?' Rehana asked, with a look of scornful incredulity. Hassanali was familiar with the look, and wished he could tell her how ugly it made her face which otherwise was attractive and pleasing. But he had never learned a way to say such things to her without making everything worse. 'What have you brought us, you and your antics? A sick man turns up from who knows where, with who knows what disease, and you bring him straight to our house so we can all die of what he is dying of? You're a man of affairs, you are. You're a man of the world, without a doubt. Have you touched him?'

'No,' Hassanali said, surprised that he hadn't. He glanced at his wife Malika and she dropped her eyes. She looked so lovely, so uncomplicated, so young. He felt a kind of agony as he looked at her, something between jealous anxiety for her devotion and a longing to please her. 'The young men picked him up and carried him in here. But you're right, I did not think of disease. I thought he was hurt. We'd better not touch him until Mamake Zaituni has looked at him. I've sent for her. Malika, keep away from him like Rehana says.'

'Now you're full of wisdom,' Rehana said sarcastically, wearily. Then looking at the man lying there, and dropping her voice as if not wanting to be discourteous, she said in a voice approaching a whisper: 'You put him on the eating mat. What were you thinking of, bringing a sick stranger to us like that, without knowing what's wrong with him? He might die,' she said, dropping her voice even further, 'and his relatives will come to blame us.'

'You can't expect me to leave a suffering son of Adam out there when we can offer him kindness and care,' Hassanali protested.

'Oh I forget, you're a man of God,' Rehana said lightly, even smiling slightly. 'Next time take him to the mosque where God will look after him. I suppose we should be grateful you didn't bring us a stinking savage. Has someone gone to call Mamake Zaituni?'

For years Rehana had treated him as if he was foolish. It was not always so. It was once she grew to be a woman that she spoke to him as if he was sluggish in understanding, as if he was an incompetent in the world. He had thought it amusing at first, Rehana playing at being grown-up, in league with their mother who had turned tetchy with age and widowhood. In the meantime, he laboured day and night to preserve their honour and put food in their mouths. That was another thing he never dared to say, that he laboured as he did and for his thanks they berated him for incompetence in the face of the world. In time, Rehana hardened into her disdainful manner and Hassanali unavoidably became resigned to her scorn. He did not know what else to do. It was not only time that made her so scornful. No, it wasn't. It was Azad and Hassanali's part in that. Sometimes her voice swelled through his body and made his eyes water with helplessness.

'Yes, someone has gone for her,' he said. He glanced at Malika, and she gave him a quick look of recognition then looked away. 'Is there coffee?' he asked her, to speak to her and to get away from Rehana.

Malika nodded. 'I'll make some,' she said, and moved in an exaggerated careful arc around the moaning body towards the braziers.

In the slow moments in the shop, when he had tired of telling the rosary to pass the time, he could not resist ripples of anxiety that swelled up from nowhere to stifle his breath. They concerned unpredictable and often petty matters. At these times, a small thing handled for too long grew large and troublesome, and one of these things was a dread he had that Malika's recognition would one day also turn into disdain.

Rehana lowered herself on to a stool by the back door and leaned against the wall with a sigh, waiting for Mamake Zaituni. Hassanali turned slightly away from her, suppressing feelings of guilt. He was too quick to accept blame. He should harden himself against these unspoken accusations. He leaned against the awning post and looked at the grey bundle of a man he had brought home. He remembered his pleasure at having him there in his backyard and it made him smile to think of Hamza trying to steal him away. Hamza could not resist that kind of thing, always competing, always showing off. Would Hamza have tried to steal the stranger if he had been a stinking savage as Rehana said? He thought not. Hamza had a mouthful of notions about the savage, among whom he had travelled and traded in his younger years: how unpredictable his anger was, how reckless his greed, how uncontrollable his hungers. An animal. Would Hassanali himself have brought him home? That thought made him grin. Of course not, they were all terrified of the savage. Everyone told savage stories all the time. No one survived out there in the open country except the wild beast and the savage, both of whom feared nothing, and of course the fanatical Somali and Abyssinian Hubsh and their relatives, who had long ago lost their reason in endless feuds. He glanced at Rehana, and saw that she was watching him grinning to himself. She shook her head slowly at him, her eyes large and awake now.

'Masikini,' she said. 'Poor you.'

'I was thinking of Hamza,' he said. 'He wanted to take him to his house. That old man, he always wants to be first.'

'And you stopped him, didn't you?' she said, sarcastic awe in her voice.

At that moment there was a call over the yard wall. Mamake Zaituni had arrived. When Hassanali opened the door, he saw that the elderly magi were settled on the rope bed to await events, and that the two young men were hovering behind Mamake Zaituni as if to protect her from harm. The healer bustled past him, tiny and tireless, reciting prayers in a steady undertone, paying out her life's spool. Hassanali had not expected the crowd waiting outside. He waved them away, making his gesture ambiguous in case anyone took offence, and closed and bolted the door.

'Is all well in there?' That was Hamza, making himself heard over everybody as usual. Hassanali opened the door again and hushed them gently, but he was pleased to see that the three

14

elderly men were on their feet, and the two young men had good hold of the rope bed and were about to lead off. He waved goodbye and shut the door quickly.

'Hassanali, when are you going to open the shop?' Jumaane asked over the wall. They wanted him out there as soon as possible, so they could get a report on what was going on.

'I'm coming, my brothers,' he called back.

'We're going to pray,' Ali Kipara called out, perhaps to tempt Hassanali to join them.

Mamake Zaituni kissed hands with Rehana and Malika, although she did not allow either to kiss her hand really, and made sure to kiss theirs. It was a trick of the humble, to kiss the other's hand and slip yours away before the kiss could be returned. It was her way to show humility even to the humblest that she never allowed anyone to kiss her hand, and it was said by everyone that this was part of her saintliness and one of the reasons God had given her the gift of healing, as He had to her father before her. Muttering prayers to herself, she took her buibui off and folded it carefully, as if it was made of the finest silk and was fragrant with sandalwood incense rather than of the thinnest cotton which smelled of wood-smoke and grease. Her old cotton shawl was tucked tight around her face and then fell down to her wrists, so that only her hands and her sharp-etched face were visible. She slipped her sandals off and stepped on the mat, then walked round the man without touching him, scrawny and bent like an old bird of prey. She said a prayer, to ask for aid and protection against the unknown. Then she asked Rehana and Malika to go inside the house, to spare the unknown man shame, she said. She spoke sharply, irritably, as if they had looked to gain some improper pleasure by hanging around. She was always like that, brisk and definite, never at a loss about what is proper.

Rehana made an impatient sound but did not resist. The combination of humility and briskness made Mamake Zaituni impossible to refuse, and she was the one who always had the presence of mind to know what was best to do. She tore the smock with a thin blade without moving the man, tearing him open from collar to ankle. He was light-complexioned and a European. His body was thin and bony, and he looked brittle and strange in the brightening light. At first Hassanali had thought he was one of those fair-skinned Arabs from the north that he had heard about, with grey eyes and golden hair, but when they took his sandals and trousers off, they saw that he was uncircumcised. Mzungu, Mamake Zaituni said, speaking to herself. A European. He was bruised and torn but had no wounds on the front or sides of his body. His belly was so strangely pale and smooth that it looked cold and dead, and Mamake Zaituni's bony hands hovered over these parts hesitantly, and Hassanali thought it was with a mixture of fascination and dread, as if she would touch out of curiosity. Those were the same tireless hands that kneaded the dough for the bread that Mamake Zaituni made and sold everyday, the same hands that rolled it and tossed it on the griddle, then turned it and later picked it out without burning themselves. The same hands that massaged an inflamed kidney or dressed a bleeding calf or plunged themselves unhesitatingly into human agony. Now they hovered over the pale belly of the man.

They turned him over on his side. He groaned and opened his eyes, and Hassanali expected a bad smell to come off him, but he smelled of dry meat and dust, of rags left out in the sun for too long, of travel. He must have been lost for several days, to judge by his starved look and the smell of dust and sun on him. There were more bruises and tears on his back, and a deep green shadow around his right shoulder but no wounds, no blood. They eased him over on his back, then Mamake Zaituni covered him with the torn smock and called the women out. She felt his face, and he groaned again, opening his eyes blearily.

'Give him some honey in warm water,' she said, speaking sharply as was her manner. 'One part honey, three parts water in a coffee cup.' She glanced at Rehana and looked away, hardly making contact. Rehana returned her glance with a sneer. Not me, Hassanali imagined her thinking. 'Then let him sleep. There's nothing wrong with him. He's exhausted and thirsty, that's for certain. He has a bad bruise round his shoulder, so there might be a break or a dislocation. Let the Legbreaker see to that. I'm going to finish cooking my bread, there'll be people waiting for it. I'll bring him some soup afterwards.'

'He hasn't got a disease?' Rehana said enquiringly, disbelievingly.

'I don't see any signs,' Mamake Zaituni said. 'No fever, or rash, or bad smells or diarrhoea. It may be the sun has dried him out and made him dizzy. Limemkausha na kumtia kizunguzungu. I'll come back later after you've given him the honey, and after Legbreaker has seen him. I'm going back to my bread now.'

It seemed that the women had no need of Hassanali any more, rattling off instructions to each other while Mamake Zaituni prepared herself to leave. Hassanali left reluctantly, hoping that the man would speak, or would look at him or in his direction. It did not seem right to leave him to other people after finding him. But he could not speak, or at least he had not by the time Hassanali finally passed into the house to go and open the shop.

'Call me if you need any help,' he called out. 'And Malika, don't forget my coffee.'

'Yes, master,' Malika said, making a parody of obedience.

And that was how the Englishman Pearce arrived, causing a sensation and a drama that he never became fully aware of.

Hassanali was a small man. He thought of himself as small and a bit ridiculous in other people's eyes, round and overweight. When the banter started he always struggled against the flow of jibes and jokes, and kept quiet to stay out of trouble. He lived in this state of self-absorbed timidity, expecting mockery and inevitably suffering it. He could not disguise his anxiety and people who had known him all his life knew this about him, and made a joke out of it. They said it was something to do with his jinsi, his ancestry. Indian people are cowardly, they said, hopping about like nervous butterflies. His father was not timid. He had been a hothead in his youth, who sang and danced and raced the streets with anyone, and he was the Indian in his jinsi. It was God who made him like this, nothing to do with jinsi, and who was he to argue. Alhamdulillah. He kept his eyes open, on the lookout for trouble, and thought that that was the best he could do. Over the years he learned a kind of wisdom about the people he lived with, although this did not always keep him out of trouble. He took their mockery kindly, pretended there was no malice behind it, just high spirits and a rough friendliness. Over the years he also learned a mild superiority over his customers and neighbours, despite his diffident airs. He was a small man, without a doubt, but he was a small, cunning man. He was a shopseller, a vocation which inevitably required that he outwit his customers, make them pay more than they would like to pay, give them less than they would like to have. He had to do this too in small ways, nothing blatant or aggressive. When he heard of the ruses and deals the merchants made and the profits that came from them, he quivered with a panicky terror and envy at the risk of it. So they laughed at him and he made them pay, a little. He thought of it as an arrangement that came with the job.

Sometimes he thought they laughed at him because they could see the pleasure he felt in the tiny advantage he took of them. Sometimes he wished he was something else, a baker or a carpenter, something useful. But he wasn't, he was a shopseller, like so many others. His father was a shopseller, and his own son, when he had one, would be a shopseller. They were small people.

When he opened the shop that morning, there were three customers waiting. They flustered him, even though one of them was only a child and the other two were the young men who had carried the injured European to his house, and were now waiting for him to thank them. We've been waiting for you all this time, the young men said, and now we'll surely be late for work. Usually he was able to take his time opening the shop when he returned from the dawn prayers, when there was no one around. It was an elaborate business. The front of the shop was a series of thick planks, each two hands'-breadth wide, eighteen of them in all. He removed the first two planks and served the child from there. A ladleful of ghee and give my regards to the house. He gave the two young men ten anna each. They accepted the coins but did not move, standing in front of him with suppressed smiles. They were good young men, Salim and Babu. They too had come to his shop on errands for their mothers, like the boy he had sold a ladle of ghee to, and would probably be his customers for the rest of his life. He gave them another ten anna each, and then another before they went away, pleased at the way they had browbeaten him into generosity. It was because everyone thought him richer than he was, and so took his thrift for miserliness. It was a terrible thing to be thought a miser, to be a sinner against God's injunction that the prosperous should be generous to the needy. People were always paying their few annas and rupees to the shopseller, who sat on his backside all day and night over the mounds of goods they desired, so they assumed all he had to do was pile up the money. That was what was said about shopsellers, that they lived like paupers and hid their wealth in a hole in the backyard.

Hassanali took the remaining sixteen planks out one at a time, and made a pile of them against the outside of the shop. Then he pulled out the hinged flaps and rested them on the platform of planks, and then arranged the display of goods in their habitual places. Then he arranged himself amid the variety of containers for oil, for ghee, for spices, among straw baskets of lentils and beans and dates, and sacks of rice and sugar. It all took time. Eventually he was done, and his thoughts turned to the coffee Malika had promised him and perhaps a bun or a piece of bread. His thought turned to the man who was lying under the awning in his yard. He felt a pang of inadequacy. What kind of man would leave his home to wander in a wilderness thousands of miles away? Was that courage or a kind of craziness? What was there here that was superior to what he had left behind? Hassanali could not imagine the impulse that would make *him* wish to do such wanderings. Was he a fool to leave a strange man, without a voice or a name, in the house with his sister and his wife? If he became violent or attempted the unthinkable, Hassanali's negligence would be unforgivable. He stood at the doorway that led from the shop into the inside of the house and called for Malika. 'Hurry hurry, come here now.'

'I'm coming, I'm bringing your coffee,' she called back, her voice muffled by the sacks and chests that lined the passageway into the house.

'Come now,' he called urgently, but he was already beginning to be reassured by the sound of her voice. She did not sound terrified, but he still wanted her to hurry, so he could tell her to take care, so he could warn her about the world. 'What's happening?' he asked when she came, bringing a pot of coffee and a millet bun wrapped in cloth. 'What's going on in there?'

'Well, it turns out that he is a demon who has taken the form of a man,' Malika said, standing in the doorway with her head uncovered and looking at Hassanali with terrified eyes. 'As soon as Rehana gave him one sip of honey and water, he turned into a rukh and is now perched on the roof, waiting for one of us to drop dead so he can steal our souls.'

'Stop playing the fool,' Hassanali said, although he quite liked for Malika to tease him. 'It can't be a rukh. I've told you before, a rukh has a name but no body, so it can't be perched on a roof.' What is more, the rukh is the indestructible spirit that leaves the body after death, not the stealer of souls. Their mzungu was a body without a name, and was conclusively not the rukh. She did not care, and wrongly repeated the things he told her just to tease him. She teased him a lot when they were on their own. One of their secret games was for Malika to scold him while he offered apologies and caresses. His life was transformed since her arrival.

'What do you think is happening then?' she asked. 'Mzungu is lying there, groaning and taking a sip when Rehana gives it to him, dribbling and burping like a baby. Legbreaker came a few minutes ago and is now looking him over. Don't make your-self anxious for nothing.'

'I'm not making myself anxious for nothing,' he said, frowning, tempted to remind her that he was nearly twice her age and she should show more respect. He did not want more respect, he just did not want her to hurry away yet. 'I wanted to know that you were all right. You were a long time with the coffee, and we don't know who that man is. I didn't know what was going on in there.'

'The man is lying there hardly living, my master.'

Hassanali nodded. 'What does Legbreaker say?' he asked.

'He hasn't said anything yet, and when he does he probably won't say it to us,' Malika said, and then added in a whisper: 'He's a frightening old man.'

'Take care now,' Hassanali said and waved her away. He could see a customer approaching. 'And tell Legbreaker to see me before he does anything.'

Legbreaker was the bonesetter, and he acquired the name and a frightening reputation because he frequently set the bone wrong after a fracture. Often he had to break the bone again afterwards and try to set it right. Sometimes more than one resetting was necessary, and to fall into the grip of Legbreaker's treatment could turn into a minor tragedy. Parents trembled when their child fell over, for fear that the services of Legbreaker would be required. There was no one else who had any idea how to set bones. He hoped the poor mzungu had no broken bones.

Hassanali liked the idea of the mzungu in his house. He had seen one before, two or or three years ago, when he had gone down to the water in town. When he was a child, he had gone down to the shore like everyone else, although there were no mzungus then. Now there was no one to look after the shop, and he bought his stock through long-standing arrangements with suppliers, so there was no need for him to chase around after anybody. Sometimes, at the death of a neighbour or someone notable, he shut the shop and joined the procession to the cemetery. And during Ramadhan, it was pointless keeping the shop open during the hours of the day when no one went out. Also, since Malika's arrival, he shut the shop for lunch and took a short rest in the afternoon. Aside from these occasions, or one or two others like that, the shop was open every day from after the dawn prayers until one hour after sunset, and Hassanali rarely left his post on the cash-box for any reason. He had even trained his body to be obedient to this inflexible regime.

The time he had gone down to the shore was the day of Idd, when it was customary to shut all businesses for at least part of the day, and he had gone to the bay along with everyone else to watch the annual boat race. There he had seen the mzungu, standing on the covered podium among the Arab nobility. He was heavy-looking and tall, in a green jacket and pale trousers, and one of the padded hats which he had heard about but never seen. He knew this was the man the sultan had sent over from Zanzibar to run the plantations, and who had unexpectedly freed the slaves and ruined the wealth of the landowners. That mzungu was so far-away when Hassanali saw him, merely a green jacket and a hat, more vivid as a figure in a story than someone real. This one was his guest, lying groaning there on the eating mat in his yard.

Guests were always exciting, especially for the first few days. Everything was happy confusion and everyone had a good time for a while. He loved it. But this guest was a different thing altogether. A European, mzungu. What were they going to do with a European? Where were they going to put him? He should have let Hamza have him. Hamza had empty rooms in his house, and the wealth and furnishings to make the mzungu comfortable. They only had two rooms and Hassanali would have to share his room with him. From what he had heard about them, the European was bound to ask to have the room to himself, or even the whole house. What were they going to feed him? How were they to speak to him? He was probably an Englishman, or a German or perhaps an Italian. Hassanali didn't know a word of these languages. Why should he? He was only a shopseller in a crumbling town on the edge of civilised life. Perhaps, he thought as he arranged the baskets and sacks in the shop, he should send word to Hamza to ask him to come and collect the Englishman or whoever he was. He was seized by this idea, his timid heart racing. He should send word straight away. Please come and take the Englishman, I have no room in my humble house for such a guest. But then what a joke people would make of it, how they would laugh at him. They would say that he was mean-hearted and a miser, that he had grudged offering hospitality to a wounded stranger when in truth he had treasure hidden away in his house, the usual rubbish. What tiny amount he had secreted away certainly did not amount to wealth.

Then, it was he who had seen the man appear out of the dawn darkness and had taken him to be a spectre stranded by the approaching light. It was he that the man's grey gloaming eyes had sought out and pursued. It was God's chance that made things happen as they did, and God did nothing by chance. This was a burden that had been chosen for him, perhaps to try him or punish him or test him, according to a wisdom which was not yet apparent to him. How could he even consider refusing the wounded man hospitality and succour? Having satisfied himself that it would be offensive to God for him to give up the European, Hassanali felt his body subsiding to the calm thrill he had felt before at the thought of the Englishman in his house. It was as if he had acquired an exotic pet that he had almost given away, but had talked sense to himself in good time.

The morning stream of customers was gently flowing when Legbreaker came out. He came through the passage from inside the house which was also the shop's store. Hassanali gave him a swift and suspicious glance, in case he had picked up something on his way through. It was an involuntary look, a habitual mistrust. They were always pilfering from him, everyone. Who told him he could come through that way?

'Yahya, how are you?' Hassanali said. No one called him Legbreaker to his face, unless he could run very fast or did not fear an accidental fracture. 'How is our guest?'

Legbreaker was a big elderly man, with a large belly bulging out of his kanzu. Stories of his youthful strength and his lust for sex were part of his legend, and even in old age he found it hard to resist strutting about like a champion warrior. The tight-fitting thick white cotton cap he wore hardened his appearance and made his head look like a cannon-ball. He glowered at everyone, and strode the streets with shoulders pushed back and belly thrust forward, swinging his arms like a soldier, hilariously unaware of how comic a figure he cut. People called him captain to please him. Yet those who laughed at him did so behind his back or at a distance from him, for he had a reputation as a crazy and dangerous man. He lived on his own in a rented downstairs room with a window which opened to the street, and many nights passers-by and neighbours heard him groaning with raucous anguish in his sleep, yet no one dared to wake him for fear of his rages.

He had been among the first Baluchi soldiers the sultan in Zanzibar had sent to guard the new plantations. The Al Busaid sultans had a fondness for Baluchi mercenaries, for some reason, and had used them from the beginning of their conquest of the coast. So when Sultan Majid decided to revive the land behind this far-off town in his dominion, he sent a Baluchi contingent with the thousands of slaves who were to work the plantations. It was there on the plantations that Legbreaker acquired a reputation as a bonesetter. Hassanali shuddered at the thought of the poor slaves who would have been his earliest patients.

Hassanali's customers, who by now knew the story of the European's arrival, waited for Legbreaker's diagnosis too. Hassanali could see the three magi Hamza, Ali Kipara and Jumaane, rise from the early morning coffee at the café across the clearing at the sight of Legbreaker in his shop. They too wanted to know if Legbreaker's frightening services would be required.

'Captain, is it true that the bones of Europeans heal themselves?' one of the customers asked Legbreaker, a skinny young man who carted produce around town for whoever paid him. He stopped every morning at the shop for a plug of chewing tobacco which Hassanali gave to him free, to win his goodwill for the odd errand he needed him for and because he felt sorry for him. He had no family and no home that Hassanali knew of. Everything about him was frantic and edgy, brittle grins, manic laughter, filthy loud-mouthed banter. Too much hashish, everyone said. None the less, smiles were poised on everyone's faces, knowing from the tone of the question that some bit of cheek was bound to follow, and that Legbreaker was bound to lose his temper and make a racket or worse.

'Don't talk such nonsense,' Legbreaker said mildly, therefore signalling that this was too important a moment for melodramatic rages. 'If anything the European has weak bones because of the cold and the wet in his country, and because he eats the raw fat of hogs. Everyone knows this.'

'Captain, so it should be easy to break and break again when you give him his treatment,' the young man said, jumping and grunting, miming Legbreaker's surgical procedures.

Legbreaker looked interested, and for a moment glared hard at the skinny young man. Then he turned slowly, reluctantly, to Hassanali who had just spoken to him.

'Any breaks?' Hassanali asked.

'No, no breaks,' Legbreaker said sadly, shaking his head at the gloomy news. 'Some bad bruising. I put a poultice on his shoulder and will come later to check. Perhaps you should send him to town to the Arabs. They'll look after him until a ship comes in. Or they'll take him to a doctor in Mombasa or somewhere.'

'Yes,' Hamza said, by now arrived in time to hear these last remarks. 'Send him to the big people in town. You don't want anything to happen to him while he's in your house.'

'That's the last thing you want,' Ali Kipara said, wagging his finger for emphasis.

'Let him rest first,' Hassanali said, not eager to part with his mzungu yet.

He measured out a quart of rice into a piece of cloth, tied it into a neat bundle and passed it to Legbreaker, who took his payment without a word and strode out of the shop. By the time the skinny young man realised what was happening, Legbreaker had him by the collar and was mercilessly twisting his ear. 'You have no manners, you filthy diseased whore, you son of a howling savage and grandson of a four-breasted beast,' he snarled, giving the young man's ear a further twist. 'You're a monkey, a baboon with no brains, a drivelling dog. What are you?' Legbreaker asked, giving the ear one final impossible twist. Then he marched off to howls of laughter and elderly cackles fit to choke, swinging his arms like a soldier on parade while the skinny young man clutched his wounded ear and shouted filthy abuse as he wept with rage and humiliation.

Hassanali dealt with his customers, and after the rush and the talk settled down, people dispersed to their work or to their homes for breakfast. He knew that the elderly sages would be back later in the morning to sit on the bench he put outside the shop for them, once the sun disappeared behind nearby houses. Then when it reappeared later in the day, they would stroll away to another bit of shade perhaps, or move back to the café, then to the mosque and then back to his shop late in the afternoon. In the cool of the afternoon and evening, the gossip would be milder, the stories longer and older. That was how things always were, from his father's days. The elderly themselves slowly changed, shuffling on and off as mutability decreed, but the bench was always there, and was never short of occupants.

In the quiet after the morning rush, he had time to think about their guest. When the man wakes up, and after he has had a rest, he would ask him if he wants to be taken to the Arabs or to the government mzungu. For now, let him rest. They had never had a guest as strange and unexpected as this one. Since his marriage two years ago, Malika's mother came every few months and always stayed too long. Their Aunt Mariam, their mother's elder sister, came every few months too, and sometimes overlapped with Malika's mother. They were old friends, and it was through this old friendship that Aunt Mariam negotiated Hassanali's marriage to Malika. All he had to do was finally to say yes to the marriage arrangement and in due course his lovely Malika appeared. It could have been worse, but it wasn't. It was a miracle.

When Aunt Mariam came, it was always with a cousin or a nephew or some such. Hassanali was convinced they pillaged his stock whenever they could. The nephews were the sons of Uncle Hamadi, who lived in Mombasa. Hassanali had only met this uncle a few times, once when he came to pay his respects some weeks after their father's funeral. They were all convinced at the time that Uncle Hamadi, who said that he had come to make sure that his sister was not left wanting in widowhood, was there to see if there were any easy pickings to be had. Another time was soon after their mother died. This time he said he had come to see that his nephew and niece were not in need. Hassanali could not mistake the way he glanced at Rehana who was about nineteen, and he feared that he was going to ask for her as his whatever-number wife. Aunt Mariam was staying then too, and perhaps her presence shamed him into silence. She was the eldest of the three and had a keen eye for the ridiculous, and would have laughed Uncle Hamadi out of the house if he had suggested marriage to Rehana. He could not really remember if there were other visits when he was younger, but they had not seen Uncle Hamadi since the time when he gave Rehana those frightening looks, all of a dozen years before.

Aunt Mariam was always welcome. Within minutes of arriving she was out of her finery and in her house clothes, distributing news and gossip, laughing laughing laughing, delivering her country gifts of vegetables and fruit. Not long after that, she would have found something to do, picking stones out of the rice, sweeping the yard, washing the bedlinen or something else as necessary. She had a gift like that. Her help was not intrusive or reproving, but companiable and unforced. When she was staying with them, all the tasks that had been put off for months somehow got done. When she was around, the talk and the laughter seemed unending, and visitors called from nearby who did not usually visit. She had no children of her own, and had been living alone for many years. She loved for her nephews and nieces to go and stay with her for a few weeks every year. Hassanali had a memory of her husband from those visits, a short, plump, friendly man who died suddenly from internal bleeding that no one knew the cause of. Aunt Mariam said Hassanali reminded her of him, and even while her husband was still alive, she threatened to give him up one day soon and marry Hassanali instead. When their own father was still alive, Aunt Mariam used to flirt with him and propose to him every few days, offering herself as his second wife. Their mother said she was shameless, but Aunt Mariam said men were allowed four wives and she wanted four handsome husbands. As soon as she tired of one she would change him for another, though in truth she remained a widow all her life after her husband died. Now she brought Uncle Hamadi's boys when they came to stay with her, or some more distant cousins who were children of a niece of hers whom Hassanali had never met. It seemed the niece divorced easily and had many children, which she distributed among her relatives for them to look after. Aunt Mariam said she wanted everybody in the family to know each other and none of them could be bothered except her. If Malika's mother always stayed too long, Aunt Mariam knew with uncanny courtesy exactly when to leave.

There wasn't a spare room in the house, so a guest meant anxious arrangements about sleeping and eating, and especially about the use of the washroom. The meals were more elaborate, the conversation livelier and full of laughter, at least at first, and Hassanali found the hectic plans and their revision exciting. When Malika's mother came, she shared Rehana's room and forced Rehana out into the yard for most of the day with her illnesses and her complaints. Some days she was sensitive to light, other days it was the heat. Some mornings she could not bear the early morning chill, and some nights she could not sleep because of the buzzing in her ears. When she was not suffering from any of these complicated and sometimes subtle complaints, she made good conversation and had surprisingly detailed recollections and stories. Sometimes Hassanali sat nearby in the yard, eavesdropping on the conversation of the women as they sat or stretched out on a mat in the dark, curbing the urge to interrupt and ask for more details. They knew he was there, and hushed each other when they came to parts that were too sensitive for his male ears. He didn't mind because he could hear their smiles in the dark.

It was even more complicated when Aunt Mariam came with the nephews. Sometimes Hassanali did not know where he was sleeping until moments before his head hit the pillow. He did not know how he would begin to explain all this to their mzungu guest. It would be easiest if they just gave up their room to him. Malika could move in with Rehana and he would sleep in the hallway. Then when the mzungu had regained his senses, they could ask him what he wished them to do.

2 Frederick

FREDERICK TURNER WAS ON his way to the estate when he first heard the news. He went to the estate every Tuesday morning, events allowing. Events were letters and reports and reading, a lot of it tedious and peaceful and all of it amenable to postponement, so really, since his posting in the town he had not missed a ride to the estate. He rode there in the morning, stayed the afternoon and evening and rode back early the following morning. It kept him informed, took him out and about so he could see things for himself, and kept the estate manager Burton on his toes, not that he came directly under his authority. It was Burton himself who had called on him in his first week in the town, when he came in to check for mail, and invited him to visit whenever he wanted. They were the only Englishmen there, so in a sense there was some obligation in addition to the pleasure of the ride. Burton was an amiable and conscientious enough fellow, medium height, big round face red from the sun, heavy build and a lumbering manner. He had the very look of a sunburned English farmer. He was very knowledgeable and inventive in his field, a bit of a scientist even with all his experimental projects, his ponds and sluices and nurseries, but he had a reluctant, burdened air about him, and a beachcomber disposition which made Frederick suspect that he would make problems for himself if left alone too long. There was that odd stare that he had at times, as if he was contemplating lunacy. Frederick thought Burton looked forward to his visits, for the company and the conversation, and a chance to indulge in some sociable drinking. Not only was he the only other Englishman in the district, he was the only other company, the rest being Bohra Gujarati and Arabs, and of course the mongrel natives. It would have been absurd not to socialise with him.

His talk was all about the Uganda Protectorate and the interior highlands and the lakes, and all the great estates that were going to be created up there when the railway was finished. According to Burton, that was the whole point of the Protectorate. Politicians and newspapers loved the grand language of global manoeuvres, so to them and the other armchair rulers of the world, the Uganda Protectorate and the railway were to secure the headwaters of the Nile against French mischief. To Burton, and according to him, many other hard-headed people like him, it was to open up the beautiful high country in the highlands, always intended for European occupation, and currently squatted on by stone-age vagrants and blood-thirsty pastoralists. Burton talked in that hard language when he wanted to show that he was unsentimental about the world, usually after a drink or two. Frederick had not been up to the highlands yet, although he thought he would go and have a look one day, just to have a look. That was the work Burton wanted to do, to manage a great sprawling estate, like the ones he had seen in the Eastern Cape in South Africa. Frederick had his doubts if Burton was made of that kind of material. That sort of authority and command, not to say cold-blooded determination, was not acquired in one or two generations, except by the immensely gifted, and Burton already spent enough time joining the labourers in their drumming and dancing sessions to indicate that he was not that manner of exceptional.

It was also a good ride to the estate. He went riding most afternoons, north along the beach which was clear for miles to the river, or south around the bay to the point, but the ride to the estate went over some rough ground and kept him in trim. It gave his stallion Majnoon a bit of work to do as well, and he needed it, the fractious devil. His groom Idris rode with him on the mare Sharifa, so both his Arabs had a good hard run at least once a week. He had brought both the Arabs and Idris with him from India and had had nothing but regrets over the matter. It was not because the horses gave him trouble, or that Idris did either, despite his lugubrious airs. It was because of the dreadful fly infestation in the area, which with horses began with fever and oedema and ended with paralysis and death. Only donkeys survived around here.

His horses were beautiful, and it filled him with grief to discover the depredations that awaited them, but by then it was too late and he had already brought them with him. It was so stupid of him not to have found out beforehand, so completely regrettable. If he had known while he was still in India he would have made arrangements, of course, and probably advantageous ones. They were a bit of a bargain when he acquired them. A Sindhi landowner had some problems with a consignment of cotton he was due to deliver to a British company, and Frederick was able to help. The landowner in turn was able to advise Frederick on the purchase of an Arab stallion, and threw in the mare at a price that was almost a gift. It was for the memsahib when she returned from home leave, he said. (Only Christie did not return.) Gracious and excessively generous, it might seem, but then Eastern hospitality and gratitude can be misunderstood, especially when extended to a government servant. There are notorious examples to prompt suspicion, of course – Clive, Hastings and Thackeray's nabobs – but those gentlemen robbed state treasuries and emptied warehouses whereas Frederick had merely expedited some procedures. The landowner's generosity was to do with a more gracious way of living, he thought, an attitude to obligation that England had lost because her rulers were querulous and envious.

Idris came with the horses, or was too besotted to be parted from them. His name meant steadfast and truthful, so his landowner told him, after a personage in the Holy Book. Frederick had not had time to study the Koran, but he could vouch that the names suited his man. He was wiry and sinewy, and not much given to smiles, but he was tender with the horses as if they were his own blood. Frederick entertained dreams of an equine dynasty for a while, but Sharifa refused to oblige despite Majnoon's best efforts. Not all was lost for the poor beasts, though. He had sent word to the Club in Mombasa, and had received one enquiry from a Mr Cowan who was stationed at Fort Smith and was down on the coast for a vacation. Frederick in turn had invited Mr Cowan to come and visit and inspect the animals himself. Mombasa was only two days' sail away.

Idris was not enthusiastic about the weekly trips to the estate, saying that the horses did not like it there because the frogs bothered them. There were rather a lot of frogs because of the irrigation ponds, but Frederick had a good idea that it was Idris, who in his Rajputana way was fastidious about the company he kept, who did not like it on the estate. He refused to sleep in the quarters for the estate workers, most of whom were former slaves, it has to be said. They had been lured away from their owners some years ago and found work with the company, while this was still company territory. Since the declaration of the Protectorate, there was no longer any question of slavery, of course. Burton was teaching them to play cricket, and had dreams of offering a challenge to the town, when it got round to making a team out of all the Indians there. In any case, Idris refused to share the men's quarters. Instead, once his care of the horses was done, he spent his evenings on the estate sitting on the veranda steps, in sight of his employer, reading the Koran by the light of the hurricane lamp or dozing, waiting for the evening to be over. A few hundred feet away, there was the sound of talk and laughter from the labourers' quarters, which every so often erupted into acrimonious banter, the conversation of men without women. Lanterns here and there burned with the soft golden glow of coconut-oil wicks. Burton sometimes tried to cajole Idris to join the men, or offered him a drink as a joke, both of which Idris declined with unsmiling courtesy. Frederick sympathised, and found Burton's fierce bantering distasteful. When he was ready to sleep, Idris slipped away to the stables which Frederick had

had specially built for his weekly visits, and which had a purpose-built platform where Idris spread his bedding.

It was Idris who hurried up alongside, soon after they set out, to tell him about the wounded man. As they turned north before the market, to avoid the stinking, winding alleyways around it, and the crowded, squalid holes-in-the-walls that served as shops, they passed the dark office of the Bohra wakil Siddiq. Frederick knew quite well it was the wakil, it was his job to know. He was one of only two wakils in the town. But he also knew that Indian wakils were slippery and rapacious, a low form of life which battened like hard-shelled ticks on the hides of the ignorant and the helpless. He had seen them at work in India, crooks and money-lenders in all but name. He was prepared to have official commerce with the unctuous being, but that did not mean that he had to know him while he was out for a ride. The wakil came out when he saw them riding past and shouted something, which Frederick ignored. He shouted again, and this time Idris said something back and stopped to listen to the reply. Frederick knew they were talking in Kutch, and heard the word Angrez, so he assumed they were talking about him, some puerile witticism or another. Then Idris hurried up alongside to tell him in his brutal English that an Angrez was very bad hurt.

It was Siddiq himself who led the way. First he shut and locked the huge studded doors of his office, adjusted his gold-embroidered cap and made a grand gesture for them to follow. Frederick sneered at the hunchbacked little man. When he saw him heading towards the warren of alleyways that led to the market, he called out for him to wait. Majnoon would live up to his name in those rutted overcrowded passages. He dismounted and handed his reins to Idris. He glanced at his groom, expecting a look of anxiety or concern that he was setting off on his own into the native quarter, with an unknown Indian as his only guide, but Idris seemed untroubled. He dismounted too, and took the reins, and then almost instantly began to walk away towards the shade of a tree. Frederick followed the wakil, smiling to himself, a tiny bit disappointed that Idris had not shown more concern. He was a hard man, Idris, which was why he employed him, but he also felt a kind of care and fondness for him. He thought Idris saw himself in some kind of an alliance with him, a pact he had agreed to when he accepted pay from him and consented to follow him as his groom. In his antique code of honour, he was nothing as squalid as a servant. Frederick sometimes caught him looking at him with a gaze that he could only describe as emotional, even devoted and steadfast, a manly love. He thought Burton caught that look too, and Frederick thrilled to hear Burton say once, That man will die for you. He wondered what Idris would do after he sold the horses. Frederick reminded himself to ask after Idris's family and to give him a gift for them.

The wakil leading the way in front of him was a thin, wrinkled, fair-complexioned man with the curved spine that Frederick assumed came from a lifetime of crooked clerking. (*A wrinkled old man of monkey cunning*, Frederick tried the phrase to himself two or three times, to lodge it in his mind until he could write it down.) He was dressed in a white cotton jacket buttoned up to the neck, tight-fitting trousers, tan leather slippers and the green gold-embroidered cap. His movements were generous and various, too many flourishes and bows and toothy grins for Frederick's liking. Something about him made Frederick think of one of Dickens's milder sinisters – quite unctuous. In a moment they had plunged into the narrow crooked lanes of the dilapidated native town whose roofs almost met above his head. His posting here was nearly four months old, but this was only the third time he was venturing into these reeking streets. The surfaces of the lanes were so eroded by rain and slimy streams of sewage, and so covered with rubbish, that Frederick had to watch his every step. As soon as they entered into the gloom, he was surrounded by a hum, a noise without words, as if he had entered an enclosed space where many people were muttering in an undertone. It was a heap, smelling of garbage and drains. The whole place needed to be knocked down and swept away, but he had no funds for such works.

He forced himself to take shallow breaths, even though his

instinct was to swallow huge heaving gulps to relieve the sense of suffocation he felt in the crowds and the alleyways. People looked at him and looked again, and he heard preceding him the cry of *mzungu*. People sitting outside their houses stood up in surprise and perhaps anxiety. One old man stepped forward and kissed his hand. Frederick was not unused to such acts of devotion. Older natives sometimes kissed his hand because they mistook him for the man who had freed the slaves some years before. Frederick did not discourage their deference. It did no harm and made some things easier. He saw grins all around him, and he could not be sure if they were kind or otherwise, if they were amused by the old man or derisive of him. The shopkeepers in their hole-in-the-wall shops called out to him, tempting him with one of their foul wares, objects which it beggared belief could provide a living for them: a tiny pile of charcoal, a couple of oranges, a handful of eggs and, least attractive of all, the ragged dirty vendor crouched over it all.

Children waved dementedly to him and tried to cross his path, calling him *mzungu mzungu*, as if otherwise he would have missed seeing them. He heard other things but could not catch anything clearly. He did his best not to. Let them shout their filthy words, why not, for all the good it would do them. Their voices irritated him, like the buzz of insects or the bleating of animals, like the whines of decrepit street-women in a London dockyard alleyway. The banyan ahead of him was waving his arms excitedly at the crowd, calling out in exasperation, making a show of urgency and impatience. Frederick was tempted to give his excitable backside a prod with his riding crop, and tell him through gritted teeth to conduct himself with rather more dignity before he made a complete fool of both of them. He strode on as best he could, keeping no less than two paces between himself and the wakil ahead of him, trusting in the irresistible force of his momentum to clear a path ahead. Frederick was not a big man, but he was well and strong, so he wasn't troubled by the crowds and their noise, not really. He was more troubled by the possibility of embarrassment and mockery, in case he slipped into the slimy gutters or was buffeted by a religious lunatic. No one needed any reminders in this part of the world about how unyielding British power could be, and if they did, the awesome events at Omdurman the previous year, word of which had spread this far, would concentrate minds anew. But sometimes native crowds were abominably and recklessly excitable, and so he found it helpful to think angry and ugly thoughts about them to keep his unease in check.

He wondered who the wounded man was. The likeliest was that it was someone from the Lutheran mission up north in the delta, which had stayed on even after the signature of the 1886 spheres of influence agreement and the departure of the German post. Some years before he came, so he had heard from Burton, there had been a Masai massacre near there, and the Methodist missionary and his wife and a score of their charges had perished. A fearless man, by all accounts, going about everywhere armed with nothing more than an open umbrella, boating up and down the river as if he had never heard of a crocodile or a poison dart. It must have won the respect of the local natives because they did not bother his mission and some even joined it. It was a less common outcome than most people imagined – missions saving souls – at least in his experience.

Still, it was astonishing that the Masai had raided that near the coast, and that they should have chosen a humble man of God and his flock as their victim. They ranged over great swathes of the interior as if it were a primeval playground for their blood sports. What was that line in Shelley's 'Mont Blanc' about the huge rocks scattered about the mountain, as if that blasted land-scape had been a playground for primeval godlings of earth-quake and storm? The Masai were the unruly godlings of the shrivelled landscape in the interior of this land. The common wisdom was that the Masai only raided for cattle, like the lion only attacked for food, but Frederick thought both had a taste for blood and cruelty, and prayed that he would never have to put his theory to the test. There could have been a Masai raid on the Lutheran mission, or if not Masai then another marauding tribe, the Galla or Somali or another wandering band of idlers. The river drew them down as if it were a funnel, as rivers had drawn barbarian tribes since time began.

He had also received word from Mombasa that the Methodists were planning another mission, nearer the town this time so they could fish more safely, and a Reverend Holiday would be on his way in due course. But when the good Reverend was ready, he would be sure to come by sea from Mombasa rather than overland. This poor devil was more likely to have wandered in from the interior.

No, the picture in his mind as they picked their way past mounds of rubbish and crumbling houses with their rotting doors, was of a bedraggled troop of loyal natives standing by a rough stretcher they had fashioned to carry their good priest to safety. It made him think of the two devoted Zanzibaris who a few years before had carried the embalmed body of the saintly Dr Livingstone thousands of miles from the great lakes to the coast in Bagamoyo. First they took out his heart and buried it in the place where he died, then they embalmed the body. How did they think to do that? Where would two native porters have got the idea for such a grand symbolic gesture from? Imagine two farm labourers or two navvies at home coming up with such a notion. Perhaps the good doctor left instructions, but even then, why didn't they drop the body into the nearest marsh and stride off home? What a saint he must have been to inspire that kind of fidelity in his people. A bedraggled troop of urchins and layabouts was at his heels, although fidelity was not what was in their minds, more like the morbid curiosity for suffering and sensation that afflicted idle and empty minds.

The lane suddenly ended, and opening up before him was a bright sandy clearing. He stopped in surprise, struck by how pleasant the open space was. Someone charged into him from behind, and without looking round he lashed out with his riding crop and felt it striking flesh and bone. There was a shrill, childish yelp, followed by laughter, and Frederick could not restrain a smile. There was a small whitewashed mosque at the top corner of the clearing with a road running beside it. The two shuttered windows and the door, which was half-open, were painted a beautiful Mediterranean blue, like the colour of the Madonna's robe in a Titian painting. At the end of the clearing nearest to them, on his right, was a grimy café with some marble-topped tables and benches outside. What were marble-topped tables doing in this neck of the woods? Beyond the café were stone dwellings, some of more than one storey, and the rest modest but clean and in reasonable repair. Another lane opened into the clearing, and now he saw that there were several other lanes that did the same. On his left were more dwellings, with door curtains gently billowing in a breeze that seemed to come from the widening road that ran by the other side of the mosque towards open farmland in the distance beyond. Frederick could feel the breeze where he stood, and wondered where he was and why no one had told him about this pleasant location in this derelict town. He tried to work out in his mind its position on the map in his office. The wakil, who had also stopped and was half-turned towards him, pointed beyond the dwellings on Frederick's left, smiling and nodding in self-congratulation.

'Sir,' the wakil said, beckoning Frederick to follow, and waggling his head with self-important urgency. The crowd that had accompanied them through the lanes pressed past them and fanned out in the clearing, facing the direction the wakil indicated. As Frederick followed behind the wakil he saw a small shop ahead, a duka, the crowded merchandise store which proliferated in Indian cities, and which Indian traders had brought to this part of the world. They weren't all owned by Indians, traders from Hadhramut also had a forte for this kind of commerce, but the idea belonged to the Indians. He wondered if that explained the orderliness of the clearing, if this was an Indian enclave. In these parts, wherever Indians went, there prosperity followed, although of course it depended on the class of Indians. In Zanzibar he had seen the street-sweeping variety that clogged Indian cities living in degrading penury and begging in the streets, whining and screeching their grating racket, and most of the vendors of the hole-in-the-wall shops were Indians. But the general idea was true: get the right kind of banyan in your district and prosperity will surely follow.

There were two or three customers outside the shop, and some elderly men sitting on a bench beside it. Frederick wondered why they were heading for the shop anyway, perhaps to ask for directions. No sign of his bedraggled troop of loyal bearers yet. He lengthened his stride so that he was beside the scampering wakil as they approached the shop. The elderly men rose to their feet and so did the dukawallah, stepping down hurriedly from the platform above his wares. They did that, apprehensive and respectful whenever a European approached, and Frederick quite understood why. Suddenly, it seemed, everyone was talking at once and casting wary glances at him. The wakil, he saw, was alternating a stern demanding tone to the dukawallah with sagacious and understanding waggles of his head. After a few exchanges at this dramatic intensity, while Frederick was still at a loss about what exactly was going on, the dukawallah went back into his shop, and through it to open the door to his yard. The wakil stepped inside and beckoned Frederick in after him. One of the elderly men kept the crowd back with his stick, but they thronged the doorway and some clambered to the top of the yard wall.

It was all so unexpected. Frederick knew, at the instant before he stepped through the door into the yard, that the wounded man would be inside, but he only knew at that exact instant and had no time to adjust anticipation. He saw a long-haired, bearded man lying on a mat under a thatched awning, covered from feet to shoulders in a cream-coloured sheet with red and white borders. There was something classical and ancient about the colours, the colours of a Roman toga. The man's head was turned to one side, his mouth slightly open, exhausted and anguished, in an attitude so familiar it was almost blasphemous. Beside him on the mat sat a woman, her legs folded and completely covered by her faded green dress. She was on the point of rising to her feet but seemed undecided, arrested in astonishment. She turned her head away as they walked in and drew the shawl across the lower part of her face, but Frederick had seen enough to know that she was a pleasing-looking woman in her thirties, perhaps, probably of mixed local production, with that shadowy brown gloss that suggested Bajun or Somali origins. He guessed she was Mrs Dukawallah, and he wished him joy of her. For an instant, hardly an instant, more like a flash, he thought of Christie in England and missed her. Hardly missed her, more like a single pulse beat stronger then subsided. He would think of her properly later.

Frederick knelt on one knee beside the wounded man and put his hand on the side of his neck. He was warm with a strong pulse, but he did not feel feverish. The man opened his eyes and let out a low and drawn-out groan. It sounded like a muffled bleat, the piteous croak of a dying animal. The woman said something, and when Frederick looked up at her she nodded, as if to reassure him. He rolled back the sheet to see if there was blood or a wound, but there was no sign on the body, only emaciation and dust. He stood up and looked around him and he was suddenly struck by the strangeness of everything, him in this place, in the yard of these people's house, standing in his waxed riding boots, tapping his calf impatiently with a riding crop, surrounded by these dark unfamiliar people that he felt inexplicably angry with and with a sick man at his feet. It was a familiar strangeness, as if a part of him was beside himself looking on, but it was necessary now that he take no notice of it. He shook himself free of this feeling, which he thought of as irresolution and weakness despite its humane impulse, and made a sign of a stretcher with his arms. 'We have to take him away from here,' he said, speaking to the wakil first and then turning to the plump, sad-looking dukawallah. 'We have to take him away from here at once. Jaldi, jaldi. Fast, fast' he repeated, miming picking up and carrying the body out of the yard.

Somehow the wakil took charge and managed the arrangements, speaking with a calmness and authority which surprised Frederick after his deferential antics earlier on. Frederick couldn't understand a word the wakil said, but he thought he managed to make everything sound calculating and crooked nevertheless. There was the usual chaos and noise, and people milling about, but eventually three men lifted up the poor fellow, mat and all, and prepared to set off. 'Where are his things?' Frederick asked. 'Property. Where's his property? His goods.' The wakil did what he could, but he could get nothing out of the dukawallah and his wife. The wakil shouted at them and wagged a finger dramatically, and Frederick guessed he was haranguing them for the robbery, or even more likely, making arrangements to ensure they would keep his share. He added a few sharp words of his own and scowled at the dukawallah, without producing the required result. Some of the crowd joined in, shouting their idle rubbish, and Frederick thought it best to get the man to safety before everyone became hysterical. They would return for the property later, he told the wakil, when the poor man could give an account of what he had lost.

When the procession had wound its way out of the lanes, Frederick found Idris sitting under the huge mango tree in the square, with an audience of children silently staring at the horses. He stood up at once when he saw the melee, but he kept his distance, waiting for instructions. Frederick liked that, the discipline of it. He pointed his riding crop in the direction of home, and Idris mounted Sharifa and led off. His presence in the procession added even more drama to the event, and by the time they reached his house, it had turned into a medieval pageant. They had some trouble getting rid of everybody, especially the wakil, but Idris and his servant Hamis managed to confine them all to the hallway downstairs and gradually disperse them, distributing coins to the men who had helped carry the sick man. He was now installed in the guest chamber and was beginning to come to. The men had put him on the bed still wrapped in the old straw mat, like Cleopatra smuggled into Antony's chamber. Frederick unwrapped him, to find him still covered in the cream and red sheet, and he now had time to notice that the cloth was hand-woven and thick, probably new. He felt the man's forehead to check his temperature, and the man opened his eyes at the touch and looked directly at Frederick.

'How are you feeling, old chap?' Frederick asked gently.

'Have you ever been to the Seychelles?' he asked, and Frederick grinned at the unexpectedness of the question and at his unmistakably English inflection.

'No such luck,' Frederick said, relieved that it was not a Lutheran fanatic.

'In this part of the world, you always have to be on the lookout for a bit of foul play, as you yourself know very well, of course,' Frederick said, and then sucked long and sweetly on his cigar. He blew the smoke out in a great gushing geyser and the sight filled him with elation and contentment. 'I must say, it's very good to have you back in the land of the living, my dear Pearce. It's something of a miracle to see you sitting there so composed after the state we found you in. You must say when you've had enough. Don't let me tire you. I'm dying to hear about your adventures, of course, but there's plenty of time. I think you've done remarkably well as it is, to be on your feet again so quickly, but you mustn't overdo it. At least you don't seem to have picked up anything. But you must have been in that terrible sun for days, and that can give you quite a headache, I believe. Well, you aren't hurt, anyway. In fact, old chap, I'd say you are pretty jolly lucky not to be. There are some fiendish brigands in that hinterland. I can only assume that somehow or the other you managed to avoid being seen by anyone in your solitary travels, otherwise you wouldn't be here. You know, when I first heard the news I thought it was one of the missionary fellows up on the river, the Lutherans. There were some deadly attacks up there a few years ago, and there are always rumours of Abyssinian levies up to no good, robbing and slaving as a way of life. You were extremely lucky not to run into them, I'd say, although a European is probably safer with them than any other kind of body. Anybody else would go straight to the slave market in Harar probably, but they know we don't take kindly to that sort of thing.'

Frederick sucked at his cigar again and then casually knocked the tip of ash off on to the floor of the veranda. The breeze had subsided after dark, but it had done its work, and the air was balmy and moist. Below them, the sea was running into the bay in long arcing swells.

'Have you been to the Seychelles?' Frederick said, chuckling. 'Funny first words. You said that when you came to, do you remember?'

'Yes,' Pearce said wearily, smiling. 'And you said, No such luck.'

'No, I'm afraid not. Do you see those swells in the sea? There is no reef across the bay, very unusual for these parts, because of the river discharging a few miles north of here. There's nothing between here and the Seychelles, due east. That's where those swells started off. I hear it's a beautifully unspoiled place, despite the French and the missionaries, a kind of South Sea paradise. Have you been there?'

'No,' said Pearce.

'The coco de mer,' Frederick said musingly. 'It sounds quite a disgusting idea, a fruit that looks like genitalia. Trust the French to discover islands where even the flora is smutty. Well, they didn't discover them, I suppose, we must have done that, but you can be sure that as soon as they saw what kind of fruit the islands produced, they knew they were meant for them to settle.'

Frederick refilled his glass and glanced at Pearce, merely a polite gesture, because he would not allow him a drink even if he asked. Pearce was lying back in his recliner, and in the glowing light of the kerosene lamp Frederick could not be sure if he had dropped off.

'Lovely,' Pearce said softly. 'The sea.'

'Yes, it is. There's nothing out there for a thousand miles, you know, until you hit your Seychelles. And yet the sea is so well-behaved. That's the Indian Ocean for you, at least this part of it, a pond compared to the beastly Atlantic. It gets quite rough before the north-easts steady, around November or so. The port is useless then, so I'm told. That was just before I came, and even now the wind is quite stiff at times. I've only been on post for the last four months, but yes, the sea, the best thing about the place. Not much else that's any good, really. The land is not bad but too sandy and shallow, the rain is adequate, but you can't get people to work as they should. You can't get them to make any effort. It's slavery that did it, you see. Slavery and diseases that sap their strength, but slavery most of all. In slavery they learned idleness and evasion, and now cannot conceive of the idea of working with any kind of endeavour or responsibility, even for payment. What passes for work in this town is men sitting under a tree waiting for the mangoes to ripen. Look at what the company estates have achieved. Brilliant results. New crops, irrigation, rotation of the fields, but they've had to get people to change their whole way of thinking to get that. We need some British estates around here, and my guess is that it won't be long before we do. The Arab landowners will have no choice but to sell soon.'

'Yes,' Pearce said.

Frederick sipped his drink and drew on his cigar in the silence, then when Pearce grunted softly, he took it that he was asking him to continue. 'The town was more or less abandoned for a century or so after the Portuguese built Fort Jesus and moved everything to Mombasa. Jolly ungrateful of them really, considering. Then about forty years ago, Sultan Majid of Zanzibar had the brilliant notion of reviving the town as a plantation colony. In theory, of course, he was sovereign over this whole coastline. So he sent over his Arabs and a troop of Baluchi mercenaries, and thousands of slaves. The harvests for the first ten years or so were excellent, so even more slaves were sent over and the locals began raiding the nearby tribes for more. The town became prosperous again and enormous fortunes were made. The Bohras came in to set themselves up in commerce, and you know I always say, if you see an Indian trader setting up in business, you can be pretty certain there is a penny or two to be made in the place. The Indians have been here a long time, or at least they were already here when the Portuguese came to plant their cross. It's even said that the pilot Da Gama, picked up from here for the final run to Calicut, was an Indian sailor. I can believe it, or more likely he was an Indian slave. Everything was done by slaves, and even the slaves owned slaves.

'It was during these years that the company was granted its charter and began its work. Everyone can say now that the company didn't have a chance, but I don't suppose it looked that clear-cut to McKinnon and his crowd. It certainly didn't look that way to the Sultan of Zanzibar. I don't think the Sultan was Majid by this time, in fact I'm sure it wasn't. Perhaps Barghash, or more likely the one after him, the mad one, Mahound, something like that. He, whichever one it was, looked to benefit from British methods and science, and so asked the company – or somebody asked for him – to send one of its managers to run the plantations here. A bad mistake. The company sent a gentleman called Tinkle-Smith, some such name, who immediately freed all the slaves on the plantations and then re-employed as many as were willing as waged labour. He fixed the price for a slave's freedom and offered to lend it to any slave who agreed to work on company plantations afterwards. This set the slaves on the other plantations off, and most of them ran away, not wanting to work at all. They all rushed off into the interior for a holiday instead of taking the paid work the company was offering. By this time even the slaves knew that the Sultan's theoretical sovereignty was only ten miles deep, after the Anglo–German agreement on spheres of influence. So all they had to do was bolt ten miles into the interior and they were safe. The result . . . impoverished Arabs. This was only a few years ago, eight or nine, but you can see the derelict plantations now if you take a look around. But those runaways are trickling back and we settle them on abandoned Arab land a little south of the town. It causes trouble, but there's nothing much the Arabs can do about it apart from grumble and decamp to Mombasa. Well, it would all have come to an end quite soon anyway, as soon as the Protectorate was declared in '95. Oh dear, you've nodded off,' Frederick concluded, as he heard Pearce gently snoring. He poured himself another drink and relit his cigar.

He would give him a few minutes and then wake him. The mosquitoes would slaughter him if he left him to sleep on the veranda. But perhaps he was used to them, mosquitoes and beetles and snakes. He guessed Pearce had something disgraceful to tell. No one travelled alone like that, unless he had been sent as an emissary from a travelling group, and even then would have been accompanied by a porter or two. He could have been robbed or been abandoned by his guides. In either case, he would have said something by now, blurted something out. Frederick had gone back to the dukawallah's house with Hamis the servant to translate, and had questioned the man almost to the point of violence, but the podgy dukawallah had adamantly, tearfully in the end, maintained that Pearce turned up empty-handed. No doubt there was an explanation, but Frederick suspected that Pearce was hiding behind his exhaustion. Not that he was not exhausted, that was evident and unmistakable. He had been sleeping all day and now there he was, sleeping again. All he had been able to eat were a few spoonfuls of the broth the cook had prepared. Perhaps, it occurred to Frederick, he was not really asleep even as he snored gently there beside him on the veranda. Perhaps he had been asked to leave an expedition for a caddish act, and was understandably reluctant to talk about it. He glanced at Pearce beside him, reclining and indistinct in the light of the lamp. He had an austere look that was probably not entirely due to his recent privations, some self-importance, something to do with labours and principles. Frederick poured himself a final drink and warned himself not to get carried away with his suspicions. 'Steady on, young man,' he whispered to himself, smiling. 'Don't let the sherbet run away with you. This may be a man returning from the extremes of experience, some encounter with the sublime, who has not yet found his way to the surface.'

Frederick was at his desk in the mid-morning when he heard Pearce in the reception room next door to his study. The doors of all the rooms were kept open on his orders, to circulate the air and keep the house cool in the morning. In the afternoons the shutters at the front of the house were closed and the veranda blinds were lowered to keep the sun out. Frederick attended to the details of his household punctiliously. He liked doing so, and even said the word to himself, over-stressing its sharp edges in self-parody. Punctiliously. He had a good idea what was purchased for the store, what was consumed, and how much slack to allow for pilfering. He wound the clocks himself once a week, and made sure that they all told the same time. He checked the specific gravity of the milk every now and then to make sure the Cambay dairyman had not watered it down too much. He liked his servants to know that he knew their duties precisely, that he was attentive to their ruses, and expected them to be considerate of his preferences. So he had warned Hamis to allow for one more guest for dinner in case Burton turned up, and he had heard Hamis going into Pearce's room at eight o'clock in the morning with a cup of tea, as he had instructed him to.

When he heard Pearce in the reception room, he set aside the report on the year's customs duties that he was working on and went out to greet him. He found him standing on the veranda, leaning against one of the corner posts in a late morning patch of sunlight. He was wearing one of Frederick's shirts and pairs of trousers, which were not the right size for him. The shirt was too large and the trousers were three or four inches too short. It gave him the look of a beachcomber, an educated idler, one of those R. L. Stevenson South Sea ruins, especially with the bare feet and the straggly beard on him. The thought made him smile, because there was something appropriate about it, something in Pearce's posture which was not to do with the clothes, some looseness or poise, a kind of self-possession.

'You shouldn't be standing in the sun there, you know,' Frederick said. 'Not after your sunstroke or whatever it was you had out there.'

'I'm sorry,' Pearce said, moving away obediently. 'Did I disturb you? Please don't interrupt your work.'

'Happy to be disturbed,' Frederick said, motioning Pearce towards the coolness inside. 'I'm writing a report on commodities duties for the year, and comparing the figures to last year's, the vital statistics of Empire but very dull going. I usually have a small respite at this time of the morning. Will you join me in a cup of coffee or some fruit? The coffee here is delicious, and Hamis lovingly roasts it and pounds it every day. It's not a very delicate bean, but full of flavour.'

'Yes, that's very kind of you. It was the smell of coffee that brought me out,' Pearce said.

'Splendid. Hamis will be along in a short while. How are you feeling? You look much better, although I think you could probably do with some more of cook's broth.'

'I am much better,' Pearce said, stroking his beard.

'We'll get Hamis to fetch the barber, shall we?' Frederick said, smiling. 'Or do you grow your beard wild?'

'No, no. I let it grow when I started on the journey, to avoid the bother of shaving every day. Yes, I'll have the barber, please.'

Frederick waited. The moment was exactly right for Pearce to begin telling his story, but when he did not, Frederick smiled secretly to himself. He would prompt him, he decided. He was ready to hear about it all. 'I'm afraid I haven't been able to locate your things,' Frederick said. 'I went back to the dukawallah fellow and asked him most firmly about it, but he is adamant. Do you remember what there was? We may still be able to force the truth out of him.'

Pearce shook his head wearily. 'There was nothing. My guides took what there was, everything. They had been debating whether to do it or not, I guessed that anyway. I got exhausted, not sleeping because of anxiety. Then the last night before they left me, I fell into a deep sleep and they took my gun. I heard them talking bickering among each other, and I woke up. One of them was sitting beside me with the gun pointing at my head. They made me lie with my face on the ground and they took off my shoes and my belt but they left me one skin of water and a bag of dried fruit. Oh, and a smock and a pair of sandals. I heard them go, arguing among themselves already. They had been disagreeing about whether to kill me or just to rob me. One of them wanted to do that, to kill me, to make sure, and the others talked him out of it. Perhaps they were still debating the wisdom of leaving me alive.'

'Damned bandits,' Frederick said. 'I must say, you're being rather cool about this business. I'd have been furious. Where did this happen exactly? Where were you headed?'

Pearce shrugged. 'This way. We were on our way here. After they left I headed due south. I left an expedition which was headed south-west, towards Uganda, you see. The three guides were to bring me to the east coast, but I suppose they didn't want to come here for some reason, or preferred to be elsewhere. I couldn't stand the killing any more.'

'Killing!' Frederick said shrilly.

'A hunting expedition,' Pearce said. 'A rather grand one. Three English gentlemen, one with his own English servant, and a white hunter to look after the arrangements. The white hunter organised everything, the camels, the guides, the provisions, like an angry quartermaster most of the time.'

Pearce paused for a moment, breathing deeply, gathering his strength. 'Mr Tomlinson. He sat on his own in his tent in the evening scribbling furiously, writing up his journal for his memoir, no doubt. The gentlemen made such fun of him, relentlessly, driving him into a frenzy with their profligacy and complaints. I met one of the gentlemen in Aden. His name was Weatherill. I don't know if you know him, he'd been in India. Quite wealthy.'

Pearce paused again, running out of breath. When he resumed he spoke more slowly, pacing himself. 'I'd been travelling in Abyssinia for four months and Weatherill was very interested to hear about that. He wanted to know if we were going in there now that Menelik had chased the Italians out. He's a man of great curiosity despite his hunting and riding ways, a man of impressive intellectual energy. He wanted to talk about Rimbaud, and whether anyone in Abyssinia mentioned him. Then he invited me to join him on his expedition to Somalia. I couldn't resist. I was feeling very well after my travels, you know how you do, perhaps slightly reckless. Weatherill invited me as his guest so there was no expense for me to bear. Only three months or so of my time. There was no urgent reason to rush back, and I had hardly travelled at all in Somalia. I really couldn't resist.'

'Has anybody ever read Rimbaud? Does anybody read him now? I think he's now better known as a gun-runner than a poet,' Frederick said. He was relieved by the fullness of Pearce's account, and he felt his doubts of the previous evening evaporate. Just then Hamis arrived to deliver rice cake, fruit and coffee, and spread it on two small tables in front of them. While they waited for him, Frederick recited:

> A maid with a dulcimer
> In a vision once I saw;
> It was an Abyssinian maid
> And on her dulcimer she played.

'There I was, warning you about Abyssinian levies when you probably count them as your blood brothers. What were you doing in Abyssinia, if I may ask?' Frederick asked after Hamis left.

Pearce took an interest in the rice cake, bending forward to study it with care, and then he shrugged. 'Travelling, working on a book. I'm a historian, of a kind. A proper amateur actually. A bit of a linguist, a student linguist. I was based in Egypt for a year, in the education service. I promised myself I would travel in Abyssinia when it was time to move on. Abyssinia always interested me, even when I was a boy. I wanted to know something of how it looked, and what its language sounded like.'

'An orientalist,' Frederick said.

Pearce smiled. 'When I know more perhaps,' he said.

'Please go on,' Frederick said, intrigued by Pearce's reticence about Abyssinia. Perhaps he was some kind of high-level spy, preparing a report on Abyssinia for a senior official in the Foreign Office. Perhaps Weatherill was right to suspect that we were going in there. He did not fancy Abyssinia.

'May I?' Pearce asked and helped himself to a slice of rice cake. He chewed slowly, taking his time, nodding slightly with appreciation. 'Delicious, such subtlety. I can taste cardamom and yeast. You can't imagine how delicate that is after my fare for the last few weeks.'

Frederick poured the coffee and waited until Pearce had a few sips. 'Please go on,' he repeated, leaning back and exaggerating his willingness to listen.

'We took a dhow from Aden to Brava in December. It was days and days of beautiful sailing, the best part of the trip. The north-east monsoons had settled fine, and then we picked up the Somali current when we rounded the Horn. We were in Brava for a few days and set off towards Dif, a small army of animals and men, armed as if for a conquest. It took us four weeks, slaughtering our way across southern Somalia. It was unbearable destruction. We killed every day, sometimes as many as four or five lions in a day, and leopards and rhino and antelope. We all reeked of blood and guts. And slaughtered meat and drying hides. Flies settled on us as if we were carrion. We ate so much charred meat that the air was nauseous with our breath and our waste. When we got to Dif I told Weatherill that I could not continue. He was furious, and his friends were too. They had been in a cavalry regiment together and I suppose they thought my objections unmanly. Weatherill refused to let me turn back. It was too dangerous, he said, and he could not spare the men. By now the plan had changed and Weatherill and his gentlemen friends were headed for Uganda to shoot elephants. I remonstrated daily with Weatherill. He was not feeling too well himself but he was inclined to see me as more profoundly feeble than him. In the end I wore him down. We went on shooting and killing our way south-westwards until we approached the Tana. There Weatherill thought it would be safe enough to let me turn back, or at least head for the east coast. He asked the headman to select three men who would accompany me. By the time we reached the coast, they calculated, it would only be a couple of months before the monsoons changed to the south-wests and the men could get passage back to Brava, and I could go to the devil.'

'Yes, you're right,' Frederick said. 'The winds are due to change quite soon, I believe.'

Pearce nodded. 'The men who accompanied me did not like the task. I don't know why exactly. I understand some Somali, a very, very tiny bit of Somali. I was learning on the journey, spending time with one of the men who gave me conversation for an hour or two every day. The men with me refused to understand when I spoke to them, and I saw early on that there was danger. I didn't think they would abandon me or kill me, really. It was very unlikely, Weatherill told me. He knew who the men were, and he had hired them. Their sense of honour would not allow them to betray me. But there must have been something else, some danger they feared in this direction. Their reluctance to travel to the coast was greater than their sense of honour, because four days before I turned up in your marvellous town, they did abandon me.'

'Somalis are the most incorrigible bandits,' Frederick said. 'My dear Pearce, they didn't only abandon you. They robbed you and left you out there in the desert to die. You should count yourself lucky to be here.'

'I don't know about that,' Pearce said, smiling. 'About being incorrigible bandits, I mean. There are people who will swear on the loyalty of a Somali. Weatherill almost did, on his word of honour or one of those sorts of declarations. Those poor young men let him down though. Maybe they will become notorious among their people for abandoning me. And it wasn't really desert, you know.'

'Pearce, my dear fellow, are you all right?' Frederick asked, half rising from his seat, for he could see tears running out of Pearce's eyes.

'I thought they would kill me. That's what I thought at first,' Pearce said. 'Then when they left me out there I thought someone on the way would kill me, or I would be attacked by a wild beast, or I would die of thirst and longing. Anything could have happened. That's all, and I so much wanted to be alive. Yes, I'm all right. Yes, I do count myself lucky to be here. What you see in my face is joy.'

'Don't distress yourself any more, Pearce,' Frederick said, pouring him another cup of coffee. 'You must be incredibly weary.'

'I am. My name is Martin. Please call me that. The people who found me, I must go and thank them,' he said.

'Martin it is,' Frederick said, raising his own cup in a toast. 'But first the barber then some lunch and some more rest. There's no rush.'

3 Rehana

REHANA KNOTTED THE THREAD tight on the button of the dress she was making and then snapped it off with her teeth. She picked another button out of the metal thimble beside her on the mat and lined it up with the next button-hole, giving the exercise her full attention. She pushed the tip of the quill through the thick material, deep enough to puncture it, and then guided the thread-carrier through the loop in the button. She had done six already, this was the seventh and then there were two more after that. Malika was sitting with her feet stretched out on the same mat under the awning, picking bruised and dead leaves out of the spinach and humming what to Rehana sounded like a lullaby. Perhaps it was to express her longing for a child, but she did not seem to know many other kinds of songs. At least, Rehana had not heard her sing anything but lullabies and some qasidas during Maulid Nabi, the ones everyone knew.

Rehana herself had no ear for remembering melodies, although when the women went wild at wedding celebrations she was as frenzied in her singing as everyone else. It was not really the words and the melody that mattered at those times, but the noise and the laughter and the dancing. No men were allowed to be present, although some young man was sure to peep over a wall or through a crack in the window planks. When the dancing began it was deliberately provocative, exaggerated swinging of hips and thrusting out of breasts, making fun of the lust that custom required women to suppress. But it became a pleasure

55

to let the body move with moderate abandon. Everything was done with smiles and laughter, and the memory made Rehana smile. Perhaps some of the women took more pleasure in the hip-grinding than others, and sometimes afterwards she felt as if they had all been children on a romp, tolerated in their misbehaviour, allowed to be naughty out of the sight of men.

'They didn't even bring the mat back, did they? Or the cloth,' Malika said, breaking off from her humming to prod Rehana's and her own indignation and revive their sense of misuse all over again. Her lower lip curled in an ugly pout, but her eyes were bright, as if her sullenness was a kind of play. 'It was the eating mat as well, and they came in and took it away with them. And they took the shuka! You went inside and you fetched a new cloth to put on him and cover his shame . . . and what did these people do? They burst into our house without greeting or anything, without one word of courtesy. Without even a salamalaikum or hodi. They burst in, took their man and off they went, mat and everything, looking neither here nor there. Not even one tiny polite word from them. That horrible Indian man, that baniani, barking like a mad dog in front of his master . . . and the man himself standing there, swollen like a ripe boil, his face red and running with sweat, with his dirty boots on the mat. Did you see those boots? Those boots could crack a bone if he kicked out at you, especially with those thighs on him, like the hind legs of a donkey . . . and the soles are probably made of metal and have poison smeared on them. They are killers, these people. He looked cruel, didn't he? . . . when he came back later to threaten Hassanali, speaking all kinds of filth. That whip in his hand and the red, angry face and that swollen neck. Wallahi, don't you think?'

Rehana thought, my father was a baniani too, but she said nothing. Instead she made a low sound of assent, thinking that Malika was playing a role, after all, putting on that voice of indignation that women seemed unable to resist at any abuse. But it was true, the government European frightened them with his return, waving his whip impatiently at Hassanali and snarling at him, turning all of them into criminals. Never mind his return, he frightened her the first time he came, bursting upon them like that as if he had caught them in wrong-doing. Hassanali had hurried past to open the yard door, in his terror only managing to say *mzungu wa serikali amefika*. The government European has arrived. Even as she rose to her feet, irresistibly panicked, Rehana felt herself resisting. What was there to be terrified about? They can have their corpse back. She had never seen one of them before, not the angry, red-faced kind that burst in on them. The sick man, somehow, had not struck her as mzungu, but was more like complication and confusion, a token of Hassanali's ineptitude with life. The one with the boots and the whip was the snarling figure from the stories, the destroyer of nations. When the Bohra man shouted at them and accused them of robbing the sick mzungu, everyone called out all at the same time, explaining what had really happened and how Hassanali had called out Mamake Zaituni the healer and Yahya the Legbreaker and neither had found anything wrong with him. Don't shout at the good man when he was only trying to help another poor son of Adam, they called out, don't abuse him for no reason. Take your mzungu and get out of here, fidhuli we.

The second time they came was in mid-afternoon, when Hassanali had not yet risen from his brief siesta. This time the European came with his servant, and the servant banged on the door and yelled out commands as if he was seeking admittance for a sultan. They had come to accuse them of robbing that ragged-looking living-death. The only thing they could have robbed him of was his soul, and who wanted to have anything to do with a mzungu's soul. But the government man was even more angry than he had been in the morning, so much that she thought he would hit Hassanali, and at one point raised his whip above his head as if he was threatening a child. The servant pleaded with Hassanali, *Mpe, mpe chochote. Humjui mambo yake mzungu huyu.* Give him, give him something. You don't know this man's ways. Hassanali thought he was asking him for a bribe, and asked how much he wanted. We don't have very much. The servant said, no no, give him the man's property back, whatever it is. So Rehana had walked over to the washing platform where they had put his rags until the next day's washing, picked them up and held the bundle out to the red-faced man. The servant stepped forward and took the bundle from her. That's all there is, she said. Then she angrily waved them towards the door, go. Leave our house.

'Poor Hassanali,' Malika said, unable to suppress a disloyal smile. 'I thought his legs were going to give way under him. You could hear his teeth rattling all the way inside the house. When that horrible man started to threaten him with prison, I thought I would burst into tears. But Hassanali stood there, shaking and rattling his teeth, and repeating humbly what he had said before. Even the Englishman knew he was telling the truth. Then when you came out and told him to go . . .' Malika put her palm over her mouth and ululated her celebration, and then clapped her hands with glee. 'Why should we want to steal from his brother? What did he have that we would want? Do we look that poor? The man came here in rags, dying for all we knew, and we took him in out of kindness. Then the government man comes and says we stole his belongings from him. What was there to steal?'

There was a book, small enough to fit in the pocket of a smock. Half of it was covered with writing, the rest was blank. Rehana had found it in his rags while she was sitting beside him, feeding him honey and water. She had put it in the pocket of her dress, and in the commotion of his removal had not found a moment to return it, although she felt the weight of it as the men were milling about. Later that afternoon, she had shut her door as if going for a rest after a long morning of shock and outrage, and had taken the book out. All morning it had bumped against her thighs every time she moved, but she had not taken it out of her dress pocket. She was not sure why she was secretive about the book, perhaps because she wanted to look at it herself first before someone snatched it away. Perhaps she was ashamed, afraid to seem petty and thieving, stealing a worthless book from a dying man. It was bound in soft leather which was sweat-stained and rough from handling. She opened it carefully and saw that the used pages were nearly full with writing. It was European writing, tightly-packed, some of it crossed out. Sometimes there were drawings of boxes and what she guessed were houses and trees. She couldn't read the writing, although she could read. She was sure it was the writing of the man himself, rather than a copy of devotions or prayers. It was the work of months, she thought, written during his travels and his troubles. She brought the pages to her face and smelled leather and dust and the sun-baked scent of the man.

'And then after that they didn't even bring the mat back,' Malika said, her face pouting again with exaggerated indignation. 'Or the shuka. What need does that European have with our mat when he has perfumed rugs on his floors? He's a thief, that's all.'

Rehana grinned at her performance, making her smile too. She often thought how lucky they were to have found Malika. How lucky Hassanali was, without a doubt, but Rehana felt lucky too, since she was doomed to live with her brother and his wife for the rest of her life. Until she knew for sure. Unless she wanted to marry again. She could have done a great deal worse than Malika. They all could have. Malika was so young and loving and joyful, and showed no impatience with her house-bound life. Yet. She was unhurried with her chores, and to Rehana it seemed she was always on the point of turning everything into play. It was irritating at times, childish, but sooner or later she made her smile and join in.

'He's not a thief,' Rehana said. 'He's a conquerer.'

'It was a good mat too,' Malika said. 'Our eating mat.'

'Ha Malika, stop all that about the mat,' said Rehana sharply, snarling with bared teeth as she bit through the thread again. 'Talk about something else, young one. This new mat is nicer anyway, lovely colours. And the government mzungu had walked over the other one with his boots, and then they'd taken the sick man away in it, so we would have had to change it anyway.'

'He wasn't sick, just tired, and it's still our mat,' Malika said stubbornly, rising to her feet with her basket of spinach leaves. 'They should have brought it back. And they should have brought your new shuka back.'

'Shall we send Hassanali to demand them back from the mzungu?' Rehana asked.

'Can you see him there?' Malika asked, laughing gaily and wobbling her knees as she mimed Hassanali's terror. She was still chuckling as she walked to the water jar to wash the spinach. She swung her hips lazily as she walked, unaware or uncaring about how she looked. It made Rehana smile to herself as she watched. 'Yes, mince away while it lasts,' Rehana said softly.

Her first thought was that it was him, her husband, that he had struggled back and Hassanali had found him and brought him home. Not because there was any resemblance or anything like that, the thought came too quickly for that. Hassanali had brought an exhausted traveller home and her first thought was that it was him. She had felt terror and anger, and the beginnings of elation, all in an instant. Now that she thought of that moment she remembered that she also thought of him, how he looked, his smile, the feel of the hair on his body, all in a rush. Then she saw that it wasn't him, and drew back in relief and disgust. The disgust was with herself, for being unable to feel only rage and humiliation at the thought of him, for being unable to stifle her body's desire for him, for the relief of having him back. Then she saw Hassanali standing in front of her, at a loss as always at what he had done, at what he had brought home, and she could not suppress her irritation with him. It was not his fault, but it also was. He had brought him home too, Azad. Rehana began on the last button, and did nothing to resist the swell of regret that passed through her at the memory of him.

He told Hassanali that he came from the same town as their father, that he knew the family. That was what Hassanali reported to her when he came in after shutting the shop that evening. He said he may even have heard of their father while still in India, as the young man who went away to the black coast and never returned. Many others went like that, but most came back in the end to look for a wife. His name was Azad. He had come to Mombasa in the last musim on a ship from Calicut. Their captain made a good profit on the merchandise he brought with him, mostly supplies ordered and paid for in India, but he was new to the musim trade and was cautious on his first trip. He also brought some cloth and jaggery and trinkets which he sold to local merchants who intended to distribute them in the interior, but he had trouble finding enough to take back on the return trip. He did not have the slack in the margin of his profit to take any risks. Other ships' captains had already made advance arrangements with suppliers, and had the reputations and connections to protect these arrangements. So the captain asked Azad to stay behind and act as his agent until his return the following year, to arrange for goods and merchandise to be ready for him when he came back. They were related in a way he explained but which Hassanali could not reproduce coherently, perhaps had not listened to very carefully. In any case, that was what Azad was doing, arranging with merchants to have goods ready for his captain and relatives. It was important, that relative part, because it meant he was obliged to be trustworthy in his dealings and his word was as good as his brother's, the captain. Not that he knew very much about purchasing, but the captain trusted him, and he was doing his best. That was what he said, Hassanali reported, smiling, pleased to be able to speak kindly about him.

Azad was in the town to agree a purchase of such and such a tonnage of simsim, because as everyone knew, this was one of the best areas for simsim. The rubber from the new European plantations was, of course, not available for purchase by people like them. That went straight into the government ships and was sent to Ulaya for their own use. But the simsim was there, and some tobacco and leather and aromatic gum, all good merchandise. While he was in town he heard about their father. To be honest, he had heard already while he was in Mombasa, because of course he used to live there, and some of the Gujarati merchants he dealt with there mentioned him. So he knew about their father even before he came to the town, and when someone here mentioned Hassanali, he thought he would come and pay his respects.

Hassanali reported all this with an excitement which surprised Rehana. She did not think India mattered that much to Hassanali, or at least she was surprised that it did. Their father, whose name was Zakariya, had always said that he was a Muslim living among Muslims, and that was enough for him. Where he was born or came from was neither here nor there, they all lived in the house of God, dar-al-Islam, which stretched across mountains and forests and deserts and oceans, and where all were the same in submission to God. He had a gift for languages, their father, and spoke Kiswahili, Arabic and Gujarati fluently. His Kiswahili was quite perfect. It was not only that he could make himself understood in this language, but that he felt it, and made his way in it with an intimacy and assurance that was like an instinct, like walking, a skill so profoundly learned that it seemed natural. From his earliest days in Mombasa, when he worked in the warehouses in the port (he too came on the musim), he made friends with other young men in the town and ran about with them as if he knew nowhere else. People used to say that if you were to listen to him speak with your eyes shut, you would not take him for anything other than a born and bred Mvita, a man of Mombasa. He even knew and recited the defiant poems of Mombasa against the threat of the sultans of Zanzibar, who seemed to be forever wanting to take charge of even the smallest town and hamlet everywhere along the coast. Everyone loved that about him, that he had so fluently and joyfully embraced the people he lived among, that he swaggered with the other young people, went to weddings and funerals with them, could be sent on errands by his elders and accepted rebuke from the usual busybodies as if he was one of their own. Perhaps some of the Gujarati merchants thought him a renegade, but they were people who admired cunning, and some among them suspected that there was method in his going native, that he was up to something. The people who loved him were forever threatening to find him a wife so he would never wish to leave them, but there was no need to because he found one for himself, their mother Zubeyda.

Rehana knew the stories of their courtship well, because they both talked about that time from their earliest days as parents. They made their meeting and marriage into a kind of myth, and no one dared or wanted to contest with them, not even Aunt Mariam, who generally did not hesitate to stamp on any foolishness. And later, after their Ba died so unexpectedly, and Rehana spent so much time with her mother in the three years that remained to her, she heard more intimate stories of the way they met and came to love each other. How he had seen her in the street and was attracted to her. She had not seen him because young women didn't dare look at men when they walked for fear of their reputations. How he was passing her house one evening, having taken to prowling nearby for a chance sight of her, and heard her singing inside, and she was unawares, and her voice aroused such a feeling in him that he knew he was in love. How he became so obsessed with his secret love that it was no longer a secret, and everyone knew and smirked as he strolled past their house for the tenth time in a day. That was when she took the chance to take a good look at him, and because she liked what she saw, she in the end let him see that she was looking. How one day she smiled at him in the street, and a few days later he sent word through the imam of the Shimoni mosque to ask for her. How her mother worried because he was only a labourer in the docks and they did not know his family, and her father said he was a courteous young man and everyone praised him even though he was Indian. Her father valued courtesy as a blessing and saw its upkeep as a moral virtue. Then she said that she liked the way he looked and would have him, and so that was that. How shy he was at first, how he sang to her in a whisper, how he made her laugh.

Well, it didn't always seem like that to Rehana when they were both alive, but those were the stories their mother wanted to remember him by. In later years he became tetchy all too easily, and demanded to be obeyed in all things, and made them all anxious and timid in his presence. His hearing began to fail, and sometimes he had pains inside his ears, which made him irritable. But their mother loved him, they all loved him. He just had to smile and say something teasing and they melted before him. He just had to speak in a certain voice and they knew that there was a song or a joke on its way. When he died, just like that, gone quietly in the night, it was a cataclysm. The house felt different, larger and emptier. The air itself felt as if something had been emptied out of it. She missed his noises, his voice, his bulk, his presence, but after that she realised how much more she missed his stories. Some of them were familiar, stories other people told, with talking animals and beautiful sorceresses, except that he told them with his own variations and additions, standing up to perform the dramatic moments and clowning the jokes. Hapo zamani za kale. In the old days of antiquity. She loved to hear him say those words, and she loved the way he told the story of *The Magic Horse*, especially the moment when the young prince and his princess soar above the town on their ebony horse and head towards his father's kingdom in Sana'a in Yemen. Some of the stories, she was sure, were his own invention, but he made them seem as if they were from the same store. When she was a child, he told her the story of Zubeyda, the wife of Harun Rashid, who sang beautifully and was famed for her generosity. She was a builder of mosques and roads and of water-cisterns, a benefactor in a dry land. 'That is why I married your mother,' he told Rehana when she was young, and because she was young she believed him. 'I knew that her name was Zubeyda, and that she was very pretty, so when I heard her sing I thought it was the legendary one come back to life.' Then one night the replenisher of graves came quietly for him and left them bereft and disconsolate in unfamiliar silences.

No, he had never seemed troubled or interested in his Indianness, so completely absorbed was he by the daily details of family and his neighbours and his business. They had left Mombasa and moved north to this town by the time Rehana and later Hassanali were born, and so as far back as she could remember him, this shop and this town were his life, and he never left it again to go anywhere. He was finished with travelling, he used to say. No one should have to travel more than a few hundred miles in a lifetime, unless he or she were driven by malice or greed, and he had travelled his miles. When they were children, he liked having them play in the shop or somewhere nearby where he could see them. Whenever possible, if there were no women visitors in the house or a crowd waiting outside the shop, he liked to eat with Zubeyda and the children. It was later that Rehana understood the unusualness of this, for a father to want to be with his wife and children rather than sitting in the shade gossiping with the men. He did enough of that too. He put that bench outside the shop and grown-up people sat on it all day, filling their lives with talk and contention and endless stories, laughing and provoking each other like children. Their father loved the talk and the raised voices and the quick-witted mockery. They all did, the men. You could hear it in the playful violence of their derision and scorn, their gleeful teasing, but Rehana found the men intimidating and scrutinising, and noticed that her mother always turned left out of the yard door and never even looked in the direction of the bench.

Twice, a long time ago when she was a child, Rehana went to Mombasa with their mother and Hassanali. Their father stayed behind, busy with his shop and the men who came to sit with him every day. She went to visit with grandparents and Aunt Mariam, and Uncle Hamadi, and though so distant, the memory of those journeys was as hard and bright as that morning's sun. She remembered the passage on the dhow, the swell of the sea and the exhilarating chill of the spray as she clung to the side of the boat, her mother silent and nervous beside her. She remembered the walk from the port Baghani to her grandparents' home, through narrow, shady streets that smelled of food and sweat and perfume, and hummed with voices and laughter and the noises of life. These were the streets women walked, the back streets away from the main roads and the shops, where back-yard doors stood open and everyone they met recognised and greeted her mother. As they walked, both then and probably at other times, her mother in her joy to be back in her home spoke about things that made her not see the half-full gutters with their green and blue crusts, or the dilapidation of the houses. She told her whose fault it was that the house they were walking past was now a ruin, how it had been lost by its old owners to a new landlord. Or whose son had grown up under its roof. She told her of childhood friends who had grown up in this house or that one, and had married and moved to Lamu or Unguja or even Ndazidja.

But their father did not come on these trips, and never returned to the town that until his last days he spoke of with pleasure and happiness, the scene of many of his recollections. Mombasa was like a home-town to me, he often said. Later Rehana wondered whether something had happened to make him reluctant to return, an argument or a disgrace. Or whether it was disapproval of his marriage to a Mswahili among the Indian notables in Mombasa that made him stay away in disgust. She was much older herself when she wondered that, and knew something herself about disapproval. There were very few Indians in their town when she was young, most of them remnants of the Baluchi troops who had been brought here to guard the slaves on the plantations. That was until the mad Sultan Khalifa of Zanzibar sent an Englishman to run his plantations for him and he freed all the slaves. There were also a few Bohra traders, and she knew that some of them worked as agents for merchants in India and Zanzibar, like their visitor Azad said he was doing. She remembered as a child how sometimes these Indians came past the shop and how they treated their father disdainfully. She knew that they did so because he complained about the way they made remarks about their mother. Rehana herself never heard any of these remarks, but she could imagine they were to do with her mother not being Indian, and she heard him ranting about the children being called chotara. She did not know what the word meant, but she knew it was something ugly. She could see that in the way the Indian men looked at her when she was a child, disdaining. Later she understood that the word meant bastard, an improper child of an Indian man with an African woman.

'I don't want anything to do with these high-handed, sneering-mouthed chewers of betel-nut badam and drinkers of sour milk,' their father said. 'See their mouths, red and twisted with ugly thoughts, sneering sneering all the time. I had enough of people like them in India, always better than everyone else, always pure, always right. Look, they live alone in the little rooms behind the warehouses, living like paupers. You see the way they walk in the streets feeling themselves up through their pants? They don't bring their families because they're afraid the natives will eat them. What do you think they do to themselves? Chinless goat-fuckers, that's what they are. Who cares about them? What do you mean don't use such words in front of the children? The children should know that these are sneering worthless goat-fuckers.'

No, he had never seemed too bothered about being an Indian, and in later years he had spoken Gujarati, when he had to, with an exaggerated voice, with his teasing voice, his voice of play. So it was a surprise that Hassanali was so excited by the connection with India that Azad offered. Perhaps their father had had different conversations with Hassanali when they were on their own, and he had been anguished about his loss, or perhaps for all these years Hassanali had felt a desire for the India which their father denied them, but it was still a surprise, a silliness. Her brother was inclined that way, anxious about the strangest things, and at times quite naïve. She was sixteen when their father died, and Hassanali was fifteen, and the day after the funeral he had opened the shop and stayed in it, brave and dutiful for them all. From his earliest youth he was counting and weighing, lifting and sweeping, hanging around the shop and listening to the idle fables of the old men who were always sitting on the bench outside. When business was quiet and their father went out and sat with the old men, Hassanali would perch on the cash-box with an air of achievement, as if this was all he wanted. Then, coming inside later, he would sit quietly and listen to their mother's ailing grumbles or eavesdrop the conversation of women, sitting with an empty gaze as if he were the victim of troubled thoughts. Why wasn't he out in the street making a racket and chasing about with the other boys? Then when he caught her eye, which to her felt hot with impatience and irritation, he looked away with his tender, guilty smile.

The next day after the funeral he opened the shop, the very next day, and hardly allowed anyone to help him. Their father would not allow their mother or Rehana to work in the shop. These people won't show you respect, he used to say. Now Hassanali stubbornly refused their help too. He was all right, he said. He didn't need to rest. 'There's no need for you to sit there all day,' Rehana argued with him. 'It's not your fault that things have turned out this way. It's as God wished it, alhamdulillah. Shut the shop in the afternoon. There isn't much business at that time, anyway. Have a rest. Go and meet your friends. You don't have to be like him, and even he had his wild times.' But Hassanali only shut the shop when he needed more stock and for Friday prayers, and only smiled guiltily when his sister or mother harangued him. Otherwise he spent his days in the shop, and the evenings in the store, arranging, weighing and packing, eyes blazing with tragic agitation. So with time she had found it harder to suppress her irritation with him, though she knew that he truly deserved better. He was silly, and afraid of things she could never understand. That was how she took his enthusiasm for the man Azad who knew their family in India. It was another silliness, a sense of obligation that was not even required of him. Why care about India, when their father, who was the only Indian among them, had wanted nothing to do with it, and the only Indians they knew treated them with disdain?

Azad came again the next day. Hassanali reported that he was full of smiles when he came, saying how happy it had made made him to meet the previous day, how moving he had found it, to meet the son of a man they thought had been lost. So Hassanali invited him to lunch after the Friday prayers. He brought him home. On Fridays, Hassanali shut the shop at noon and went to the Juma'a mosque for prayers. After prayers he came straight home to eat and did not open the shop again until four o'clock in the afternoon. It was his only half-day off in the week. Rehana always tried to make something of an occasion of the Friday meal, which they ate together, as they did every meal, even when they had guests. On Fridays, every Friday, Rehana made a chicken pilau, flavoured with cardamom and ginger and littered with raisins. She served this with a plate of fried red mullet or changu and a salad of white radishes, an onion cachumbar, a freshly made chilli sauce, a pickle or two, and a platter of whatever fruit was to be had, to eat before, during or after the meal. On this Friday, she swept the back-yard, watered the plant pots and started chopping and cooking in mid-morning. She would serve the men on their own. They never had men to eat, had never had anyone who was not a relative or a friend of their late mother's, and she was sure Hassanali would be embarrassed if she sat down to eat with a man who was a total stranger.

When they came, Rehana was wearing her best shawl, covering her head and her neck, standing beside the backyard door to greet the guest. He took her hand briefly, grinning with pleasure, and moved his head from side to side to indicate his delight. She served them and then withdrew inside, from where she listened to Azad's animated voice with a smile on her face. He came to the shop every day the next week, as Hassanali reported, and the following Friday he came to lunch again. Only this time he insisted that Rehana join them, since he had found out this was their normal practice. His face was lean and beautiful. He was almost tall, and well-built, half a hand's-breadth taller than her, who was slight of build. His beard was neatly trimmed and his whole appearance was handsome and clean, and Rehana thought he carried himself with the knowledge of his attractiveness. It was not very pronounced vanity, but she saw his slow contented smile when he thought his appearance had pleased. And he pleased her, he could not have helped but notice that. When he talked, she sometimes found herself sitting still, a smile on her face, listening, but really watching the movements of his face.

He spoke to them in a broken Kiswahili which they tried not to laugh at, at first, but which Azad turned into good-natured comedy with his gestures and the over-zealous repetition of their corrections and promptings. Sometimes Rehana recognised his unmistakably thin voice among the ones that came over the yard from the shop. He seemed to be there very often, and Hassanali spoke about him every day, sometimes with a sly look at her. Friday after Friday he came to eat with them, not every Friday but often, over several weeks, and then afterwards he sat in the shady part of the yard with Hassanali until it was time to open the shop again. Hassanali had never had a friend like this, with whom he could sit for hours screeching with laughter. Rehana could not stop herself from thinking about him, and when she heard his voice and could not see him, she felt a pain in her chest that she could only think of as longing.

Then one Friday, three months or so after he arrived among them, after their meal, and after Rehana had cleared away the dishes and left the men to their talk, and after they had finished talking and Azad had gone on his way, Hassanali stood outside her room where she was lying down and called her to come out. Azad had asked for her, he said, unable to stop himself grinning, unable to disguise his pleasure and anticipating hers. She felt the blood rising to her face, and her first thought was the madness of it all. How could such a wished-for thing happen to her? Look at you, Hassanali said laughing, reaching for her. Then, because it was what she wished for so much, she felt herself drawing back, squirming out of Hassanali's embrace, saying to him, Wait, wait, let's think about this.

She saw Hassanali's impatience, mild, good-natured, still smiling, but his smile lined with faint dismay. She had turned down other offers before. 'Yes, of course, you must pause and think about this,' he said. 'But . . . I thought he . . . Doesn't he please you?'

She nodded, humbly, made shy by her admission. 'He does,'

she said, and felt her face becoming warm again. 'It makes me happy that he has asked . . .'

Hassanali grinned with pleasure and reached for her again. 'Wait, wait,' she said, leaning back from him and retreating into the doorway of her room. 'It's not conceit . . . not vanity which makes me hesitate. It makes me happy that he has asked. He is a good man, joyful and courteous and . . . pleasing. But we don't know very much about him or his people. We don't know . . .'

'I know he feels like a brother to me already,' Hassanali said stubbornly, his smile fading. 'I know that he has been a cheerful and kind friend from the first day he visited me. I believe I have seen enough of the world to know that he is a truthful and . . . sincere man. I feel ashamed that you should doubt him when he has shown us such friendship. Has he been discourteous to you in any way? No, he has been proper and honourable in every way, even though anyone could see how much he admired you.'

'Yes,' Rehana said, and could not suppress a smile.

'Well then, and even a half-blind man could not miss that you liked the look of him,' Hassanali said, triumphant now, his case made by the sheer force of his own feelings for Azad, and by the fugitive smile on Rehana's face.

'Yes, but we don't know anything about his . . . obligations,' Rehana said.

'What obligations? Why don't you accept him and then we can ask him any questions you like? I don't want to offend him. I think he's a good man, I don't think you'll find another one better.'

'His family,' Rehana said, becoming impatient herself. 'Does he have a family . . . of his own? Is he married already? Is he required to return or will he live here? This is not a small thing he is asking.'

'Married. I didn't think of that,' Hassanali said, at last understanding. The three marriage proposals that Rehana declined had all come from men who were already married and wanted her for a second, and in one case, a third wife. But they were all older men, with children from their existing wives, who wanted to renew and replenish the pleasure of matrimony with a new young wife. Azad could not be much older than they were, and seemed so carefree and cheerful that it was hard to imagine him married.

'If you don't want to ask about these things, we can send word to Aunt Mariam. We can get someone else to ask these things which you fear will complicate your friendship.'

'No,' Hassanali said quickly. 'She will torment him with questions and drive him away. And it will take days to get word to her, and days for her to get here. It's not right to keep him waiting that long. No, I'll ask him. I'll talk to him. But can I say that you're happy to be asked, as happy as I am?'

'Say I'm happy to be asked, yes,' she said cautiously, already uncertain about how seriously Hassanali would press for answers.

He left her to open the shop. She went into her room and shut the door, then she lay down on the bed and involuntarily gasped. She felt a kind of terror, as if she was being asked to agree to something that would have unknowable consequences, but she also smiled at the thought of Azad, and shivered slightly as she imagined touching him, on his arm or his shoulder, and then shut her eyes to feel his breath on her body. She kept her eyes shut for a long time, her body melting in the detail of his embraces.

She understood why Hassanali was so anxious, so eager for her to accept. She was twenty-two, old for a woman to be unmarried. She was sure he worried for her and for his honour, in case her unattachment made her vulnerable to impropriety. In his eyes, and in everyone else's opinion, he would have failed to protect her if she succumbed to something unseemly and then both of them would be dishonoured. There were men who made a kind of profession out of seduction, and their victims were generally widows or older single women whose families were lax in their surveillance. Well, things hadn't got that desperate for her yet, but she thought Hassanali worried. He had said something like that to her when she turned down the second offer of marriage. With the first he had laughed at her refusal, the very idea of Abdalla Magoti marrying his sister was ridiculous, above all because he could not imagine her married, she thought. Then there was something ridiculous about Abdalla Magoti himself. His name described his knees, which were large and bandy, and which made his walk unmistakable and comical. He already had a wife and three children, and they all lived at the back of a gloomy one-room café down one of the lanes. That was soon after their mother died, and perhaps Abdalla Magoti thought she would be feeling vulnerable and would accept the protection he offered. Hassanali himself giggled when he delivered that offer, and smiled understandingly when she declined.

The second time he wasn't so amused, which made Rehana want to laugh at the way he was giving himself such airs. It was while Aunt Mariam was staying with them on one of her long visits. Whenever she came, she made her rounds of visits to all the numerous people she knew in the town, was invited to weddings, attended the wakes for the dead and received more visits in a few days than Rehana did all year. Of course, Rehana had no choice but to accompany her. It would have seemed peculiar and unsociable of her not to, and Aunt Mariam would not have allowed it. One day they visited the house of one of the Omani notables in town, who owned land here as well as in Takaungu. Aunt Mariam had a weakness for these grand connections, and when she was in their houses she behaved as if this was her milieu too, and not the modest dark house (but with a spacious walled yard where she grew rose bushes and jasmine) where she had lived throughout her adult life, through marriage and widowhood, and all her busy aunting. Rehana was always surprised at how many people lived in those huge houses, wives, relatives, servants. Some of them were slaves, or were children of slaves and now considered themselves part of the family.

They were sitting with one of the wives of the household and her servants and relatives in an upstairs room with a veranda. A sweet breeze blew from the bay, so that even though it was mid-afternoon and trembling with heat outside, in the room it was as cool as the shade of a tree at sunset. A man's voice called from outside the room, announcing himself. One of the women called out that there were visitors, but she was not quick enough to stop the man stepping into the room. The women hurriedly pulled their shawls over their heads, all except Rehana who was not quick enough, and in any case was not as punctilious with a shawl as these Ibadhi women who covered themselves even in front of their own brothers, or so she had heard. The man who walked into the room was stocky and dark, in his late thirties. He stood immobile with embarrassment in the doorway. His eyes rested on her for a moment, and then he retreated with apologies. The wife returned their visit a few days later, and then invited them to call on her again, and visited them another time before the matter was brought out into the open. The man, whose name was Daud Suleiman, had asked for Rehana after seeing her that one time. The offer was relayed through Aunt Mariam, who asked all the questions and delivered a full story to Rehana and Hassanali. He was related to the wife of the notable they had visited, and Aunt Mariam conveyed the details of the relationship with such complexity that Rehana stopped listening. She thought she already knew her answer. Now that she knew what was in the offing, she remembered that something about the worldly and appraising look he had given her had repelled her. Was repelled too strong? Had made her flinch and turn away, and although at the time she did not examine her reaction, she realised now that she understood his look and was intimidated by it. He managed one of the landowner's farms near Mambrui, and yes, he was married and had four young children, but the house on the farm was roomy and there would be plenty of space for everybody. There would be the pleasures of living in the country, fresh fruit and vegetables and eggs, and the patronage of their landowner meant that they would never be short of life's necessities.

Aunt Mariam nodded quietly when Rehana said no, and asked her to explain so that she could convey an answer to the notable's

74

wife. 'Do I have to say something? Can't I simply say no?' She did not think she could say that from the look of him she feared he would constrain and crush her. He looked an assured and respectable man, who understood his duties in their tacit subtleties and was careful to fulfil them, and would require her to fulfil them too. She didn't know that, couldn't know that from a brief glance, but she felt it, and felt that he would want to dictate and direct, the way her father used to and Hassanali thought he had to. She didn't want to be anybody's second wife. She had never heard her father say anything about taking a second wife. What did anybody want a second wife for? 'I don't want to live in the country,' she said in the end, because she could not think of anything better.

'Who do you think you are? A princess?' Hassanali snarled, quite unlike himself, unable to control his rage at what he took to be her frivolity. Then he stood up and made for the yard door, storming out. After a few steps he stopped and turned around. 'What is so good about living here like this? You'll say no to this man, who saw you and liked you, and who can provide for you, and then no one will ever ask for you again. They'll say you're too proud.'

'You, child, keep your voice down,' Aunt Mariam said sharply.

'What are you shouting about anyway? It's my life,' Rehana said.

'Yes, it's your life, and it will always be your life, but if you go on like this, it will end badly,' Hassanali said, lowering his voice to an angry whisper. 'No one will come to ask for you because they will say you're conceited, and you have nothing to be conceited about. Then one of those evil men will get the better of you and you'll bring dishonour to all of us.' That was when he said it, and then stormed off while Rehana glared and Aunt Mariam in an undertone asked God to forgive him the malicious thought.

Then what happened some months later confirmed to Hassanali that he had been right in his ugly foresight. A messenger came from Ali Abdalla the trader, whom everyone called

Msuwaki for some reason, offering marriage to Rehana. She saw when Hassanali conveyed this message to her that he felt vindicated and sad at the same time. Perhaps he even felt ashamed for her. In their eyes, Ali Abdalla was an old man, sixty, white-bearded, a trader in whatever came his way, and with two wives and a grown-up family somewhere in Arabia. A whiff of scandal was attached to his name, which Rehana did not know the details of and did not want to know, and in any case it was none of her business. People were always making scandal out of scraps. He probably made his offer because he wanted a woman for sex, and he was too old for the indignity of paying for it with someone off the streets. She understood that. Older Arab men made a show of their piety with such marriages, picking up widows and divorcees when they were going cheaply, or even sometimes a luscious young girl from a family overwhelmed with debt. The dowry in such marriages was usually only nominal as the families concerned were eager to have the woman taken off their hands and given some respectability. And it could all be done in the name of piety and esteem, rather than lust and greed. That was why Hassanali was ashamed for her, and perhaps of her, that she should receive such an offer, as if she was ruined or hapless.

'I shall say no, shan't I? Thank you but no,' Hassanali said, looking down into his coffee cup. They were sitting on the mat in the ill-lit yard after a cold supper of lunch-time left-overs, and Rehana felt dispirited and discontent, and thought Hassanali felt the same. She could not understand why she felt useless and alone, at fault, and why Hassanali should look so dejected, as if they had both failed at something, at life. She should have cooked something, even some beans or spinach. She determined after that that she would never give them cold supper again, never allow the weight of congealed rice and vegetables to sink through them like inadequacy.

So when Azad turned up in their lives in the middle months of that year, it was like an unexpected gift, a blessing. Hassanali would have considered himself fortunate to have him as a friend, and was made proud by his admiration for Rehana, and incredulous that he should wish to be married to her. He was so excited by Azad's proposal that he had to struggle to restrain himself from embracing him and making him part of their family at once. Azad was young, friendly, open, daring. He had sailed hundreds of miles in a boat to an unknown land, that was daring. Then he had stayed on to act as a business agent when he could only speak a few words of the language, that was even more daring. Yet he was at ease and happy, and had given them unstrained affection and made no demands. Hassanali had watched him and Rehana with sly and unbelieving anticipation, noting their interest in each other with wary hope. Really, it was more than he could ever have hoped for, and that was what he told Rehana when she said they should wait, or think, or ask Aunt Mariam to come and ask questions. You'll never find anyone better, he had said, and she knew he was right. When Hassanali reported that he had put her questions to Azad, and he had replied that he was not married and that he desired nothing more than to live with her in happiness, she smiled her consent and sent word to her aunt. They were married the day after she arrived.

Perhaps it was more than she deserved. For months she was lost in him, as if he had possessed her and transformed her. She felt herself beautiful and ample, smiling to herself when she thought of him, and tolerant of so much that had seemed aggravating and paltry before. Day after day she rejoiced at the miracle of his body beside her, at his embraces and his laughter. He travelled for his business, but not unbearably at first, and every time he returned she felt he possessed her even more. It was so unexpected, the feeling of intimacy and closeness, as if he were part of her flesh. When the musim finally came, and his captain returned, Azad became very busy, travelling and supervising the gathering of all the merchandise he had negotiated. They did not see very much of him in those last weeks.

He said he would have to go back with the captain, to make sure he would get his cut of the profits when the merchandise was sold. Business is business, and you had to look after your share or you would be cheated. Yes, of course the captain was a relative, and he would make sure there was something for him, but wealth is a corrupter of the most pure of souls, and even the captain his relative, who was by no means the purest of souls, might be tempted. When he had seen to his affairs, he would return as soon as he could, and by then his Rehana would be big with their first child, he hoped. She was reluctant, she begged, but he consoled her. This is how people like us make a living: travel, trade and make our way in the world. I will go and I will come back, and if we are blessed I'll bring back something of God's bounty for us. Hassanali told her to stop being a fool, and to stop giving Azad a hard time. That was how it was for so many people in these parts, she knew that. When the musim turned that year, he went to join his ship in Mombasa, and then not another word for the next five years or probably ever.

They thought he would send word if he could, and when he didn't Rehana feared that the ship had met disaster. Their father Zakariya used to tell them that that was how his own father had died, drowned on a return musim trip when his ship perished in a storm in the Arabian Sea. It had taken his mother weeks to find out, and it was only when the merchants decided that the ship must be lost that she had no choice but to admit his death. His name was Hassanali too, and when Zakariya was old enough he himself went on the musim trip, perhaps to look for his father. Luckily he found his little Hassanali, so he did not bother going back and therefore did not drown. So Rehana's first terrible thought was that the ship was lost on the way back to India. Hassanali asked people how he could find out, and some of the people asked for them among traders and merchants. No, the ship had not met disaster, so they could expect their young man with the next musim. But he didn't come, and after a while Hassanali was ashamed to ask. He had abandoned them, abandoned her, and gone back to his Indian life laughing at her love and her hunger, chuckling at their gullibility. Yet she could not be sure that he had not met some misfortune, and might not turn up one day and speak of the trials that had befallen him and kept him away. That was how it was, although she had known somewhere inside her within the first few months that he would not be back. She had dwelt on his departure for years, so that now all that was left was bitterness. She hardly allowed herself to think of the exhilaration of those early months. It made her feel a fool, and as memories of him turned into bitterness, she found a need to blame Hassanali for the way he had talked her out of her caution about him, although she never said this and resented her restraint. Her life became a muddle in this way, resentful, depressed, sleeping late, missing him. She could not stop herself missing him, even when she hated everything about him, his existence, his name, his voice. She did the work in the house as she had always done, but more listlessly and intolerantly now, and part of her congealed into something heavy and sour.

Aunt Mariam came to visit them every few months as she had used to before Azad came. She had kept away in those seven months or so after Rehana's wedding, to give her the time and the space to be happy she said, but after he left on the musim she started coming again, to keep her company and, Rehana suspected, to be on hand in case of a pregnancy. But there was no pregnancy, and as his absence lengthened, she abandoned her probing questions and made reassuring noises when Rehana lamented. It was she in the end who took things in hand. After nearly two years of Azad's disappearance, with Aunt Mariam coming and going every few months, Rehana and Hassanali were still captive to their misery. So she stayed. Stayed on. She stayed from Mfungo Mosi until Mfungo Mosi, a whole year. She spent Muharram with them, Maulid Nabi, Miraj, Ramadhan, Sikukuu Ndogo and Sikukuu Kubwa. She even sang a satirical song about the guest who stays and stays until she is removed by force, inviting them to protest that her presence was no imposition.

As always when she was around, and the passing of years seemed to make no difference to her, she made everything about her hum and buzz. There were visitors, of course, and visits to be returned. They had the mattresses unpacked, the kapok dried in the sun to rid it of smells and bugs, and then repacked in new marekani calico. She had the windows in the yard repaired and the walls whitewashed. Hassanali grumbled at the expense but he smiled as he did so. It made the yard clean and new, and made the plants seem lush and shapely in contrast. Aunt Mariam started a business, frying samosa and bajia which she made to order for functions and some for Hassanali to sell in the shop. Fishermen turned up at the yard door with strings of fish for sale, and she argued and debated with them as if she intended buying enough for a banquet rather than the handful they needed to accompany their rice or cassava or bananas. But the fishermen still came the next day, setting up a clamour by the yard door and sometimes handing over a fish without being asked, just for the pleasure of bargaining with Aunt Mariam.

Rehana could not stay in bed while all this was going on, she did not even want to. Aunt Mariam moved into her room with her, and bustled her out of bed at the same time as she got up, charming her irresistably into activity. She asked Rehana to read her a few pages of the Koran every day, because her eyes were going now, and she had never really been able to manage the big suras for herself, and she, Rehana, was such a good reader. At the age of ten Rehana could read the Koran from beginning to end, and some of it she knew by heart. (Although soon after that age she had to stop attending classes as she began to bleed and was therefore at peril.) Aunt Mariam persuaded Rehana to make dresses for her, as she used to for herself, and then praised the results to such an extent that other people wanted dresses made too. Finally, she persuaded Hassanali that it was time to think of taking a wife. She didn't say so, and perhaps she didn't even think it, but a wife for Hassanali would also be company for Rehana, and would lift both of them out of the muddle they had sunk into. She knew exactly the person, she told Hassanali, whenever he was ready, though it was best not to wait too long to decide. 'I would marry you myself,' she told Hassanali, 'if I didn't have so many other proposals from rich bachelors to think about.'

So Malika came, and brought happiness to Hassanali and allowed their lives to change. Rehana learned to think of Azad as a mistake she had made. She had no means to do anything about that mistake. She could try to have the marriage ended, but what would be the point? Time was against her. It was ten years since their mother died, and she was twenty-nine years old. Old. And there she was, Malika, the spinach all cleaned and now starting on dressing the fish, humming her lullaby or whatever it was, probably thinking of what she and Hassanali would be doing to each other when he came in for his rest. For now that Malika was there, he had taken to shutting the shop for a couple of hours after lunch, for a rest. It made Rehana smile to herself, even though she also felt envious of them. She rose to her feet and held the finished dress out away from her, turning it round to see that all was well. She felt some satisfaction at the thought of the woman who would come later in the afternoon to collect the dress she had brought to her for making. She thought she would be pleased. She folded the dress and sat down again, and as she did so she felt the book she had taken from the wounded man bump against her thigh. She could not believe that she had thought he was Azad, the man who taught her longing and loathing in equal measure, and taught her to loathe herself even more than him. He is not coming back, thank God, because what would she do if he turned up? What was she to do with the mzungu's book? She couldn't even read the words it was written in, and it was certain to be in his language. She couldn't throw it away now, because the man who collected their rubbish for burning always rummaged to see if there was anything worth saving for sale, and when he found the book would take it to the government European and report them as thieves, in case of a reward or a handout. She could bury it, although if that was discovered it would look like sorcery or the malicious fantasy of a disturbed woman. She would have to carry it around like a burden, hiding it until discovery, or until her death, when people would mock her for her petty spinsterish pilferings.

4 Pearce

T HEY SAT ON THE veranda after a supper of goat-stew and rice. Burton, the manager of the estate at Bondeni, had come to meet the invalid and make acquaintance. He was a thick-set man, with tangled black hair and a sternly trimmed moustache. The care of the trimming made him seem fussy, Martin thought. In his baggy clothes, he looked lumpy and perhaps unwell, but had looked worse when he arrived in his khakis. Since sunset, they had been steadily consuming, gin and lime juice for Burton, Scotch and water for Frederick and Martin. He kept pace with them for a while, although without their thirst and relish, and drank so as not to appear unfriendly or tiresome. Once they were well set in their bickering conversation about the future of the Empire, their voices raised as they became heated, Frederick lost interest in topping up Martin's glass and left him to his own devices, only calling upon him now and then to take sides with him on some issue or another.

Burton wanted no allies, quite sure that the future for British possessions in Africa was the gradual decline and disappearance of the African population, and its replacement by European settlers. It would happen inevitably, unavoidably, in his firmly-held opinion, so long as events were left to themselves and there was no interference from busybody officials, or at least not obstructive interference of the kind that prattled on about responsibility for the welfare of the native.

Martin thought there was something staged about the

exchanges, Englishmen in the colonies talking seriously about public issues. Burton's voice even became crisper, raised in register, precise with authority. It could have been for his benefit, but perhaps it was also for their own, to make themselves feel significant and present in the world. Never mind the loneliness or the servants or the illnesses or the nagging anxiety about being where they were and doing what they were doing. There was the world to worry about. It was the way men talked after a drink or two, suppressing the petty discomforts of every day with talk of grand affairs.

'This continent has the potential to be another America,' Burton said, speaking with stubborn emphasis, as if he expected to be received sceptically. 'But not as long as the Africans are here. Look at this region. The niggers here have been corrupted by the Arabs, by their religion and their . . . their perfumed courtesies. The Arabs themselves do not amount to much. They are mostly bluster, not capable of a day's work unless their lives depended on it or there is a bit of loot and pillage in it. Before we came this way, this was pirate country. When the winds were right, the Arabs came raiding all along the coast, kidnapping and looting at will, making slaves. When the winds turned they sped back to their caves to play with their booty. The sooner they are impoverished and expelled, the better.'

'Maybe so,' Frederick said, conceding the point about the Arabs, but looking for mischief. Martin had already heard enough to understand that Burton said the ugly things and Frederick deliberately provoked him into excess. 'But you'll have to admit they brought a bit of order to these parts. You'll have to admit that.'

Burton took his time, swishing the gin in the glass contentedly, and when he spoke his voice was mild, resisting Frederick's prodding. 'Despite the pretence of order that the Sultan of Zanzibar represents, without our presence here this would return to pirate country in one season. The savage African in the interior, now that's a different animal altogether. He is doomed, what's left of him. He will just pine and starve and die off in the encounter with civilisation. No need to bleat to me about morality or responsibility. It's inevitable, it's scientific. There is no cruelty in this outcome, and it has happened everywhere, again and again, in exactly the same way.'

'I'm inclined to think you derelict in your duty as a servant of the Empire,' Frederick said in a pompous voice that was meant to signal that he was not serious about the charge. 'To tell you the truth, I'm inclined to think you derelict in humanity. I do have a responsibility to the natives, to keep an eye on them and guide them slowly into obedience and orderly labour.'

'That is precisely what I mean, obstructive interference. The more we do for them,' Burton said, his voice rising again, 'the more they will demand, without having to work for any of it. In time they'll expect us to feed them while they carry on with their barbarisms. They will hate us and still expect us to have their welfare as our obligation. They will see it as their entitlement. You won't get much orderly labour out of them, not left to themselves.'

'That is why I said guide them,' Frederick said. '*That* is our responsibility.'

'Force them, you mean,' Burton said. 'You can only make them work by coercion and manipulation, not by making them understand that there is something moral in working and achieving. For us. They won't understand that. That's why they still wear skins and live in huts made of leaves and dung. They are quite content with that, and will kill to defend that way of life. You can talk as much as you like about responsibility, but if you want prosperity and order in Africa you have to have European settlement. Then we can turn this into another America.'

'We'll have to murder to achieve that,' Frederick said, glaring, and then took a large gulp of his Scotch. 'Though the way you're talking, it doesn't seem that you think that is such a terrible thing.'

'No, yours is a position deficient in intellectual manhood,' Burton replied amiably. Martin saw that Burton had slipped away from Frederick's provocation and was now provoking him in his turn. 'We are already murdering them. We murder them to make them obey us. In reality we simply have to leave them to their own devices without interference and they will do their dying themselves.'

Martin listened silently to their unwearying reiteration of their difference from the niggers, which had now come to mean more or less everyone they had forced to submit to their rule. It was not only the British. He had listened to similar exchanges between other Europeans, the French and the Dutch, or even Poles or Swedes who had no natives to rule over or pronounce imminent doom upon. He had a reaction to this kind of talk. It made him feel ill. It made him feel nervous of being overheard. He wondered if Burton had sensed his distaste for what he was saying, and was exaggerating to irritate him, or whether it was the gin.

'Come, come, Pearce, I mean Martin, old fellow,' Frederick said, slightly drunk and slightly tetchy, perhaps because Pearce would not take sides against the vulgar fantasy Burton was entertaining. 'What think ye of all this? Here we are, 1899, what thought of the new century? Will we do better than our resolute predecessors? Will this place be cleared of its natives, and be turned into a kind of America, or will we see these chumps become civilised and hard-working subjects? Come, let's hear from you, my good sir.'

'I think in time we'll come to see what we're doing in places like these less heroically,' Martin said. 'I think we'll come to see ourselves less charmingly. I think in time we'll come to be ashamed of some of the things we have done.'

'An anti-Empire wallah,' Frederick said delightedly. 'Come now, Burton, let's hear what you think of that.'

'As for these beasts we have come so far out of our way to improve,' Martin continued, at the same time wishing he had not spoken at all, 'we owe them care for the way we have intruded in their ways of life.'

Burton turned away with a look of sneering disgust. 'We don't owe them anything but patience,' he said, 'until their time comes. Like the same patience you would show a dying animal. We didn't make them live and die like beasts. All that we owe them is the patience to allow them to put themselves out of their misery.'

'Burton, you sound like a beast yourself sometimes,' Frederick said, making a face of distaste. 'I have no doubt you're right, Martin, especially when we come to recall these ugly prophecies Burton is so fond of. I don't expect it'll be any better than the century we're limping out of. You can't expect much of any century that closes off its account by snuffing out a mind like Oscar Wilde in the way that it has.'

'Oscar Wilde!' Pearce exclaimed, laughing. 'Oh, we've done a lot worse than that.'

'I tell you, if I thought Burton was going to turn out right in his predictions,' Frederick said, stumbling slightly over his words, 'I'd pack up and go home tomorrow and to hell with the Empire. These are fantasies of those lunatics Burton spent so much time with down there in South Africa. Greedy Englishmen and Dutch fanatics have fuddled his sharp scientific mind with their predictions of extinguished races. That is *not* what the empire is about. You never heard any of that kind of talk in India.'

'Africa is not India,' Burton said. 'And even there, what the empire has shown is that Indian ways are antiquated. There is no point to them any more. The best they can do is allow themselves to be superseded by us, to imitate us as best they can. But even that is better than what we have here. India is an antiquated civilisation which has come to the end of its useful life. Here there is nothing but beasts and savagery.'

'You are such a ranter,' Frederick said, filling up the glasses. 'If you think they're such beasts, why are you teaching them cricket?'

'For the comedy. It's certainly not because I think there is a Ranjitsinhji among them,' Burton said, smiling at his own struggles with the name.

Martin got up late the following morning, feeling exhausted from the effects of the drink. His early morning tea was cold by his bed, and Hamis had rolled up the mosquito net without waking him. He found Frederick at his desk, in white shirt and baggy khaki short-pants, knee-length stockings and shiny brown shoes, still writing his report on the previous year's customs and tax returns. Burton had left for the estate at first light. 'On his donkey,' Frederick said, leaning back, smiling. 'You get all sorts in the colonies, don't you? He'll be back on his estate this morning, striding about and pitching in as if he's one of them, up to his thighs in muddy ditches. If he's in the mood later this evening, he'll sit with his workers and have a sing-song, or tomorrow afternoon he'll turn them out for a game of cricket. Then in a few days he'll be back here on my veranda saying how they are all dying from encountering civilisation, and we simply have to wait for them to perish like dying animals. He likes to act the hard man, the practical and unsentimental technician who is only interested in efficiency. Yet he's something of a thinker, very serious about his work. How're you feeling? You look a bit . . . under the weather. Still exhausted, I should think. Terribly hot this morning.'

'I don't think I'm made of the same stern material as you two when it comes to drink. There you are, clean-shaven and blooming, smiling happily and dutifully turning the wheel of Empire, whereas I feel like something evacuated by a beast. Hamis brought me my tea and rolled up the mosquito net, and I didn't even wake,' Martin said.

Frederick laughed. 'Oh, I'm sure it's only because you're still exhausted. We'll have you hardened up in no time at all. Actually, I'm not sure I can take this stuff quite as I used to. It wears you down in the heat. Yes, Hamis can be quite subtle about his duties. Do you think there's anything in this idea that blacks have a natural instinct for such things? Who was it who said something about the black man being ideally suited for the avocation of one's person? Was it Dr Johnson? No, it was Melville. That story about a slave rebellion. He writes a rough-hewn prose, I think, but perhaps appropriate to his subject. Ha, try getting one of those Masai warriors to avocate about your person. It will be short of one or two vital items in no time, if the stories are to be believed. I was thinking about your trudge across the wilderness out there this morning, and all the terrible ordeals you had to go through. No, no, my dear Pearce, there's no need to make light of them, although I would've done the same thing myself if I'd had the fortitude and courage to survive such ordeals. I was thinking about those murderous cut-throats who were your guides and protectors, and their thoroughly disgraceful treachery. Who can fathom the minds of these people? I remember you said something about struggling through that terrifying landscape on your own, and I know then, at the time, I thought of Browning's 'Childe Roland', you know, and that terrible passage to the Tower. I don't like Browning, do you? I can't get on with him, all that enjambment sticks in my throat. But this morning I thought no, not Browning at all. Not 'Childe Roland', but Swinburne. Swinburne is the one. Are you a poetry man, Martin? It was something you said last night about the new century. I had a look at Swinburne this morning and found these lines. They are quite improbable, you might think, and nothing to do with what you said, but I hear an echo there. I hope you don't mind, I marked them to read to you:

> Only the wind here hovers and revels
> In a round where life seems barren as death.

The poem's nothing to do with landscape, I know – all about the death of love and so on, good old Swinburne – but it was that image of a forsaken place, a wilderness parched and cruel when once it must have been otherwise. I wondered whether you were right, whether despite all our efforts, what has been eating out the heart of this continent will eat out the rest, and there'll be nothing left here after us.'

Frederick looked at Martin for a long moment, his eyes round and molten. Martin looked back silently, unable to think of anything to say. He saw that Frederick was moved by his own words, his own thoughts, and he felt he should say something in return, but he was struck dumb by the self-regard in Frederick's expression, nothing left here after us. Frederick smiled, 'You're right. There's nothing we can do about it so we might as well do our best and, well, make the most of it. I think I can smell the coffee. So Martin, what are you planning today? Shall I lend you Swinburne? Do you think he's a great poet? He's incorrigibly gloomy and a pukka grumbler, but by God he can write. Would you care to put your feet up and wallow in a bit of penance and remorse?'

'I thought I might go down to the water and take a stroll along the beach,' Martin said, glancing over his shoulder towards the veranda. Frederick rose from his desk and the two of them walked across to look at the bay.

'The sun's too strong for a stroll, I think,' Frederick said. 'Plenty of traffic down there as well, people have been sleeping on the beach. Look at that beach, look at the filth on it. I'll have to put some notices up when they've cleared off. Do Not Litter, by Order. Or Off With Your Heads. Too late this time. The monsoons are beginning to turn, that's why those boats are turning up from Mombasa and beyond, loading up. When you lift your eyes the bay looks lovely out there, doesn't it? No good for real shipping, though, especially when the monsoons begin. The swells can drive a ship aground in no time. Apparently it's worse when the north-easts are blowing. They had just finished when I arrived. The debris on the beach then had to be seen to be believed. They blow right into the bay and the sea comes up to the road there, and any ship caught in the bay then ends up on the beach or worse. Only those Bajun dhows and other local craft can manage around here. The rest have to anchor out in the roads round the headland. These winds beginning now are the south-wests, and the headland cuts out some of the swells. The dhows, they can snuggle into the curve of the bay safely. Do you see them? They'll load up there and take all the trade goods to Mombasa and Lamu to wait for the winds. It's been a good year, I'm told, and those are our customs duties down there. Except for the wretches who smuggle themselves out in the dark, the miserable malcontents. Can you see, down there in that shed? They're weighing everything that is being loaded on those boats, to make sure Her Brittanic Majesty gets her share in return for our calming presence here among them. It's quieter in the afternoon. We can go for a stroll then, and the sun is not so oppressive.'

'Thank you, this afternoon will be a perfect time,' Martin said, because he guessed that Frederick did not want him to go out into the crowd of people, but was too polite simply to forbid him. Could a District Officer forbid him from going for a walk? Frederick the Tyrant, in the antique and benign sense, who knows best and expects to be obeyed, even though he disguises caprice by understatement and self-deprecation. Well, his disapproval as a host so far-away from home was a kind of forbidding, especially when the guest had arrived in such a needy state. It would be ungrateful not to comply. Though what Frederick thought would happen to him in that throng of busy people Martin could not tell. Perhaps he feared he would be offended as he picked his way through the sparse bits of litter and the scattering of dead ashes from the cooking fires. Or perhaps he wanted to accompany him, to show him his dominion himself.

'Ah, here's the coffee. Then a good dose of Swinburne for you while I finish this damned report, then lunch,' said Frederick. 'I like lunch.'

They went for their walk in late afternoon, Frederick compact and blond in his baggy short-pants, the hair on the bare parts of his legs thick and golden like a pelt, a pipe gripped in his teeth through the lush bronze moustache. Martin assumed this was the public figure of the strolling colonial officer, a figure of relaxed authority. Martin himself was clean-shaven and had had a haircut but was still in borrowed long trousers that were not long enough for him. The frantic activity of the morning and early afternoon had subsided, and they passed people sitting outside houses, or strolling or sitting under a tree, and boys running on the beach or swimming. 'It's only a tiny dilapidated town,' Frederick said, frowning, ignoring the remarks shouted at them from amidst a group of young men sitting in the shade of a tree but returning the greetings of the older men with a small salute of his own. 'But it has a lot of history. Some of it is pretty fanciful, I must say, Egyptians and Greeks sailing down this way for ivory in ancient times, that kind of thing. There's a persistent one of a runaway Persian prince who establishes a kingdom which founds the mongrel Swahili *civilisation*,' Frederick bared his teeth as he said the last word but it was not clear whether he was smiling or snarling. Perhaps he was only wincing at the word, to indicate its inappropriateness in the context. 'The Persian came down here on his magic carpet, no doubt. There's some truth in it, I'm sure, but it's dressed up in exotic rubbish to beguile idlers. I suspect the people who built these old towns were the same ones that Burton was calling pirates last night, and not runaway princes of any kind. What we do know is that when the Portuguese arrived here this was already a prosperous place, a rival to Mombasa. There was trade with China, so it's said, although I have my doubts about that. If the Chinese came all this way in the fifteenth century, why did they then turn around and go back? It's a long way to China, why didn't they stay and take charge down here?'

'Perhaps because they decided that there wasn't anything here that was better than what they had at home,' Martin said.

Frederick looked at him with a grin and then nodded. 'Well said, old chap. Anyway, by the time the Portuguese finished with this town, it was not much more than a decaying coastal settlement. You know what they were like, plunder and loot and fanaticism. Then the town almost disappeared, under assault from the Galla and the whatnots from the interior, who camped and defecated on the ruins for centuries, until the sultan in Zanzibar decided to revive it. The land is poor but productive enough, and we're introducing new crops all the time. There's a future, I think.'

As they walked past the mosque on the seafront, Martin hesitated. A group of older men were sitting on the baraza outside, all bearded, some eminently grey, some turbanned. The court-yard door, which was painted with a green wash, was open, and

Martin saw two doors along the side of the wall of the mosque proper. He took a step backwards and saw that there was a third door, and when he saw that he smiled, recognising the traditional architectural style even in a mosque of this modesty, even this far-away from its origins. One of the men said something and Martin's smile broadened, and then Martin said something back. The men shuffled interestedly, smiling and exchanging gleeful surprised looks while further exchanges followed. Martin waved to the men and they walked on.

'My dear Pearce, I am most thoroughly impressed,' Frederick said. 'What were they saying?'

'Oh, the first man said it's a good time for a stroll, and I said perhaps he should join us. Then he said he has already had his exercise. Just pleasantries. I'd love to see the inside of the mosque, another time,' Martin said, glancing at Frederick's short-pants.

'How come you speak the language? You're not some kind of . . . er, government . . . representative, are you?'

Martin laughed. 'Do you mean a spy? He spoke in Arabic, and I've been in Egypt this last year and a bit, advising in the department of education. Interfering, rather. And intefering in the department of antiquities whenever they let me, looking at buildings and charts. I think I learned a great deal more than the unfortunates who had to listen to my advice.'

'Of course you were, silly of me,' Frederick said, leaning back to give Martin a frank admiring look. 'I can stir a bit of Hindustani myself, especially if I don't have to understand what the other fellow is saying. Well, it's impressive nevertheless. I should commandeer you and keep you here. Burton can push a bit of Swahili, but I don't think he could describe the destiny of British possessions in Africa in that language. It's more carry that, bring this, and don't ever do that again. It doesn't sound right when you hear him in spate. How he gets that estate to function as remarkably as it does is a mystery. And talking of Burton, he insisted that we visit him on the estate as soon as you feel up to it.'

'Yes,' Martin said softly.

'Oh, he's all right. He lets off steam after a drink, and gets frothy about the white man's destiny, but he's all right. He gets abrasive like that to provoke. I think he's a bit of a beachcomber, you know, ha ha ha.'

'I don't think I know what you mean,' Martin said.

'Well, you know, beachcomber. Those chaps in R. L. Stevenson who abandon ship for a bit of a fling with the native girls. Or am I thinking of Melville again? But R.L.S has plenty of beach-combers as well. I imagine Burton gets up to a bit of that up there on that estate. Oh God, I mustn't slander the poor fellow, take no notice of me, I'm just making it up.'

They followed the curve of the bay, leaving the edges of the town to their left. Soon, some thick gnarled vegetation forced them inland for a few yards, and when they rounded that they saw ruined stone buildings between them and the sea. 'Here you are,' Frederick said. 'The tomb and the mosque of the sherif. I can't tell you very much. You're the antiquities man. I'd say sixteenth century, after the Portuguese had finished with this place.'

The mosque had three arches along the side wall. Martin smiled again and almost said something to Frederick about Persians on a magic carpet but he did not. Some of the mortar had perished and there was no roof left, and the back wall had collapsed, but the mihrab wall was still standing, the mihrab itself in perfect condition. The surround of the mihrab was a square arch, within which was the pointed arch of the qibla. Above the mihrab was a tablet of a different stone, perhaps marble, with writing on it. The late afternoon sun reflected off the bare coral floor and glowed golden in the qibla enclosure. He stepped through the single arch of the other side wall, and saw graves and collapsed walls, and beyond that, partly in the shade of a huge mimosa tree, the pillared tomb of the sherif. Compared to the graves and the walls of the outbuildings, it was clear that the tomb was maintained. The pillar was whitewashed and unblemished, standing several metres high, higher than the lower branches of the mimosa. It rose from the head of the tomb, which was rectangular and open at the top. Each corner was formed into a small cupola, topped with a knob of brass or bronze. The tomb itself was not quite so well-maintained as the pillar, the repairs had not been whitewashed and some of the mortar had gone black with moss. Martin saw a porcelain plate set in the wall below the pillar, with ornate writing in Arabic script, too ornate for him to decipher at a glance. Martin again remembered his notebook, and wished he had it with him to make a drawing of the ruins and the tomb. It had been with him throughout his time in Abyssinia and Somalia, and even after his guides abandoned him, but he must have lost it in the scramble to safety.

'The tomb of Sherif Himidi,' Frederick announced, waving his pipe at the tomb. 'People come to make offering here. Take a look inside the tomb.'

Frederick smiled and nodded, encouraging, confident that Martin would find the invitation gratifying. The walls were too high for Martin to peer over, so Frederick made a step with his two cupped hands and Martin leaped up and sat on the side wall of the tomb. Rough grass grew in the tomb, and lying on it were several packets wrapped in cloth, some blue, some crimson, some cream, and some old and colourless and perished. Some were tied with twine. There was a miniature boat, three or four inches long, with a tiny mast and outriggers. Inside the boat was a round pouch wrapped in a strip of dried banana leaf. At the top end of the rectangular space, the pillar end, a carved piece of dark wood lay in the same alignment as the body might be expected to lie. Martin shifted on the wall and then leaned forward to take a closer look. As he did so, he felt a sharp stab in the side of his left buttock and thought he must have pressed against a broken piece of masonary. The carved piece of wood had some marks on it, crescents and lines, but no shape he recognised.

He leaped down from the wall and felt his knees give way under him as he landed on the ground. He was still so weak. Frederick looked at him with a suppressed smile, anticipating his surprised report. 'You thought there'd be some nasty bits of flesh, didn't you? Disembowelled rodents and crucified crows and that sort of thing. But no, only those bits of things apparently, and people pray to get better and to have sons and for safety at sea, that sort of thing. I'm tempted to purloin one of those packets, in the cause of science, of course, to see what's in it. But when I came this way before it was with my groom Idris, and he became thoroughly distraught at the idea, as if I proposed to interfere with the whole course of human destiny. What do you think is in them?'

Martin shrugged. 'Prayers written on parchment. A piece of quartz. A rosary.'

'Mumbo jumbo,' Frederick said. 'Nothing of any value, that's for certain, and it does no harm, I suppose. Did you know the original mumbo jumbo was bits of cloth tied to branches of trees? Mungo Park brought the phrase back from his travels in West Africa. Mungo Park. What kind of name is that? Mungo sounds like one of our native friends, doesn't it? Mungo jumbo. He sounds a bit of a wild Jock, old Mungo.'

It occurred to Martin to wonder how Frederick might describe himself: as a colonial idealist, something of a scholar of poetry, a bit of a rake, perhaps as a man of wit and subtle humour. 'I thought I saw a pouch of tobacco in a miniature boat,' Martin said, turning and beginning to walk back. He thought he would return later to try and decipher the writing on the porcelain plate in the wall.

'Perhaps the sherif was fond of snuff,' Frederick said, grinning. 'Is a sherif allowed snuff? He was apparently a bit of a poet, our sherif, which I think is a jolly good thing. It's all devotional chanting, I expect, but you might look into that, Pearce.'

'Yes,' Martin said.

'It's remarkable, isn't it, that these people have got by for centuries without writing anything down,' Frederick said, bending down to remove burrs from his stockings. 'Everything is memorised and passed on, and they have to wait until Bishop Steere turns up in Zanzibar in the 1870s before anyone thinks to produce a grammar. I think I'm right in saying that this is true all over Africa, am I not? It's a staggering thought, that no African language had writing until the missionaries arrived. And I believe that in several languages the only piece of writing that exists is translations from the New Testament. What a thought, eh? They haven't even invented the wheel yet. It shows what a long way they have to go yet.'

By the time they reached the house, the pain in Martin's back and hip was almost unbearable. His face was covered with sweat, and he dragged his left leg slightly. It took Frederick a while to notice Martin's increasing distress, and when he did they were only a short distance from the house. Frederick put an arm around Martin and helped him hobble the last few steps. They found out that Martin had been bitten. Hamis said it was a kenge, and by the gesture he made with forefinger and thumb to indicate the animal's jaws, they assumed it was a scorpion. The area around the bite was discoloured and darkening and beginning to swell. Martin lay on his right side while Hamis unhurriedly cleaned the bite with a rag and cold water, seeming untroubled by Frederick's urgings and questions. Is there an antidote? How dangerous? Pearce, dear fellow, you really have been in the wars, one thing after another. Then the cook came in with a bowl of greenish pap which he had prepared while Hamis cleaned the wound, and applied it as a poultice on the bite. It smelled strongly of mint. The cook propped Martin's body with cushions so he should not roll over, then Hamis tore a clean piece of rag and wiped Martin's sweating brow. He sighed with the relief these ministrations gave him and shut his eyes.

To Frederick's amazement, Martin was on his feet in time for supper. He called it another miracle: a day or two to recover from sunstroke, and only a few hours to shake off a scorpion bite. 'But perhaps it simply wasn't a scorpion bite,' Martin said as they sat on the veranda after supper. 'In any case, scorpion bites are not as lethal as their reputation, and the cook's cold compress was the perfect antidote. I think it was probably a centipede. Anyway, I must find a way of rewarding your servants . . .'

'No need, I've given them some coins in your name,' Frederick said, his hand held up, palm outwards to discourage any protests. 'Not much you can give them at the moment, is there, shorn as you are of your worldly goods. I told Hamis where we were when you were bitten, or rather where you were sitting. He was shocked. Apparently it's very bad manners to sit on the sherif's tomb. And what's worse for you, my dear Martin, is the prediction that if you are bitten by an insect while so sitting, you will be unable to leave this place. I do hope, for your sake, that the prediction is no more than gentle hocus on Hamis's part. Incidentally, there are some ruins a few miles south of here which we must visit when you're better. When you see them you'll wonder again, I'm sure, about civilisation. How could the people who made this have turned out as they have? I used to think this in India and I'm sure you must've thought it in Egypt and in your various travels. How could this chaotic, infantile host have descended from the builders of these magnificent monuments? It seems as if when inspiration deserts you, it deserts you completely.'

'Perhaps we should heed those words ourselves,' Martin said softly, reluctant to be drawn into Frederick's pronouncements and summaries.

'Ozymandias,' Frederick said, nodding. 'The hubris of empire, that's what you mean, isn't it? What seems massive and powerful today will be dust and ruins tomorrow. But Ozymandias was an oriental despot, my dear Martin, quite unlike our good rational selves. Would you not suppose this was what Shelley meant? That in the moment of our greatness we should remain true to our traditions of liberty and not be tempted into despotic hubris. Although when he wrote the poem he would have had no idea how much greatness lay ahead.'

After some minutes of silence, Frederick recited the whole poem to the cooling night breeze, having spent those few moments refreshing his memory of it. He delivered the final lines with prophetic emphasis:

<pre>
                              Round the decay
Of that colossal wreck, boundless and bare
The lone and level sands stretch away.
</pre>

And then he sighed. 'I don't think so, you know. I don't see much knocking our little edifice down. I think this will be the order of things for a long time to come. So don't visit your doom-mongering on us, my good sir.'

Martin smiled. 'Talking of visiting,' he said, weary now in an uncomplicated way. 'Tomorrow I would like to go and see the shopkeeper who found me, to thank him and his family for their kindness.'

Frederick looked doubtful, but nodded none the less. 'I'm not sure about kindness. They probably hoped for a bit of reward.'

'I would reward them if I could, although I would prefer to think it was kindness,' Martin said.

'There's a lot to be said for kindness,' Frederick said amiably. He put his glass down and scratched distractedly at a bite on his wrist. 'It's good of you to be so generous. Of course you must go and see them, if you wish. And if you'd like to reward them, I can advance something towards that, though I hardly think it's necessary. We got there pretty soon after they found you, a moment before one of their witch herbalists was about to start on you, in fact. Do you know what passes for medicine here? Mumbo jumbo pap and cauterisation. Slap the mumbo jumbo on or put a red-hot poker iron on it.'

'I'm happy to go on my own,' Martin said tetchily. 'I asked Hamis for directions this morning and it seems quite uncomplicated.' Hamis, Frederick's servant, had given him directions in his laconic style. Turn into the lane opposite the big tree near the tomb of the sherif, follow the street until you come to open ground, and there on your left is the shop, on your right is the café and opposite is the mosque. It sounded simple enough, but Frederick would have none of it. 'My dear Martin, my good fellow, you've already had one near miss, and you do seem prone to accidents and mishaps. Maybe more caution is advisable in the interim, at least until you recover your strength. Out of the question to go on your own into that filthy maze. We'll go together tomorrow morning.'

Martin would have preferred to make the visit unaccompanied, to stroll through the lanes without hurry until he found the square with the shop, the café and the mosque. 'I don't wish to make a ceremony of it,' he said mildly, too tired to argue.

'We won't,' Frederick said cheerfully. 'Just thank you chaps, and keep up the good work. Then back home for lunch.' He smiled with generous goodwill, offered Martin another drink, who declined, and filled up his glass. 'Concerning your affairs at large . . . if I may be so bold, dear friend. I'm expecting a mail detail any day now from Mombasa, and I wondered whether you had any post yourself, any arrangements you wished to make. You are welcome to stay here as long as you wish, rest and chat about Swinburne and the Empire to your heart's delight. I feel contented with your company and am delighted to discover a new friend, if I may be so brash.' He raised his glass in a salute, genially tipsy.

'Thank you,' Martin said, and felt his eyes prickle at the ingratitude of his earlier impatience. 'You have been very kind. I'll write a letter to the consul in Aden. He knows of the arrangements I made with the luggage and effects I left behind, and he can also arrange to have funds sent to me in Mombasa. If I may impose on you until the funds . . .'

'Don't mention it. I am grateful for the company. And now it looks to me as if you're ready for bed,' Frederick said, then slapped himself irritably on his left ear, spilling some of his drink. 'Damn them. The bloody mosquitoes are busy tonight. It's the fault of all that ragamuffin sleeping on the beach, no doubt. They must've brought them with them. Their voices irritate me, all that tuneless wailing and shouting, such a racket.' He relit his pipe from a splinter he kept beside the parrafin lamp, and leaned back with a sigh.

As it turned out, the mail boat from Mombasa arrived the next morning. The messenger was a neat, courteous Mombasan, in white shirt and khaki trousers, a clerk's habit, who stood with hands crossed behind his back while Frederick frowned about what to do. In the end he was forced to excuse himself from accompanying Martin in order to complete his paperwork, so that the messenger, who had expressed a wish to return as soon as possible because of the changing winds, could leave early the following day. The messenger offered his thanks and left, smilingly refusing offers of food or bed. Martin had written the letter to the consul in Aden before breakfast and was otherwise unencumbered except by Swinburne, but he was not to be left to his own devices as he had begun to hope. Frederick sent for the wakil who had taken him to the shop the first time.

'I've had some more to do with the character,' Frederick said, smiling wickedly. 'And I'm beginning to think he might be useful. He has been calling at the office downstairs every day, to enquire after your health and to offer his services. He stands there, hand-wringing and cork-screwing, but with a sharp glint of cunning behind his deferential airs. I liked the no-nonsense manner he dealt with the crowd at the shop when we came to collect you. It was merely display, of course, seeing as the little pest has no authority at all, but I'm beginning to think I can make use of that display for government's ends. He also speaks some kind of English and is educated up to a fashion and understands the nature of process. He thought himself cunning, but I think I can be even more cunning than him. I hope you won't think me boastful for saying that, but my experience has been that native cunning only goes so far. And I imagine that the unctuous gentleman will be a useful tool now and then.'

So, Frederick sent for the wakil and asked him as a favour to the government to accompany Mr Pearce to the dukawallah who had found him several days ago. It was late in the morning by the time they set off. The wakil had had no dealings with Martin, no acknowledgement of his visits to enquire after him, and was not certain of the nature of this visit to Hassanali, so he smiled and led off. Martin could see that he expected to make himself adaptable to whatever was required. It was a hot, bright morning and the wakil had brought an umbrella with him, which he opened and held over Martin's head like a canopy.

'La la, ma'esh,' Martin said, stepping away.

The wakil gave Martin a quick look of surprise, and no doubt made some adjustments. He replied in Arabic, and it was Martin's turn to be surprised. Yes, he spoke some rough Arabic, a tiny amount of terrible English, and some Swahili. You can't do business without Arabic here. But how is it that you speak Arabic? the wakil asked. Martin explained that he had lived in Egypt. Ah, the wakil said, Britannia is everywhere in the world.

The wakil was right, it was a very hot still morning, but since Martin refused to have the umbrella held over his head, the wakil did not protect himself either, out of politeness. It was cooler when they turned into the lanes, and Martin stopped for a moment in this comparative gloom to get accustomed to the light. He walked slowly after the wakil, who had stridden ahead several paces before realising that Martin was not hurrying. There was an unusual but familiar smell in the alleys, the smell of age and human paltriness: the open gutters, the blackened streams of waste, the dilapidated houses tumbled over each other and penetrated with decades of condensed sweat and human breath. It was a smell of something like healing flesh, drying mud, a smell about to turn to illness and decay, to bubble up a balloon of dead gas. It was malarial air. People sat in the midst of it, and lived and traded, and suckled their young and sang them to sleep. So Martin took a deep breath and bid himself to become accustomed to it. Children smiled shyly at him and called him mzungu. He smiled back. Older men looked him up and down without saying anything, at his sandals, his baggy clothes, his cropped hair, and could not restrain a smile. Mzungu hafifu, one of them called out. A feeble European. Everyone laughed, and so did Martin, which made them laugh even more, because they assumed he had no idea they were laughing at him. Other shouts followed, ugly names which made everyone chortle and splutter: kelb, sheitan, majnoon, punda. Dog, devil, madman, donkey. Most of the words were borrowings from Arabic.

'Anafahamu,' the wakil shouted out, waving his umbrella at the nearest revellers. He understands. There was more laughter, and people came to the doors of their houses to look at the mzungu who understood. There were more shouts and more laughter, but the ribaldry was now beyond both of them, Martin guessed. Certainly he could not understand more than a word now and then. The merriment sounded as if it was still good-natured so he shrugged to show his bewilderment and waved, the village idiot pretending not to take offence in order to disarm his tormentors. One or two waved back, and then suddenly the children turned their attention to the wakil. Kumbaro, they shouted. Martin did not know the word, but he saw the wakil take firm hold of his umbrella and glare at the children. Kumbaro, kumbaro, anakumba uharo, they chanted, dancing out of the reach of the wakil's umbrella. A woman came out of a doorway, took hold of one of the children and gave him a mighty slap on his cheek. You don't have any manners, she yelled, and gave the boy another mighty slap on the same cheek. The boy burst into a heart-broken wail and ran in the other direction, stumbling and slipping in the rutted path, blinded by tears. The woman ran after him, calling him by name, herself distraught.

They stepped into the square and Martin glanced at the wakil to see if he shared his sense of relief. It was as if they had walked through a large house and witnessed its domestic intimacies. So for a moment he did not take in the openness and orderliness of the square, the proper and fitting dimensions of the mosque in one corner, its blue doors open now in mid-morning, the fields beyond, the café with marble-topped tables, the neat houses and the billowing curtains that screened the doorways. When he did, he made a small noise of pleasure, a hum through his nostrils that was both recognition and approval. This is what we mean by beauty, he thought, this composure, this balance, and he felt his eyes smart with homesickness even though nothing in front of him looked like England.

The wakil pointed to their left with his busy umbrella, then waggled his head gently and smiled. Even before they reached the shop, Martin saw that their approach was causing consternation. One of the men sitting on the bench rose to his feet and looked towards the shop, shouting a warning, and some of the children who had followed them out of the alleys raced ahead to find a good place to view the forthcoming spectacle. The other men on the bench were also on their feet when they reached the shop. They shook hands with the wakil and then with Martin, who had no choice but to give himself up to the melee of greeting and hand-shaking, as if he was an honoured guest at a wedding. He turned towards the shop, with its display of baskets and chests of goods arranged in a cascade of rice and beans and twists of ginger and lumps of salt and gouts of tamarind, and when his eyes became used to the gloom, he saw the shopkeeper on his feet, shoulders hunched, braced for misuse. Martin raised his hand in greeting and the shopkeeper saluted back. The crowd had now formed a tight arc around him, despite the wakil's best efforts with his umbrella. Martin reached across the merchandise and offered his hand, and he saw a smile appear on the shopkeeper's face before he reached forward and grasped it. The shopkeeper climbed down from his platform and opened the side door to his shop and stepped out. The crowd loosened and spread out, the tension in them beginning to slacken, and Martin realised that they had all expected him to arrive with hauteur and demands, a repetition, perhaps, of Frederick's earlier visit. The shopkeeper shook hands again, smiling with a kind of modesty, relieved. But Martin saw that even as he smiled and shook his hand, his eyes were distracted by the closeness of the crowd to his unguarded merchandise, so he turned towards the crowd and waved to them to leave, asking them to show favour, please. Anafahamu, the wakil explained, and waved his umbrella at the crowd as if it was a magic broom that would sweep them all away. After a few such sallies the crowd retreated reluctantly but refused to disperse. The three old men returned to their bench and the shopkeeper was able to turn to Martin with a less troubled smile.

'I came to thank you for your kindness,' Martin said. 'I am Martin.'

The shopkeeper nodded to show that he had understood and gave his name, Hassanali, and Martin nodded back. The wakil nodded too, approving these exchanges. Perhaps it wasn't what he had expected but Martin guessed that for a man as worldly as he took the wakil to be, there was always method in everything, and the possibility of some advantage in anything. Mashaallah, mashaallah, the old men said, marvelling at Martin's Arabic. He loved the way his halting knowledge of the language had always won him friends in his travels, and now here too. He was not at a loss to understand why. After a few minutes of such cordial exchanges, Martin was seated on the bench with the old men, who made room for him when normally, perhaps, they spread themselves out more luxuriously, and submitted himself to an interrogation. The bench was in the shade and a breeze blew from the direction of the mosque, but Martin felt himself sweating heavily. The wakil waved his umbrella furiously at the crowd, and each time he waved another small section of the crowd dispersed. Martin saw that Hassanali was reluctant to leave them and serve his customers, and that the wakil stayed nearby, leaning on his umbrella in front of the bench, keeping an eye on things, reluctant to give up charge of him. The self-assured craggy-faced man with a stubbly grey beard led the proceedings. He touched Martin lightly on the thigh and told him his name was Hamza bin Masuud, and this one was Ali Kipara and that one there was Jumaane.

'So,' Hamza said, speaking slowly in Arabic so that everyone should understand, 'Mashaallah, you have amazed us, o sheikh mzungu. I have travelled from Lindi to Kismayu and even to Aden, and I never came upon a mzungu who spoke Arabic or Kiswahili. If you had spoken when we found you a few days ago, looking like a corpse, and had spoken to us in Arabic, and had spoken thus at that dangerous hour, I think we would have taken you for a servant of the infernal one. Tell us, ya Martin, how has this come to be and what brought you this way, walking in rags and so close to death. Tell us.'

It could have been an opening to a new episode in *One*

Thousand and One Nights, an invitation to begin a tale. So he did, keeping everything brief although he could see that his listeners had plenty of time and were eager for more details. He had been travelling with a hunting expedition in the interior, but they wanted to go even further to the west, so he then decided to come down to the coast.

On his own?

No, no, but on the way he had been separated from his guides and had had to get here on his own.

Who were these guides? They must have robbed him and abandoned him. Were they savages?

Somali.

A Msomali never gets lost. They must have robbed you. You are very lucky to be with us, ya Martin. God looked after you, say alhamdulillah, say thank you God. And your health? Is it restored? Your brothers and your children will be very relieved to hear that.

It was the shopkeeper he had come to thank, who was now back in his shop, glancing towards their conclave with some anxiety. He saw Hassanali call for someone inside, and saw the shadow of a woman in the gloom of the doorway at the back of the shop. He wondered if that was the woman Frederick had said was feeding him some kind of muck when they arrived to rescue him. A while later, when Martin was politely listening to tales of other wanderers who had been lost and how they had found their way home, he saw the woman in the shadow of the door again and saw Hassanali rise to collect a white porcelain jar from her, which he passed on to the wakil who passed it to Martin. It was lime juice, he could smell its freshness. Only one jar came out and Martin hesitated, but the wakil waved him on officiously. Drink, drink. He offered the jar to the men on the bench, all of whom wordlessly refused, making graceful gestures of gratitude. So Martin drank the lime juice greedily, and was himself grateful for the contentment it gave him. At that moment, the muadhin began the call for the noon prayers, and the old men and most of what was left of the crowd started on their way towards the mosque or home. Hassanali came down from his perch and invited Martin to join them for lunch. Nothing very lavish, only their usual midday meal, and the wakil too can stay if he wishes. Martin protested that he had put Hassanali and his household to enough trouble, that he had simply come to thank them for their kindness and not to impose on them further, that he was already too deeply in their debt. No need lunch, the wakil said in English. This man asking good politeness. No sir, lunch with DO.

But Martin wanted to stay, and had made his reluctant flourishes out of courtesy, to give the shopkeeper the chance to withdraw. Would they have enough food? He guessed the instruction would have gone out some time back when the woman first came to the door. He wanted to stay because of the way Frederick told the story of his rescue from their hands, his suspicion of them when Martin knew there was nothing for them to rob him of, the disdain with which he imagined Frederick treated them. The story of how Frederick returned to shout at them and shake them filled him with embarrassed anguish. How he had raised his riding crop at the shopkeeper and said to him: If you're lying to me, you black dog, I'll whip the skin off your back. Frederick himself had told the tale, making mock-thunder and terrible operatic faces, standing up on the veranda to demonstrate, right hand raised, still clutching his cigar, while the left held a glass. The buffoonery on the veranda may have been an exaggeration, but Martin was sure the ugly threats were not. He wanted to stay and do something that was uncomfortable to him, to sit with them in their modest house and eat their modest food, and struggle to find conversation with them. Not to shake hands and leave a few coins, thank you chaps, but to show them that he felt nothing but gratitude, no suspicion and no disdain. So in the end he sent the wakil back with a message to Frederick that Hassanali the shopkeeper would personally deliver him home later in the afternoon.

Hassanali shut the shop with deliberate care, or perhaps was taking his time in the great heat, and then he took his guest into the house through the backyard door. He called out and pushed open the door, and ushered his guest into the yard. There was no one in sight. The yard was white and green, whitewashed walls and green windows and lush bushes growing in pots: roses and lavender and a pale green bush with leaves like geraniums whose scent, he knew, would fill the night air. On his right was a thatched awning on poles, with a mat in interlocking patterns of blue, green and pink spread out underneath it. To his surprise, the food was already laid out on the mat, and covered with a cream cloth to keep off the flies and dust. How had they prepared for an additional eater so quickly? Hassanali showed him the washroom at the end of the yard, which to Martin's relief was dark but clean. He had no idea what they would have managed to get together in the hour or so since his invitation to lunch, but in such matters the thought was weightier than whatever splendour was on offer. He thought he had smelled rice and fish, and there was bound to be fruit. He had never seen such a variety of fruit as there was in this town.

Hassanali invited him to sit on the mat, smiled to see him remove his sandals first and then went to the washroom himself, while Martin sat on his own, conscious of being watched by the woman who must be inside, looking out at him from the gloom of one of the windows. When Hassanali came back out from the washroom, his grey-flecked moustache glistening with moisture, he went inside the house and returned followed by two women. His first thought was that they were his wives. Hassanali pointed at him and said his name, a smile on his face. The younger woman smiled too, but the other one looked at him with beautiful glowing brown eyes and did not smile. That was what he saw first, those eyes.

'I hope it will not offend you if we eat together,' she said to him in Arabic, correctly, not unfriendly. 'We always do.'

'This is a great kindness, thank you,' Martin said.

They sat down on the mat, Martin struggling with his knees and ankles and feet, which seemed to jut out at all angles while his hosts seemed effortlessly comfortable with their joints. When the cloth was removed, he saw a platter of rice, and a variety of other dishes served separately: spinach, fried fish, a vegetable stew, potatoes cooked with rosemary, and flat bread sprinkled with sesame seeds. Hassanali poured water from a brass kettle for Martin to wash his hands and then offered the same service to the other two. They all ate from the same platter, using their hands and reaching for handfuls of the side dishes as they wished.

'It's delicious,' Martin said after a mouthful. No one responded so he too kept quiet and concentrated all his faculties on making as little mess as he could. He was distracted by the closeness of the women's hands and wished he could glance up at the elder of the two wives.

Once the initial rush was past, Hassanali interrupted his rapid and efficient consumption with conversation. His Arabic was halting, and he had to make many appeals for help to his sister Rehana (ah!), who had a gift for the language, as their father did. When Hassanali appealed to Rehana for assistance, Martin too had a long look at her. She had pulled the shawl off her head and thrown it across her shoulders, like a scarf, so it would not get soiled in the food. At times Rehana had to take over the conversation for a moment or two when Hassanali faltered, and Martin gave her his full attention with a kind of disbelief at the anguishing beauty of her eyes and the delicate movements of her face. She did not smile much, and did not look down or away when he stared at her while she spoke, so he did not either. He felt a charge growing between them, and looked away reluctantly in the end, in case he gave offence. He guessed that they all saw him staring at her, and felt his colour rising at his discourtesy. What would they think of him? To go into these people's house and stare at the women.

'Was it you who was giving me food when they came?' he asked her, starting again what he had really come here to do. Oh my God, get out of here if you can't behave with courtesy. She nodded. He continued: 'I came to thank you all for your kindness, and to apologise for the suspicion that fell on you. It was a human thing you did, and I am for ever in your debt for your kindness . . .'

'No, no, apologies are due from us,' Hassanali interrupted. 'We did not even come to ask after you, for fear of causing offence to your government brother, when keeping away was a greater offence to God and the kindness He asks that we extend to each other. We did not know how we would speak to you either. So we kept away out of fear of the angry mzungu when we really wanted to know that you were recovered and getting better.'

And so on, in a happy few minutes of generosity and mellifluous courtesies. But Martin was all the time aware of Rehana beside him, and turned to look at her at every opportunity. She listened to Hassanali's enthusiastic friendliness with an ironic and mildly disbelieving smile. How could he find out about her? What did he want from her? Was she married? Was it right? How could he see her again? Did he dare? Stop this ridiculous nonsense. What had come over him? If nothing else, just to see her, to look at her and watch her face move and her eyes glow, to take pleasure in seeing her. When it was time to say goodbye, he said: I hope I'll see you again soon, but he said that in a way which included all of them, when what he really wanted was to say it to her.

An Interruption

I DON'T KNOW HOW it would have happened. The unlikeliness of it defeats me. Yet I know it did happen, that Martin and Rehana became lovers. Imagination fails me and that fills me with sorrow. I had thought that even without knowing the details of their affair I would be able to get to the truth of it, for imagination is a kind of truth. I do not mean that as a Romantic solipsism: it is only what I am able to imagine that is true. I mean that even with very incomplete knowledge, we can imagine what might have been, and how it might have come about and proceeded, but I find that in the case of Martin and Rehana I cannot settle on a sequence of events that seems likeliest.

Or perhaps I am reluctant to imagine it, as I have found myself doing with the events that preceded this moment, out of a squeamish reluctance to intrude into affairs that could only have been constructed out of unlikely subtleties. Perhaps I am reluctant out of fear that I will find myself unable to resist repeating the cliché of the miraculous in imagining such an encounter. I don't want to find myself saying they fell in love as soon as they caught sight of each other and the rest followed, that they looked into each other's eyes and into each other's souls and abandoned every other demand that circumstances made on them. Can that kind of thing be true? Do such things happen? And even if they do, how can they be written? The predictability of such a banal explanation makes me squirm with disbelief. It's our age. We think we know that the miracle is a lie and we always look for the hidden or suppressed explanation. We would rather have greed and lust as motive than love. We are reassured by slyly mocking references to our squalor, our smells and our expulsions, than to our trembling modesty, or to our quivering desire for affection. We are not even allowed souls any more, and our secret inner spaces are merely sites of unresolved turmoil, raw with throbbing wounds.

None the less, whether I am able to imagine it or not, I know that Rehana Zakariya and Martin Pearce became lovers. I have no choice but to try and give an account of how their affair might have happened. Martin arrived back at Frederick's house, his head pounding from the glare and the heat. His mind was turning on Rehana's fluid face, the movements of her features and the complicated depth in her dark eyes. He shook hands with Hassanali, who had insisted on accompanying him to the door, and thanked him for his hospitality and for his kindness. He had not, after all, been able to hand over the gift of money that he had borrowed from Frederick, sensing that such a gesture would cause offence, or at least a scene, and in either case would diminish the generosity of their hospitality. It would have made him seem petty and mean-spirited, as if he thought he had found a value in money that was commensurate with human kindness. He wondered if he should do it now, between men who understood the regrettable value of the commodity in this imperfect life. It was not repayment for their generosity, but a generous gesture in itself, a reciprocal kindness. But something unmistakable in Hassanali's manner prevented him, something sensitive and fragile.

'Thank you for visiting us. You're welcome any time. Our house is yours,' Hassanali said, and then the glare swallowed him.

That was how it started. He could not let matters rest there. He could not say to himself that Hassanali and his neighbours had been dutiful to their sense of responsibility and had looked after him as their custom and humanity required. He could not say: consider that in my gratitude for your succour, I will not fail to return your kindness to someone else in need, and thus the human chain will have one tiny link added to it. Nor did he remind himself that he, in turn, had done more than was required of him as one of a suzerain people. He had gone to offer his thanks for their dutiful care of him and his regrets for the clumsy and unnecessary suspicion and abuse they suffered. That should have been that, and Hassanali and his neighbours would have returned to their medieval niceties and Martin would have continued with his convalescence while waiting for a ship to take him home. (If he had been a medieval prince, he would have sent a purse of gold and jewels after his safe arrival among his subjects, and he would have become a legend in these parts.)

Only he could not forget her. Perhaps he said to himself, I cannot resist, I cannot stop myself. As he thought about her, his yearning (it very quickly became that) picked up strength with every recollection. There were moments in the days and nights that followed when he shut his eyes and deliberately evoked her, and felt her as if she was very close to him, felt her gaze on him and a slight tremble of her breathing on his face. In any case, he had not been grateful enough for their kindness, and it was smug and complacent of him to think that a single visit was gratitude enough for the open-handed welcome they offered him. Hassanali had been insistent on this. Our house is yours. They would think him ill-mannered and self-important if he did *not* make another visit.

A few days after the first time, he went back to the shop, to sit with the old men who were flattered to have the mzungu come back for a chat, and called the coffee-seller over to serve their guest. They were not used to such simple and unexpected courtesy from a mzungu, that he should call by for conversation and a sip of coffee. They were not used to Europeans. The ones who had lived in the town or passed through in recent years had had no time for such trifles, going about their important affairs with stern absorption, impatient of delays, impelled by some desire which made them intimidating. The ones a few of the townspeople had seen in Mombasa seemed the same, deliberate and purposeful, always watchful, easy to irritate. This one was unhurried, was happy to listen and spoke casually, making conversation in his unexpected Arabic.

Perhaps Martin had had the craftiness to send Hamis with a gift of fish and bananas to Hassanali's house a day or two before his visit, announcing himself an intimate of the family, or at least one in its debt, and thus making possible another invitation to visit. Hassanali watched jealously from his perch in the shop, straining to hear the old men's incorrigible chatter, and then invited *his* mzungu to lunch again, to show those chatterbox sages whose friend Martin really was. That was how Martin saw Rehana again, and then found a way and opportunity to approach her. But would Hassanali really have invited him again? Once was impulsive hospitality, a generous gesture that the moment called for, twice would have been complicated and calculated, like a design. Even if there had been a second invitation, because the generous impulse had not yet worn off, how would Martin have approached her? How would he have found an opportunity to say anything to her that would have led to such an unimaginable outcome?

He wrote her a letter declaring his passion for her and arranging a meeting. He wrote in Arabic, labouring with the unfamiliar script, because although he spoke Arabic after a fashion, he had no practice in writing in it. A love letter in Arabic, or perhaps in any language, required a command of convention and metaphor which was quite unlikely to be within Martin's grasp of the language. But he had spent all that time in Egypt, and he probably knew Edward Lane's *Modern Egyptians* and his translations of *One Thousand and One Nights*, in both of which he would have found many hints and examples on how to proceed in matters of love. This was not Egypt though, nor the fantasy land of Haroun al-Rashid, nor was this a matter involving glittering princesses of Persia and China, and so Lane's florid prose might not perhaps strike the right note. None the less, Martin wrote a letter in Arabic, and however clumsy the effort, it signalled his intent and purpose. To a woman's guardians, intercepted correspondence was conclusive evidence of improper advances, and therefore the danger of discovery confirmed the seriousness of the desires the letter expressed. It was, furthermore, a time-honoured method of conducting a courtship where casual meetings were not easy, especially among the wealthy and the literate, of course, but even among the less fortunate. It was the kind of transaction whose meaning was impossible to mistake, even if you could not read a word of the letter. Perhaps Martin Pearce would have said to himself again and again, I cannot resist, I cannot stop myself. Oh God, why will you not teach me restraint?

In any case, the intrigue proved irresistible for Rehana, who had found herself unable to stop thinking about the Englishman. She replied cautiously but not discouragingly, waiting for a second letter or a third before agreeing to a meeting.

Hamis was the messenger, of course. Martin had taken trouble over Hamis, addressed him courteously, flattered him politely for avocations upon his person and rewarded him generously (with Frederick's money) for various necessary errands. He knew how susceptible powerless people were to such banal gestures, how much they valued appearance of generosity and humility. So after eating at the house for the second time, Martin sent another gift of tea and fruit to the family, and when Hamis delivered that, he also slipped a square of paper folded small into Rehana's hand. Or if Hamis took exception to this request to be a messenger of passion, as some men do however lowly their circumstances because they see such services as degrading, maybe the cook would have done it. In fact, cooks were ideal vehicles for such traffic, because theirs was women's work, carried out in parts of the house where men who could employ cooks did not always bother to visit and where carefully folded notes could be transferred safely. And because their work was unmanly, it made them *seem* less threatening to women's virtue. Perhaps it was this appearance which made some cooks so ferociously aggressive and foul-mouthed.

Or the wakil! No, the wakil would not have done it. He was

too respectable for that, and neither Martin Pearce nor Rehana were important enough for such a risk. Discovery would have been too damaging for a man whose profession depended on an appearance of integrity and propriety, even though everyone believed that lawyers had none. Nor would he have had the access to the house and the women that a servant would, and would not have been able to deliver the letters to Rehana. It had to be Hamis or the cook.

How would an Englishman, so visible in that place, have found a ruse to do any of these things? The people he was among would have been curious of how he went about his affairs. They would have kept their eye on him. They would probably have talked about the unimportant things he did which they found unusual and strange. How could he have done anything *so* unusual without the whole world knowing his every move? Perhaps the whole world did know and Martin did not care. Frederick knew, because Martin told him after his second visit. Frederick remembered the beautiful woman who had chased him out of the house, and nodded cautiously at Martin's enthusiastic report. He resisted asking if Martin had lost his mind, but he did say that he hoped he knew what he was doing. Martin explained that he wanted Frederick to know so that he would not be embarrassed. Nothing may come of it, but he had written a note to her, and he wanted Frederick to know in case of trouble.

'So long as this Residence and this office are not involved,' Frederick said. 'Take care, old chap. These characters take such things seriously. Well, everyone takes such things seriously. Let me tell you a story about a fellow in India. He got into a situation like this, a local beauty caught his eye and he went along with it. Soon he was in it so deep that it needed a considerable settlement to extricate him from the rage of her relatives. The Divisional Secretary was not the slightest bit amused, and the fellow was transferred with the ludicrous scandal preceding him. And do not waste your sympathy on the local beauty. Aside from the fat gratuity she earned for her family, she promptly made eyes at a tea-planter sahib and went off to keep house for him in the hills.'

'Yes,' Martin said.

Would Frederick have dared lecture Pearce in this way? Would it have exceeded some latitude that gentlemen, even of their unaristocratic, middle-class ilk, have allowed themselves? In any case, that evening (perhaps) Frederick talked for the first time about his wife Christabel, Christie, who had gone back home from India, refusing to return. Indian voices grated on her nerves. He told her native voices grated on everyone, but she would not hear of it. She said they made her unwell. Those grating, whining voices, made her want to scratch the inside of her head with her nails. And she thought the empire was evil, making them greedy and cruel to those pathetic people who could not know better. 'She is a poet,' Frederick said, 'and something in her revolted at the way the rigours of empire degraded finer feelings, the way it made us into charlatans and bullies, as she put it. Brought out the worst in us, she said. She would not relent,' he said, and nodded tersely. After a moment's silence he added: 'I don't know if she might not be right about that charlatans and bullies.'

But still, even if there was a way of doing it, what would have made Martin reckless enough to want to begin an affair with a woman like Rehana? These were not sophisticated and worldly people, Rehana and Hassanali and Malika, not aristocratic idlers whose indiscretions were screened by luxuriant gardens and high walls. They lived behind a shop, under scrutiny of their neighbours, all of them squeezed up against each other and in the grip of an anxious ethos about women's sexual honour. The women only went out to visit each other or to go to the market when they had to, or to go to a function: to a wedding or a reading after a funeral, to commiserate and congratulate a neighbour after childbirth, or to wheedle a loan in time of need. They were not people who had any knowledge or interest in clandestine love affairs, and who punished each other mercilessly for any indiscretions in such matters, with ridicule and shame and worse.

This was 1899, not the age of Pocahontas when a romantic

fling with a savage princess could be described as an adventure. The imperial world observed some rigidity about sexual proprieties. The empire had become an extension of British civic respectability, and while that allowed for some high spirits and adventure, it no longer included dalliances with subject floosies, at least not from its officers, at least not officially. There were wives and mothers to consider, and missionaries, and public opinion and dignity and the effect of everything on commodity prices on the Stock Exchange. Martin Pearce was not a naïve young sailor from a rural backwater or a swaggering urchin emboldened by imperial pride, who was overwhelmed by the strangeness of his surroundings or was touched into impetuousness by the beauty of an exotic jewel or a muscular amazon. What would have made an Englishman of his background – university, colonial official, a scholar – begin something like that with the sister of a shopkeeper in a small town on the East African coast?

Perhaps he wasn't the one who began it at all. Perhaps she was the one who followed up their first meeting. Rehana could not help smiling when Hassanali came to tell them that he had invited Martin for lunch again. She smiled because he was so pleased with himself. Mwengereza wetu kaja kututizama, Hassanali said, smiling back. Our Englishman has come to pay us a visit. While Malika hastily removed the washing from the line and swept the yard and sluiced the room of necessity, Rehana washed lentils and salad to extend the dishes on offer and make the lunch seem suitable for a guest. He sat with them so comfortably, friendly and at ease, treating them as benefactors to whom he was obliged, looking at her with unsettling frankness. She had not expected anything like that. After that second visit with them, and his friendly gifts, keeping his notebook from him seemed like a kind of malice. Two days after his visit, in the afternoon, she set off with a tense heart for the government mzungu's house. She was tense out of fear of the government mzungu and his accusations, but she was also tense in case there was an embarrassment, in case the man she had come to see rebuffed her or treated her slightingly. She had considered whether to ask Hassanali to accompany her, but she thought she would do this better on her own. She was won over by Pearce's modest manner, and she thought he would not make a fuss about the notebook, would take it back quietly and keep the matter to himself. She also wanted to see the immodest longing in the way he looked at her one more time.

When she got to the government house, she found the office was shut and the front door was bolted from inside. She followed the wall round until she came to a garden door, which was only pushed to. She stepped into the garden, calling out hodi, announcing herself. It was a shaded yard, with a young palm tree in the centre and some bushes along the walls. While the street outside trembled with the heat, the shaded yard was cool and fragrant even that early in the afternoon. Across the yard from the house and screened with a trellis of flowering vine were the servants' rooms and the kitchen. There was no one in sight. She called out again, thinking she would go after that if there was no answer. After a moment, his astonished face appeared at an upstairs window.

Perhaps she thought she had nothing to lose, that all that remained for her was a lifetime in that bright yard behind the shop, making clothes for women who only paid her a pittance, or only offered her affection and promises in return. That does not sound so intolerable, really, not for a woman who had lived her whole life in the back of a shop in that town, and who was used to women's lives such as hers. Perhaps she was much more reckless or courageous or wilful than I imagine her. Azad's abandonment had made her stubborn, less sensitive to what others thought best for her, slightly more indifferent to opinion. Men left while women stayed behind and died after a lifetime of wheedling and scraping. So when she reached out with the notebook, and Martin took it and then grinned, and then after that held out his hand to invite her into the house, she took his hand and followed him in.

What did Burton think about it all? What did Burton have to

say about Pearce? Would one beachcomber have felt a stab of sympathy for another? He would have seen it as an amusing and uncomplicated affair of lust and its gratification, perhaps, and would have thought less of Martin for his lack of restraint and discretion, for making a fuss about such an ordinary matter. That would have been at first. Later he would have sneered at the ardent self-delusion of such a love-affair, no doubt. The man has gone too far, he would have said. He really has gone too far this time. Did the affair result in a quarrel between Rehana and Hassanali? It must have done. He must have berated her for losing all sense of what is proper or bearable. He must have ranted at her for the embarrassment she had brought upon him. He must have suspected that she had lost her mind.

What I know from my brother Amin is that it did happen, that Rehana Zakariya and Martin Pearce became lovers, that Martin Pearce left for Mombasa, and that a short while later, under pretext of going to visit relatives, Rehana followed him there. She lived with him in an apartment he rented in the leafy district near where the hospital is now, which was where Europeans lived at that time. Martin and Rehana lived openly together, for a while, until he left to return home. At some point, Pearce came to his senses and made his way home.

My brother Amin knew this story because it had consequences for him, but he could not tell me much about it for various reasons, the most important of which was that I was not there when he could have told me. He could have written about it in a letter, but he chose not to mention it, not for many years. There are some things you cannot simply write in a letter, that require intimacy, that need an encounter. Then in a letter some months ago he mentioned Jamila for the first time since I left. I had thought often about Jamila and Amin and what had happened between them and what it still meant. In some ways, his silence about her made me understand things I would not have thought about him, and made me think about obduracy and anguish. When I wrote to tell him about Grace, he replied to say that my news filled him with sadness and made him think of Jamila. That was the first time he mentioned Jamila in any of his letters, the first time in all that age since I left home, and the suddenness with which he brought her back into our lives made me want to write their story, Jamila and Amin. Perhaps it was a way of not thinking about Grace. I don't know. I had time on my hands. I had no one to placate and wheedle affection from, and I wanted to think about Amin, to bring him closer, to remember the things that were now lost to me.

At that time, I thought there was something tragic in Amin's life, a profound sorrow, whereas my own life and its glooms were the result of mismanagements and timidity. In any case, the impulse to write their story did not go away, and after putting the idea off for some while, I decided to make a start. But when I began to think about these events and that life, I found I had to give an account of how they might have started. I could not begin without imagining how Rehana and Martin might have come together, and all I had of that were a few scraps of gossip and scandal. I decided that the Englishman's first appearance was where I would start. Now that I have arrived at the critical moment, I find myself suddenly hard up against what I cannot fully imagine.

There is, as you can see, an I in this story, but it is not a story about me. It is one about all of us, about Farida and Amin and our parents, and about Jamila. It is about how one story contains many and how they belong not to us but are part of the random currents of our time, and about how stories capture us and entangle us for all time.

PART II

5 Amin and Rashid

early 1950s
Zanzibar

Across the road from them was a huge crumbling house. The outer rendering had eroded in places and exposed the coral and earth filling. The wooden shutters on some of the windows hung on by a miracle, and tattered rags of cloth fluttered in the heat and gestured towards privacy. Sometimes fishing nets hung out of the windows. The men in the family were fishermen, and sometimes brought their nets home and hung them out of the windows for some reason. The crowd of people who lived in the house went in and out without seeming to notice anything precarious about the building, and the chickens which roosted in all corners and angles of the stairs did not seem concerned either. To Rashid the house smelled of ruin, and his senses could already anticipate the clouds of dust as the floors collapsed in on themselves. It also smelled of fish-scales and chicken-droppings, and of human breath, like the inside of something living. It had no electricity, and after a few steps into the gloom it felt as vast as a cave. When it rained hard in the musim, he expected the house to be washed away, but it wasn't. It stood like that, year after year, on the point of collapse, obdurate like history.

Their house was light and airy, because their mother liked it that way. The first thing she did when she came home was to open all the windows to let in the breeze, regardless of anyone's wishes, all the time asking questions, and getting everyone on the hop. *Do I have to do everything in this house?* She liked it like that too, a bit of confusion and chaos around her, at least for a while.

There were three of them: Rashid, Amin and Farida. Rashid was two years younger than his brother Amin, who himself was two years younger than their eldest sister Farida. Two years, one month and twelve days. Amin liked to number, to count and chant the days to annoy Rashid, when such things still had the power to irritate and diminish. Two years, one month and twelve days, and it will always remain like that, whatever you do, whatever you say, for ever and ever and ever. At some age, Amin could say that again and again, tirelessly and pitilessly, for ever and ever and ever, and for some reason, Rashid found this chanting painful, until in the end he would throw himself on the floor and sob. Then Amin would fall silent and watch his brother sobbing, awed by the depth of his anguish. That such pain should result from his teasing words, that such heaving sobs were even possible in Rashid's little body. He would pat him gently to calm him down, and sit beside him and soothe him, smiling at the sublime drama.

Amin had other ways of tormenting his younger brother, but most of them gradually became known only to the two of them as the intervention of their parents or Farida forced these tortures into secrecy. They were not really tortures, no bruises or contusions, no degradations, just mocking words and laughter, or sometimes a brutal shove or daylight robbery (marbles or sweets), and an unrelenting desire for primacy which was non-negotiable. Rashid understood very early that the torments were unavoidable, the price he had to pay for his brother's love, necessary to the ritual of intimacy. It was not always enough that Rashid was compliant and obedient for the most part. There were times when Amin wished to make a display, to make an exhibition of his omnipotence, to have his every demand met, even if for most of the time he was satisfied with having the upper hand. This regime was at its most brutal when they were very young. As they grew older, and Rashid became less pliant, Amin became more composed, more subtle and more adept at disguising his dominion, adroitly dispersing the moment of revolt. Other people made it harder for Amin to give up his complicated ascendancy because they treated the two of them as if they were utterly unalike. For a while, Farida tended to do the opposite and at times pretended to mix them up. Everyone else, from their parents and relatives to the most distant neighbour and the vaguest of street acquaintances, treated them as if they were unlike each other.

It was a small place, and no neighbour was that distant nor were any acquaintances that vague, and everyone knew who everyone was. In any case, none of them were willing to give up their right to talk about and interfere in other people's lives, to be aghast at that one's infraction and the other one's dereliction, and to expect yet another one to bring calamity down on his family, you mark my words. Some of them were merely familiar faces in the streets to the two brothers, without names or connection, yet even these people did not hesitate to offer an opinion or discriminate between them. They were different, no doubt, in the little ways that make us speak about our individuality and uniqueness while we trot with the herd, but there was something of a crude formula in the treatment they received. Amin was the elder and Rashid was the younger. Farida did not count in this equation since she was a sister, and therefore had to be spoken about differently and to a different timetable of change and expectations. For the brothers, that was what it amounted to at first, the elder and the younger, but out of it grew a story of their difference whose consequence was a tight body of petty entitlements and prohibitions which became awkward to change as they grew older.

At home Amin was always Amin, but Rashid had to answer to a variety of diminutives. When he was very young, he was Shishi or Didi, or even Rara, all carelessly coined by his own thick tongue when required to pronounce his name. From an early age he learned to supply the means with which to burden his life and invite mockery. Then he became Kishindo, which means a commotion, because he was thought noisy and restless.

Kishindo kishafika. To some, such names are an expression of affectionate kinship, and those who have never had to answer to some such may even envy ones who have, seeing themselves as unloved or loved reservedly. But Rashid chafed under them, felt the mockery in them more than the affection, and hated the orchestrated laughter that followed any protest he made. Most of all he hated that he could not shrug the names off, or laugh at them too, join in the fun. He had to struggle to restrain the impulse to run out of the house in a wail when they started. Later, he was Mtaliana, the Italian, which was the name that stuck the longest.

This was how he acquired that name. His Uncle Habib, his father's brother, worked as a consignment clerk in the Customs House on the waterfront. Amin and Rashid sometimes stood in the great doorway of the Customs House just to see him sitting there at his section of the counter, the great clock on the wall behind him, the ceiling fans whirling into a blur high above them. It would be on a detour from Koran school, perhaps, taking the long way home through Forodhani and along the waterfront. Or it would be during school holidays, when idle children and youth wandered into every nook and cranny of the town. Then, if the doorway was not choked with merchants and scribes, they would go in and stand in the tiled hallway, dwarfed by the pillars and the huge windows that filled the chamber with an underwater light. If it was quiet, and he saw them, Uncle Habib beckoned them over and leaned over the counter to shake their hands while they grinned with pleasure and self-importance.

They had several uncles, but he was the most glamorous because he had been to war with the British forces in Abyssinia. At home they had a framed studio photograph of him in his KAR uniform, the brim of his hat folded back against the crown like a European settler, the chin strap biting into his cheeks. It was he who gave Rashid a pocket Italian phrase-book.

It had been given to Uncle Habib as a gift by the agent of a motor company that was beginning to specialise in the Vespa scooter. This was in the days when such a trinket was adequate to win the goodwill of petty officials, when such offerings were made openly, standing under the green pillared canopy of the Customs House itself, in front of its huge studded doors, in sight of the main waterfront promenade. (The Customs House is still there, I should think, though by now it is probably a café for tourists called The Blue Parrot or the Blue Marlin or the Blue something else.) In those days, the agent from Kapadia Motors could offer an Italian phrase-book, and a poster of a Venetian canal, or one of cypresses on a Tuscan hillside, and expedite his dealings with the customs official. If there was any furtiveness in such exchanges, it was because these trinkets were valuable. They were tokens of the big world, which was always cleaner and brighter than the dark, familiar one of every day. This big world did not have to be European. It could be a Japanese calendar, with pictures of delicately-lit paper houses and minia-ture bushes of blazing azaleas. Or it could be Lebanese grapes nestling in tissue-paper, in fruit boxes stamped with a silhouette of a cedar tree, or Iraqi dates in packets illustrated with a painting of an oasis. Nothing Indian, that was part of the odorous every day. European was best, though. The European world was remote and intimidating in a complicated way, and these tokens were like parts of its sprawling body, handled and consumed with some hunger. The agent did not want to be relieved of these valuable trinkets by any bright-eyed passer-by who would do nothing for him.

In our hungrier times such gifts would be offensive. They would only expedite irritation and delays. The official would remember urgent business elsewhere, and when at last he was available, he might be awkward. He might undertake a deliberate and metic-ulous search of the consignment, and observe a punctilious adher-ence to the bureaucratic form, perhaps even muse over a threat of prosecution for customs infringement under a previously unknown regulation. This is not to say that the gift required had to be substantial enough to deposit in a numbered Swiss bank account, not for a customs clerk, although that depended on where you were and what you were consigning. It did not need to be that substantial at all, and often was only expected to be a gracious offering, a gesture of gratitude, a hand-out, which was necessary for the official's self-esteem and for the petty luxuries which his meagre salary made impossible. For, of course, the extended family never ceased in its demands, and even cigarettes were expensive.

What has changed so much that our times are so unruly now when they weren't before? What is so different that Uncle Habib could accept a phrase-book and a poster with a thrill of pleasure then, and expedite the business of Kapadia Motors with a smile, when now he would be greedy and probably mean? The British have gone, that's what. When they were here everything was run like a school for monkeys. This is not allowed, that is not allowed. Wrong, wrong, off to jail. Backward, corrupt, childish, only us British are honest and intelligent and efficient. The most honest, most fair, most efficient rulers since the dawn of time. Then they left to go back to their own unmanageable corruptions and the monkeys took over. The petty greed of the customs official is nothing like the flagrant syndicates which the President and his Ministers run, of course, but the example is there for all to profit from.

In any case, in those more moderate times Uncle Habib accepted the Italian phrase-book and shook hands with the agent of Kapadia Motors on the steps of the Customs House, in view of anyone who might have been strolling by the sea. Then later that afternoon he gave the book to his nine-year-old nephew, Rashid. He kept the poster of cypresses on a Tuscan hillside for himself.

Rashid was not sure what it was exactly, but something about the phrase-book appealed to him. Perhaps it was the idea of a box of statements that could see you through all of life's contingencies that appealed. Or perhaps it was the look of Italian, or what sounds he was able to make from the phrases on the page, for there was no one there who could tell him how to say the words he saw there. No one he knew spoke Italian nor had ever heard it spoken, except for Uncle Habib himself, who must have heard several Italians begging for mercy. Perhaps it was the association of the book with Uncle Habib's glamour as a soldier against the Italians that made it attractive. No one could ask Uncle Habib anything about the war. If anyone did, he frowned or laughed or ignored the question, so Rashid could not try out the phrases on him.

Rashid practised and learned several of the phrases, and when he could, replied to questions in Italian, or what he thought Italian sounded like. It was a spectacularly popular trick. At first he only spoke Italian at home, making everyone laugh at his incomprehensible gibberish. Then as his fame spread, people would fire questions at him in the streets just to hear him spouting off. He became tedious at home when he refused to answer questions except in Italian, but everyone still laughed despite their irritation. Once Farida stole the book and hid it somewhere (under her mattress as it turned out), because she said she could not take any more of his gabble, but Rashid made such an irresponsible fuss, refusing to speak, refusing food, refusing to look his mother in the eye despite the most dire threats, that the book had to be produced. Then the torrent of Italian resumed, now delivered with triumphant malice whenever Farida was around and there was someone else nearby who would offer protection from her irritable pinches and smacks. His father took the book from him sometimes when he was in this mood, to see if he could identify the phrases, and to see if Rashid was really saying them or only making noises. He announced to the family that indeed he was speaking Italian. That was how he became Mtaliana. But even that, which was a name he brought on himself for his exhibitionism, and which for so long made him smile, he came to hate when he was an adolescent, when little children shouted it after him in the streets.

But it wasn't only names and teasing. It was the way he was made to feel irresponsible and feeble by everyone. If there were instructions to be given, they were addressed to Amin. If there was money involved, to go to the market or to convey to someone, it was entrusted to Amin. Sometimes it was even money for

Rashid, but still it was given to Amin: this is for your brother, to buy his sandals, to go to the cinema, to pay for something at school. Look after the dreamer.

To make matters worse for him, and perhaps to justify these reservations about him, the very first time Rashid was trusted with money, he lost it. He was only eight at the time, but still, he should have done better. He should have realised that his reputation was at stake, that history was made up of such continuous moments and that everything counted. It happened like this. His teacher gave him a note to take to his mother. No, he didn't think it was anything to do with what he might have done wrong at school. That was not how such things were done. For a start, most parents probably could not read, so it would be the culprit himself who would have to deliver his own denunciation. Even children would know the wise thing to do in that circumstance. For another thing, the teacher was capable of letting a child know of any wrong-doing himself, in no uncertain terms. In fact, teachers often seemed to enjoy this part of their duties most of all. No, Rashid didn't think there was anything suspicious about taking a note from a man to his mother. He was too young for that, and in any case, the teacher was known to write notes to selected parents to ask for a loan now and then. Usually it was towards the end of the month, and he paid back promptly, using the children as his messengers. Also, the children were terrified of this teacher, who never smiled at them but sometimes laughed unnervingly, and at other times raged at them unpredictably, whirling his arms in exasperation and landing knuckly blows on the backs of nearby heads. So it never occurred to any of them to wonder about the meaning of his instructions, ever. They knelt and obeyed, which was how the teacher wanted it.

In addition to the loans from parents, the teacher had other ways of augmenting his income. Every school morning, he instructed the class to stand up and chant a times-table first thing, one of those delightful practices that came unchanged from the English elementary school system. The chanting may have been done in a different language, but the moral effect was the same. The children stood up behind their desks, their arms by their sides, and waited for the teacher to announce the number for the day by saying the first line, for example Tatu mara moja, *Three times one*. Then he stood facing the class while they sang the numbers, smiling with pleasure at their taut childish voices, shutting his eyes briefly and swaying slightly as if to the rhythm of a sonorous qasida. If a voice uttered the wrong words, his eyes flew there unmistakably, and fixed the offender in a glare that promised pain. Tatu mara moja tatu, Tatu mara mbili sita, Tatu mara tatu tisa and so on. Sometimes, if he was not satisfied, or if he had not had enough of the straining little voices, he ordered another number. Then he took a collection.

As he called the names out of the class register, each child had to walk up to the teacher's desk and put a five-cent piece on the plate there. He was then marked present. The teacher never said what the money was for, but you didn't need to be a child prodigy to guess that those precious pennies were going straight into his belly. He knew that most of the children were given a few cents to take to school, for a fruit juice at break, or a small cone of nuts, and to feel good about school. He relieved them of some of these cents before they became a nuisance to them. If a child had no money at all, he was instructed to borrow from another child, one of the rich ones. There was always someone who would be too frightened not to hand over his spare cents. The biggest boy in the class ran a syndicate of his own, every week forcing someone to buy something useless from him and requiring a payment of five cents a day, which he duly handed over to the teacher at registration as his own contribution to their teacher's happiness.

Five cents is nothing these days, or even less than nothing. The coin for it does not even exist. Then, in the early 1950s, you would have bought a handsome mango for that money, and for ten cents you would have bought a loaf of bread or a plate of spinach or a roast cassava or a dish of Adnan's potato na urojo, or even a small stick of grilled meat. Five cents was not a pittance to an eight-year-old at that time. Now a small mango costs twenty shillings. You would have bought four hundred mangoes for that then, and the fruit-seller would probably have added another dozen as bakhshish for your custom. Never mind. By the time the teacher had made his daily collection from forty or so children in his class, he had more than enough money for his dinner. Usually, immediately after the collection, he picked out a few coins and sent one of the children to a nearby café to fetch him a glass of milk, so he could make a healthy start to his working day. Other teachers knew he did this, the parents knew he did this, every day, yet no one said a word. He was a teacher, a figure of respect. He was allowed to be eccentric, and the stories of his whimsies and idiosyncrasies would swell into a myth that would seem less oppressive with time. All the teachers were like that, famed for one quirk or another. The quirks were sometimes cruelties or oppressions they inflicted on the children, insult and intimidation and violence, no laughing matter when you looked at them closely, but none the less everyone laughed, or at least smiled, at these excesses and somehow made them seem harmless. That was how things always were. For a parent to confront one of them over such matters was to show ingratitude, to humiliate the teacher, and to do so over a few cents would have been unbearable.

Anyway, Rashid was given a note by this teacher to take home to his mother, and the next day his mother gave him an envelope with some money in it to give to the teacher. A few days later the teacher called him back at the end of classes and gave him two folded notes to give back to his mother, whispering his gratitude. For despite the way he was with the children, he was a man of courtesy. If you only saw him in the streets, you would see a smiling man of manners, as we have a way of saying. You would not imagine the charge of terror he generated in class.

It was a Friday afternoon, when school finished half an hour earlier so that the children could go to prayers. Rashid hurried home, threw his school shorts on the heap of dirty washing without a second thought for his mother to wash, and then changed into his Friday mosque clothes and went to join the other boys under the banyan tree at the waterfront until it was time for the Juma'a prayers. He only remembered about the money when he came to put on his shorts on Monday morning and felt a coagulated lump of paper in his pocket. He had not mentioned the errand to Amin. He wanted to do the errand himself, without Amin's interfering advice. If he had mentioned it, Amin might have reminded him about giving the money back and he would not have had to shuffle up to his mother with the dried pellet of paper in his hand and with tearful and pathetic excuses. 'What did I tell you?' his mother said. 'This boy would lose his head if it wasn't attached to him.' Mothers are the same everywhere in this respect. They use the same clichés and say the same hurtful things to their younger children. After that it was back to business as usual: Amin, make sure Rashid hands in his homework, goes to the barber, comes home immediately after school, and so on.

There were some advantages to Rashid in this otherwise unhappy arrangement. If there was any scolding to be done, for some silliness in the streets, for loitering at a busy crossroads within striking distance of hurtling hand-carts or careering cyclists, or for throwing rotten fruit at each other or for arguing too loudly, the busybody who would take on the task of correction would address his righteousness at Amin, and even blame him for being negligent of his younger brother. At home Amin bore the brunt of any reproaches for their joint misdemeanours, and on these occasions Rashid made sure to stand safely out of harm's way, grinning and making woe-begone faces at his suffering brother, and throwing in a tiny snuffle if anyone looked his way. Such scenes ended in one of three ways. One: Amin took his berating quietly, eyes lowered in shame and contrition, and everything ended well, concluding with agonised pleas from the parent not to allow whatever it was to happen again. A coin might even change hands at the end of such a scene, to make up for the hard words. Two: Amin would be unable to prevent himself from grinning back at Rashid's antics, in which case the parent concerned would be enraged at his levity under torture, and would conclude with cuffs and slaps and acrid abuse. Three: if Farida was around during the scene she would betray Rashid instantly, and stern parent would turn around and catch Rashid's facial contortions. In which case the cuffs and slaps would land on him while he yelled and screamed extravagantly. But on the whole, if there was any hardship to be borne, it was Amin who was required to volunteer. If there was an errand to be run, it was almost certain to be run by Amin. If there was only one juicy morsel of something left, then it was he who was expected to be self-denying and leave it for his little brother. These rules did not apply to Farida who was a sister, and therefore had other rules to follow, and in any case, she knew how to protect her own.

The scolding and cuffing and slapping only lasted while they were young, of course, but the pattern remained. Everyone treated Amin as if he was nearly grown-up, expecting him to be calm and responsible, and treated Rashid as if he was a bit of a child, impulsive, dreamy. The brothers knew this about themselves, about how everyone thought of them and treated them, and they benefited in a variety of mildly self-gratifying ways. They never discussed this treatment openly, but they worked out strategies that took account of the assumptions of their natures, and then smiled when they were able to have their own way. It was important to them that they were brothers. They were in it together. They were used to each other's ways. So they found themselves cast involuntarily, and later more willingly, in these roles of responsible elder brother and impetuous younger brother, but as they grew older it became clear that there was a truth in it. It was an apt and pleasing coincidence, an alignment of contingencies. Either that or socialisation worked more profoundly in their case than it does in the wishful thinking of the rearing of other children. Amin the trustworthy: Rashid the dreamer.

As the children grew older, so their parents' opinions of them became more set. They saw Amin and Rashid largely as above, making their way in the world as they were equipped to. Farida, on the other hand, was a real worry, especially to their mother. She was easy-going (lazy) and always smiling (silly). All she seemed to want to do was play with her friends or visit the neighbours in their crumbling old house. Getting her to sit down to schoolwork was a torture, which their mother appointed herself to endure. She threatened, and when that did not work she cajoled, and when that only partially worked, she sat down and more or less did the homework for her. 'This world is not kind to women who don't look after themselves,' she told Farida, who looked tragic because she knew this was what was expected of her when her mother talked about how the world treated women. When her confinement was over, she was full of smiles and ready to go round to the neighbours or sit and chat with anybody who was willing. She loved chatting, and when there was no one around to speak to, she chatted with a cushion or an umbrella or the empty chair. She was even happy to help with the housework, and sometimes managed a conversation with the objects she was cleaning or washing. She only did this when she was on her own, or when she thought she was on her own. Her mother eased off as time passed. She herself had had to struggle hard to become a teacher, and could not conceal her disappointment in Farida's lack of interest in school.

The time came when Farida finished school, or rather school finished with her. She was thirteen years old. She failed the examination to the state secondary school for girls. There was only one in the town, in the whole island, in the entire country, which consisted of several islands and a population of half a million people. Every year, hundreds and thousands of girls sat for the examination, and thirty of them were admitted into the school. For most of them, it was their first and last public examination. The names of the successful children were read out on the national radio, to disseminate the news as quickly as possible to all the far reaches of the tiny country, but also to mark the magnitude of their achievement. They sat in a tense silence around the radio while the announcer read out the names in the solemn voice used to announce the death of someone eminent. Farida was one of the thousands whose names were not read out.

Although Farida had never seemed especially urgent about competing for the scarce chance of being one of the chosen, when she was excluded, she was full of grievance and anger. She burst into tears and fell gratefully into her mother's embrace. She had been expelled, she said, denied any chance of making something of herself. There was no future for her now, nothing at all. There was a co-educational convent school run by nuns and attached to the cathedral, but that was for Christians. No sane parents would send their children there, especially not girls, to be corrupted and degraded and bent into unbelievers. Then there was the Aga Khan School, for Ismaili children. Non-Ismailis were required to pay fees and to achieve a high pass in the examinations. Farida's passes were not high enough for the school. There was nothing for her now.

Her mother contemplated giving up teaching to be at home with her, to teach her herself and look after her, but everyone told her what an absurd sacrifice that would be, after all. Her husband argued against it, her sisters, her brother, even Farida herself.

Their father Feisal said to their mother, 'You have worked so hard, and now your reward is to do what is useful to others and what brings respect to you. People like you are an example to others, a challenge to the bullying ways we have to learn to change. People can look at what you've done and say, Alhamdulillah, things can't be all bad if you can learn to be what has been denied you, if you can manage to bring some satisfaction to yourself and to be useful at the same time. How can you even think of giving it up? We'll find a way.'

Their mother's sister Halima said: 'Let her come to me until you decide. I need the help. There's no reason for you to give up your work, not after all the trouble you've put everyone to over this job of yours. Lo Mwana, calm down. She's no worse off than thousands of others.'

'That's what everyone said to me when I was her age,' their

mother said. 'And if I'd listened I would have been staying at home cooking and looking after children for the rest of my life.'

'Like me,' Halima said, chuckling and snapping her fingers at the same time, to show how unmoved she was by her sister's belittling comparison. 'But then you'd have had time to enjoy looking after your children and cooking for your husband, and even spend some time going out to see people, instead of rushing around like someone with a madness risen in them.' *(A multitasker, as in the rest of the world)*

'I look after my children,' their mother said, as always stung by this irritating accusation. 'And I look after my husband. Ask them, see if they have any complaints. Ask them.'

'I don't need to ask them,' Halima said, sighing at having arrived at the familiar impasse. 'Of course they don't have any complaints. How can they? Don't make such a fuss, that's what I'm saying. Send her to me until you decide what to do.'

So Farida was sent to her mother's elder sister, Bi Halima. Bi Halima had a large family but she refused to have a servant, for reasons she could not be forced to explain. She did not like to have a servant around her, she said. She did the washing, cleaned the seredanis, swept the house, did the cooking, the ironing, all herself. She bought what she needed every day from the shop nearby, and her husband Ali brought what was needed from the market on his way home from work. What would a servant do? Farida was sent to help her out during the morning and learn to do the domestic chores which it was necessary for every woman to know. Her parents were distraught at falling back to these old incarcerating ways, but there was no school to send her to. To leave her at home on her own all morning was, of course, unthinkable, not at that age, when girls did not know how beautiful they were, and how much yearning and turmoil they aroused in men if they seemed within reach, and how defenceless they were against those who could arouse their vanity. At about lunch-time, Farida returned home to help her mother prepare the food.

They had been young radicals in their day, their parents. Not political radicals, marching in the streets and delivering speeches, and making fists in the air, not that kind of raucous radical. There was no space for that kind of thing then. The British would not have stood for it. They were very sensitive about marches and speeches, always on the lookout for what they called sedition. The Omanis would not have allowed it because they trembled at disorder, although they did not always mind raised voices and whirling canes among men. The sheikhs of religion would have prohibited it, because they prohibited any contention or challenge to authority, unless it was one of their interminable feuds among themselves. Their parents were radicals because they both defied *their* parents to study at the new government teachers' college. Their father was forbidden to go to the college because his father was suspicious of colonial education: 'They'll make you despise your people and make you eat with a metal spoon and turn you into a monkey who speaks through his nose,' he said. Their father's father threatened and ranted in the way only a father of that generation could. 'They will turn you into a kafir, and we will have failed in our duty to God. You might as well escort us personally to the gates of Hell. You will not have my blessing, I will disown you. Stop this nonsense at once, you stupid child of sin.'

Their mother, on her part, was forbidden by her parents too. Her parents were different in many ways from his, part of a larger and more dispersed family, but they were the same as his in this respect. She was already a young woman, her parents told her, and to allow her to roam abroad unattended was to invite the world's predators to visit disaster and dishonour upon her and her family.

Defiance is a sin for people who are required by God to Submit, first to Him and then to their Fathers and their Mothers. But both their parents were defiant. They insisted on continuing with their studies, together, already known to each other, already in love. They bickered and cajoled and begged with their parents, who themselves were also acting in their best lights. They recruited relatives and neighbours to their side, and gradually wore their parents down with the seriousness of their desire and the goodwill of so many among them. It is hard to resist the massed opinion of relatives and neighbours in such matters.

Then they defied their parents again by refusing to marry, when everyone suspected they were lovers, until they were both qualified as teachers and about to start work. In the end they exhausted their parents, who agreed to a betrothal and some discretion. Sometimes, when she was in the mood, their mother told the story of their fights with their parents, often when their father was also around. Perhaps it was to relive with him the memory of their happiness that she told the stories, and to admit their children into it, to recruit them into their content. Then, in the telling, they shared smiles at certain moments, or their father would frown and remonstrate with their mother for making the telling too melodramatic, too heroic.

'You're over-salting the dish again,' he would say, then as always preferring restraint and calm.

'I'm over-salting nothing,' their mother would say. 'That's exactly how it was. You're getting old. You've forgotten, that's all.'

To parents like them, for whom school education had been a personal quest, an undertaking into which other unspoken ambitions had been displaced, the route to a new and enlightened world, their daughter's exclusion felt like a small tragedy. That they had no choice but to accept Aunt Halima's offer to keep her at home and out of harm's way felt even worse, like a kind of treachery to the dreams of their own youth. So when parents of a few of the girls who had failed the examination paid a teacher to start a class for their daughters, they were eager for the scheme, especially as Farida was happy to join them. The teacher, who offered private classes at her home in the afternoon, worked in the state secondary school in the morning, the same one that had refused thousands of girls along with Farida. They may not let the girls into the school, but the teacher was the same and the books were the same, the parents said to each other. Farida spent the morning at her aunt's house, doing her assignments and helping out when she was required, and then went to classes in the afternoon. It was better than school, she said, as the routine was more friendly and the work more manageable. It was embarrassing to walk to classes when ordinary school was over, marked out as one of the failures going to a private school, without a uniform and where anybody with the fees could attend. But there were so many other failures that, after a while, she felt reconciled to be part of this stubborn experiment, to be one of those who had refused to sit in the corner allotted to them.

'I don't want to stay at home doing nothing,' she told her Aunt Halima. 'That's what women are expected to do. Well, I'm going to do something for myself.' It made her aunt smile, the thought that she stayed at home doing nothing, when so much of her day from first light to midnight seemed an accumulation of chores, worry and exhausting labour. That was Mwana's talk, quarrelling and bustling for what she wanted, as if the whole world was desperate to prevent it.

The classes lasted for a few months and then both teacher and students gave up in mutual recriminations. The teacher said the students did not take the work seriously, and probably were not up to it. There were moments when she sat in aghast silence, which was slightly exaggerated for pedagogic effect, at the students' failure to grasp elementary ideas in algebra or chemistry. The students said the teacher did not know the subjects she was supposed to teach them, as her subjects at the school were domestic science and Kiswahili. They said she spoke to them as if they did not know anything, when the truth was that she did not know how to teach the difficult subjects. It was a waste of money, they told their parents, who themselves probably thought the same, for how could one teacher in her own home offer as much as a whole school with its troop of teachers, its books and its laboratories. They may also have thought, but certainly would not have said, that they too wanted those luminous European teachers that the girls at the state school had, and not this one like themselves, who could not suppress grateful smiles when she met the parents in the streets.

So Farida was back to the old routine. She went to her Aunt

Halima in the morning, helped her with the sweeping, washing clothes, chopping vegetables or whatever, chatting and laughing with a contentment that was more revealing than she realised. For a while she still took her books with her, as if she still had assignments to complete, but she never touched them. There was never time. When lunch-time approached, she went home, collected what Bi Aziza, their neighbour in the big house, had sent for them from the market, and started the cooking. By the time her mother came home, everything was under way, so Mwana had time for a cool glass of water and perhaps a brief sit-down before taking charge. Food was ready in good time, and its consumption became less frantic and less haphazard. Her father smiled at this new arrangement, though his smile was at times troubled. Her brothers were able to satisfy their enormous appetites before being chased off to Koran school, and Mwana had time for a slow grateful wash before going to lie down for a rest. Everyone felt the benefit.

Farida's arrangements grew more assured as months passed in this way. She took the family washing with her when she went to Aunt Halima and did it there, and then brought it back when she came home the following day. She did shopping errands for her mother, and sometimes went to the market for a particular ingredient that her mother had forgotten to mention to Bi Aziza. She was already wearing the buibui by then, the black robes which all women wore, all except those hardened by foreign ways or by perversity. She went to the market if she wanted, or to the shops, or to call on friends, and came home in time to begin lunch. In the afternoon she cleaned the dishes, swept the house, perhaps did a bit of her own ironing (she left the rest for her mother), and then washed and went out again to call on friends. She went about these uninspiring chores with a smile and a kind of excitement. It worried her mother.

'What's wrong with her? She shouldn't be content with this,' she said to Feisal. 'She's fourteen years old. She should be wanting things. She should mind all this drudgery. We haven't taught her to be like this.'

'She seems happy,' Feisal said carefully, reluctant to inflame her worries when he could not think of a way of diminishing them. They were lying in bed in mid-afternoon, the quietest time for them, their best time in all the years of their married life. Nobody called at that time of day, and the children were either at Koran school or were old enough to know that this was a time to leave them to themselves.

'You don't suppose she's mixed up with someone, do you?' she asked.

'Nuru, why do you say that? Don't even think such a thought.' He was the only person who called her by her real name.

'We can't let her turn herself into a servant like this,' Nuru said. 'It's not as if it's necessary. I was managing perfectly happily before. I'll have to find a way of stopping her from doing these things.'

'It would be odd to forbid her, when she thinks she's helping,' he said. 'It seems to make her happy. All these cakes and pastries that she's learning to cook. She's very good at them. Maybe she has a talent in that way.'

'That's Halima, she's been teaching her all that,' she said. Then she turned and looked at her husband for a long moment. 'I hope you're not suggesting that she should do that for the rest of her life, cook samosas and pastries.'

'No, of course not.'

Of course not.

There was one last attempt to educate Farida. At the end of the school year in December, their mother took Farida with her to see relatives in Mombasa. Her eldest sister, Saida, had married there. Also, their mother's mother had come from there, so there were cousins without number as well. Their mother had written to her sister, asking her to make enquiries about schools for Farida, who was eager for the plan, and could not wait to go and stay with her Aunt Saida and go to school in Mombasa. Their trip was to see what had come of these enquiries, to see if Farida would like Mombasa, to see and make up their minds, to work out the delicate financial arrangements which could not be discussed by letter, for neither family was wealthy. At the end of three weeks, their mother returned on her own, leaving her daughter behind to repeat the final year of primary school at the age of fifteen before making another attempt at a secondary school entrance examination, this time in Kenya.

While Farida was in Mombasa, Amin passed the same examination that Farida had failed two years before. Boys had two schools to go to, but it was still a tall order for them too. In any case, Amin's name was second on the list, so even if they had taken ten students he would still have been one of them. Farida arrived back soon after this success. Mombasa had not worked either. That January, at the end of a year which Farida had enjoyed in so many ways, and memories of which would stay with her for the rest of her life, she returned home defeated. She had not been chosen in Kenya either, and the cost of a private school in Mombasa was beyond her parents. She had tried her best, she said, but she was too stupid.

She took up where she left off, helping her Aunt Halima in the morning, washing, cleaning, making lunch for the family. She volunteered to oversee Amin at his homework, now that he was at secondary school and everything was so hard, though in truth she distracted him more with her chat and laughter. She drew up a working timetable for Rashid's revision, for the same dreaded examination, citing her own lack of organised study for the tragedy that had befallen her. Rashid dutifully pasted the timetable to the inside cover of his revision exercise book and then completely ignored it, preferring to play cards and football with his friends to falling in with his sister's orders. She noted every single infringement of his timetable in a notebook that she kept, and threatened to report him on each of these counts to the powers that be, which had some effect. When it came to it, he too duly passed at the end of the school year. But despite all these labours and chores, Farida was smiling with the old happiness, or something like it, for there was a subtly knowing twist to her smile, a trembling at the corners of her mouth as at a secret joke. Perhaps it was nothing more than age and a growing self-consciousness. The year in Mombasa gave her a new glamour, and it was impossible now not to see the way boys and young men looked at her, but she smiled at them all with such uninhibited carelessness, and responded with such laughing assurance when they spoke to her, that no one dared approach her. It was as if she was a grown woman beyond flirtation and intrigue.

Her brother Amin, in the meantime, was effortlessly becoming all the things that were predicted of him. He was courteous, reliable, truthful and kind. He's a good boy, his mother sometimes said, with a catch in her voice. He was more silent than he had been as a child, and was inclined to speechless stares for no obvious reason, but this was hardly a blemish compared to his virtues. His silences and the increasing inexplicitness of some of the things he said made him seem deeper, wiser. He was successful at secondary school from the beginning, even at subjects and procedures that were new to all of them and in which so many of the students at first struggled. He understood instructions, and worked competently to deliver what the assignment required. He did not chafe under the rules of this new learning, and did not try to find short-cuts to the tasks he was set. His teachers delighted in his unfussy thoroughness. Despite this diligence and excellence, he was a relaxed and unflamboyant member of his class. The teachers never expected any obstinancy from him, yet also looked upon him as one of the leaders. They relied on his acquiescence as an endorsement of their authority, and as an example to others. Amin was not exceptional in this role, but he was among the exceptionals. They had all been schooled in diffidence. They all knew how fortunate they were to be where they were, and had not arrived there by obstinancy and rebelliousness. He was healthy, strong without being intimidating, graceful in a youthful way, and with a devastating smile. Everyone was proud of him, especially his parents, of course, who looked upon his achievements with relief and gratitude. Who knows how children will turn out? How many examples are there of progeny who guzzle on parents' love to satiety and then turn into tireless wasters and relentless demons, blighting every waking second of their parents' lives?

Rashid was proud of him too. Rashid loved him, although he would not have thought to say either of these things to Amin, and perhaps would not have said them to himself until much later. He followed two years behind him, enduring comparison with his elder brother with equanimity. He felt party to Amin's distinctions, was intimate with the effort to achieve them and so did not think them remarkable. When a teacher told him that he was not as good at some task as his brother had been, he only suffered a pang for the disparagement, not because he wanted to compete with Amin. In any case, it was not as if Rashid was hopeless in comparison. He too was successful at school, but in a different way. For a start, it was not a universal opinion that he had a talent for academic work, as it was with Amin. In the eyes of some of his teachers, he was opinionated, inclined to over-reach himself, unrealistic and reckless at times. He was not as thorough, and sometimes just went through the motions. Some thought he would burn himself out with all his show and racket, and amount to not very much. He was intelligent, his teachers thought, but flawed in many small ways. He was noisy, a chatter-box in class, had poor concentration, was enthusiastic on the sports-field but without skill, unlike his elder brother who did well in all the sports he took up. He was a hot-headed debater, which may sound like a good thing but was not. Not in a school debate, when a bit of logic and strategy was required, a bit of stateliness and decorum and sagacity, a bit of guile and show, otherwise what is the point of a debate. In such situations Rashid was likely to rush in with indignation and scorn and bloody-mindedness, putting people's backs up or making them laugh, playing to the grumblers and the malcontents.

There was also his fervour for all things Italian. To tell the truth, aside from the phrase-book and a few pictures and posters from the same source, some magazine cuttings and photos of Giacomo Agostini on his Vespa and a bio-comic of Garibaldi that his sister brought back for him from Mombasa, his fervour was not based on much substance or knowledge. But in any debate about style or beauty or poetry, especially in his adolescent years, his champions were always Italian. Shakespeare is well and good, in fact phenomenal, but bears no comparison to Dante. Why aren't we given a chance to study Dante? Silvana Mangano is the most beautiful film actress in my view. The Italian football team is almost as good as Brazil. When he was younger, his primary school teachers had taken his Italian pronouncements as a bit of high spirits, the inevitable exhibitionism of a bright boy. In any case, most people at that time thought of Italians as slightly comical, from the stories that came back of their antics during the war in Abyssinia, so Rashid's championing of Italy was also taken as a perverse comedy in itself. But by the time he was an adolescent, almost all his teachers at the government college were British, and some of them saw his fervour as an absurd affectation. The history teacher was unreasonably irritated by Rashid over the Italians. He always looked at Rashid before quoting something by a Roman scholar or notable, one of your ancestors so-and-so said such and such. The literature teacher quoted him lines in Italian, and smiled icily as he informed the uncomprehending little fellow that *that* was Dante. He bade him consult the Everyman translation, which was in the library and which in his view was the most accessible to a beginner, before he continued with his pointless flauntings. Perhaps he should learn to walk before he tried to run, the literature teacher wisely advised.

It happened that Rashid really did have a passion for poetry, reading it in the school library and buying battered anthologies from the second-hand bookshop. When he was younger he had loved singing qasidas, and had known several by heart. People loved to recite passages from the Koran or lines from a qasida or a story. Those who had the skill, slipped in a line or a passage on the most casual occasions, and recited their lines with a fluency which never failed to impress and give pleasure. Sometimes, when in the middle of speaking, someone began to recite beautiful lines, others joined in in a delighted chorus, showing off and enjoying themselves. But at his age and in the school he was in, he no longer sang qasidas. Poetry meant Shakespeare and Keats and Byron and Longfellow and Kipling, and it was into this poetry that he threw himself with zeal and pleasure. It was what education meant. It did not mean knowing what everyone else knew, and it did not occur to him to lament any loss in the process. He even had his own copy of Dante at home, although he had not got round to finishing it.

At some point he started writing poems of his own in English, mostly to amuse friends, jokey and excessive verses in the style of *Hyperion* or *Childe Harold's Pilgrimage*. They went on interminably and were deliberately mock-sagacious. He learned a few of the lines by heart and declaimed them to the world with florid gestures as they rode home from school. One of the friends told the literature teacher who had been irritated by Rashid's Dante affectations, and the teacher was even more irritated by this new information, as was the intention. He demanded to be shown the *opus*. Rashid gave him the exercise book reluctantly, anticipating scorn. It was not his idea of a joke, and even though the poems were lightly done, he felt a kind of tenderness for them.

'The poetry is altogether immature,' the teacher reported to the whole class afterwards, as if they had all eagerly sought his opinion. 'When it isn't tedious cut-price *Arabian Nights* mysticism, it is copious, rambling, imitative blather in the style of Byron in satirical mode. Confused and meaningless, as attempts by Africans to write evocatively in English usually are. Even to attempt to write in this way indicates an overweening temperament, an unrealistic estimate of your abilities. Pull up your socks, young man. Your homework for today is a character analysis of the captain in *The African Queen*, and I expect something clear and organised, unlike this froth.' *The African Queen* by C. S. Forester of *Hornblower* fame was the great work their teacher thought suitable for their talents. Rashid was too intimidated by the teacher's disdain to think of any reply. It was at this stage in his life that the name Mtaliana started to become a burden to him.

So his teachers' opinions were divided about Rashid in a way that they were not about Amin. His parents were proud of him too, of course, but their minds were not as easy about him as they were with Amin. His mother, in particular, worried about him. Sometimes when he sat in the kitchen while his mother was preparing food, and chattered as if he would never stop, she glanced at him between her tears of laughter and wondered if he would always be well. Not like that, not illness, not instability, God forbid, but whether he would always have the strength to carry on. His enthusiasms were so obsessive, his wit sometimes disrespectful, his confidence so reckless that she wondered if he would know how to deal with disappointment. As he grew older, she saw a growing stubbornness in him, a willingness to disobey and to ignore what he did not like. He was smaller than Amin, small for his age, always on fire. Burning. She thought she saw something of herself in him.

This was in the late 1950s, when the world was as full of ironies as ever and almost all of Africa was ruled by Europeans in one way or another: directly, indirectly, by brute force or by strong-arm diplomacy, if the idea is not too illogical. A British map of Africa in the 1950s would have shown four predominant colours: red shading to pink for the British-ruled territories, dark green for the French, purple for the Portuguese and brown for the Belgian. The colours were a code for a world-view, and other imperial nations had their own colour schemes for their maps. It was a way of understanding the world, and for many who studied such maps, it was a way of dreaming about journeys that could only be pictured in the imagination. Maps are not read in the same way now. The world has become much more confusing, and full of people and names that obscure its clarity. In any case, nothing much is left to the imagination now, when the picture has become the story.

In the British maps, the red was a gesture to the English national banner, and it represented the willingness to sacrifice in the name of duty, and all the blood spilt in the name of the Empire. Even South Africa was still red shading to pink then, a dominion like Canada, Australia and New Zealand, places where Europeans had travelled half the world to find a bit of peace and prosperity. The dark green was a joke at the expense of the French, to suggest Elysian pastures when most of the territory they ruled was either desert or semi-desert or equatorial forest, so much useless territory won with arms and a grandiose hubris. The purple was for the anxious self-regard of the Portuguese and their obsession with royalty and religion and symbolisms of empire, when for most of the centuries of their colonial occupation they had been plundering these lands with barefoot brutality, slashing and burning, and transporting millions of the inhabitants to the slave plantations in Brazil. And the brown was for the stolid and cynical efficiency of the Belgians, who came late into the festivities but whose gift to the people they ruled turned out to bear no comparison to any of the other Great Powers of that mean-spirited era. Their legacy to the Congo and Rwanda will keep the rivers and lakes of those places muddied for a while to come yet. The Spanish had their territories as well, marked yellow on the British maps as a gesture to their national colour, which signifies an obsession with plundered gold. Later in the decade, the colours would be toned down to pale pink, light green, mauve and beige. This was to signal a gradual relinquishing of colonial rule, perhaps, an evolution to self-government, everything under control, here today gone tomorrow.

The 1950s map would also have shown the exceptions to European rule. Egypt was nervously free, and had been since 1922, but had no choice about playing host to the British Army, Navy and Air Force. Liberia had never formally been a colony, but had come into being as the liberated land where freed African slaves could be sent *back* from the United States of America to build a New Jerusalem, and what a fine job they made of it. Ethiopia had held out against the shambolic Italians twice. In the nineteenth century, when every European army that wanted to managed to grab a piece of Africa and slaughter thousands of its inhabitants, Emperor Menelik's army defeated the Italians at Adwa. You can be sure that it was buffoonery that led to this unnecessary defeat, although some authorities give the credit to Rimbaud's efforts as a gun-runner to the emperor. Later, Mussolini's armies were expelled by partisan and British and colonial African forces, Uncle Habib among them. Then there was Sudan, an independent military dictatorship since 1952; and Libya, a theocratic kingdom under British protection since 1951. These were ironies about which such a map had no comment to make. Otherwise everything was in the hands of the Civilising Mission, from Cape Town to Tangier, and that included all of East Africa, where these events were taking place.

The reason for indulging in this glimpse at a 1950s map is to recall how different the world looked then. No one really understood what a panic was in the offing, that in a few years most of these European administrations were going to break camp and dash off home, leaving behind them a series of paper-thin treaties and agreements that they felt no obligation to honour. So the way that young people like Amin and Rashid thought of themselves and their future had not even begun to disentangle itself from the expectations of a colonised people, living in a small place, in the interregnum (although they did not know it) between the end of one age and the beginning of another. In his last years at school, Amin was convinced that he wanted to go to the teaching college where both his parents had studied, and no one argued with him or discouraged him, or suggested that he should consider other possibilities with independence only seven or eight years away. No one knew independence was that near, and not many had even speculated on what opportunities it would make available, and in any case, there was no reason why Amin should not aspire to the useful and contented life that his parents lived, useful to their community, fulfilling to themselves and their dependents. Except that it *was* all going to change in a mad scramble out of Africa, and no one seemed able to imagine that, at least not anyone Amin knew. Not even his father, who listened to the news on the radio every day, had mentioned anything about independence being on the way.

*

His father was a well-known and respected teacher at a school in town, although all teachers were respected, as we know. In the streets people addressed his father as Maalim Feisal, addressing him by both his profession and his name, and went out of their way to greet him and wish him well. Whenever he went to a government office, or to the docks or to the hospital, wherever he went to feed the hungry bureaucratic machinery of state, he ran into a former pupil who was only too glad to be of assistance. It thrilled Amin to hear them praise his father for his kindness and for his cleverness, and to hear them tell their favourite stories about him. Do you remember that time, Maalim? Amin knew that wherever in the world he himself went and whatever he did, he would never have a greater importance or meaning than his father did in his community. Even though his mother too had been a teacher until Amin's last year at school, her former students did not populate the public world in the same way because they were women.

It was a wonder to see them together, his mother and father. He was thin and tall, and she was ample and getting ampler with the years. Perhaps he was not tall compared to the well-proportioned giants in other places. It was a small place with small people, and he was tall for there. His face was thin too, made more ascetic by the greying beard he trimmed to a point. His shirt-sleeves were always buttoned-down, and in everything he did he seemed measured and neat. It was an appearance which could not possibly be true all the time, but that was the impression he gave. He walked with a slight stoop and often wore a slight frown, but when he spoke his voice was clement and his face was on the brink of a smile. Some people called him Msafi, clean, especially as the word had a vague rhyme with his name. In another place he would, perhaps, have been called fastidious.

She, on the other hand, was short and plump, more likely than not to look dishevelled and hurried, straggles of her stubborn hair evading the pins that were meant to keep it in check. Her manner often seemed overstated, her look of surprise too wide-eyed, her indignations over-acted. She bubbled with schemes, with unfinished business, but she also had a gift for listening. When she was at home, all conversation and observation was inevitably addressed at her, everything focused and dispersed through her. She knew exactly the moment to stop what she was doing and give someone her full attention. People called her Mwana, because she was the youngest in her family. Mwana means child. Her real name was Nuru, which means Light, although now only Feisal called her that.

At the age of nineteen, Amin duly enrolled at the teaching college, which itself had been established only a generation or so before, to prepare for a career as a teacher. One among his peers at school had been sent to study medicine in England by parents who could afford the expense, others were sent to study in India, in Egypt and perhaps elsewhere. Several others had dispersed to seek a future among the network of family and relatives up and down the coast and in the interior. That was how it always was. People got up and left when the opportunity came. But Amin did not look for opportunities. He did not wish to leave. He had made his decision, and had every anticipation of being a teacher for the rest of his life. Perhaps it was a way of thinking which is only possible in small places, and perhaps the world has become more restless than it was at that time.

Farida too had made a decision about her life. A couple of months after she returned from Mombasa, she apprenticed herself to a dressmaker in Vuga, Mrs Rodrigues, a Goan woman with pretensions to fashion because some of her customers were wives of the colonial officials. They only brought in repair work, adjusting hems and loosing waists, but their custom was enough to allow Mrs Rodrigues to write on her name-plate: By Appointment to Her Majesty's Government. The bulk of her business was making dresses for all sorts, but the Europeans gave her prestige. Farida worked there in the mornings and afternoons and took work home to finish off in the evenings. She received no payment of any kind for the first six months, and only a pittance after that. Mrs Rodrigues, who was a quiet, smiling, soft-spoken woman with hard and inflexible opinions, told Farida that really she should be grateful for the advanced skills she was teaching her, and the quality of client she was introducing her to, and not to expect any payment at all until she was fully trained. The money that she gave her was done out of kindness. Did she not give her tea and a slice of cake every morning for gratis? Farida planned to start her own business when she was ready, and thought she had no choice but to put up with the meanness.

Her mother Mwana loved sewing, and had her own sewing-machine, not an unusual acquisition in that time and that place. So she helped her with the tricky tasks that she brought home, sewing on the lace and ribbons, stitching the button-holes, and so on, crouched over the pool of light under the bulging forearm of her machine. It was recreation and a pleasure for Mwana, so she said to her daughter. Sometimes they worked late into the night because Farida had promised her employer to deliver the work the next day, and she could not bear the scolding that would follow if she failed. Her mother often complained of strain in her eyes.

She worked for Mrs Rodrigues for three years. Every time she suggested leaving to take in her own work at home, Mrs Rodrigues talked her out of it, offering her more pay, frightening her with the risks. Farida allowed herself to be persuaded and stayed, but after three years she had learned enough to start taking in work at home. At first she did this for friends. They brought a picture cut out of a magazine and said they wanted a dress like that, and Farida would do her best, working on weekends or in the evenings. It took a long time to complete a dress, and the friends called round, and complained and chatted and no one minded. If the result of this labour was not exactly like the picture in the magazine, it none the less looked good, for Farida had a talent for cutting and sewing, and could study a picture and produce a dress not too unlike it in the end.

The pace of the house was completely transformed when Farida started to work from home. In the morning, Farida did not appear until after everyone had left, but when they came home at lunch-time, it was to find her firmly in charge. One by one they went to the kitchen to pay their respects, the mother to enquire and interfere, the father to hand over the fruit which it was his special task to buy on his way back from work, the brothers to sniff the pots greedily and get in the way. After lunch, everyone milled around helping. Then Feisal and Mwana retired for their afternoon rest, and Amin and Rashid went off to their consuming round of adolescent activities: sports, homework, wandering the streets, playing cards, and Farida got started for the day on her sewing work.

It was at this time, when Farida was beginning to gather customers for her sewing, and Amin was confidently in his examination year for the School Certificate, and Rashid was following less assuredly in his wake, and Maalim Feisal had refused his first offer of a headmaster position, that Mwana collapsed at work and was advised to retire at the age of thirty-nine. She was diagnosed as suffering from glaucoma and suspected hypertension. She was distraught at the thought of how much trouble she was going to be to everybody, weeping silently and unexpectedly in company. 'I will go blind and you will have to look after my useless body,' she said. 'O yallah, alhamdulillah.'

They sat with her and comforted her, crying themselves because they too had no doubt that she would go blind. The doctor had only mentioned the possibility, but the horrific prognosis was like a curse to Mwana and her family. So their mother stayed at home and started again. She was irritable and becalmed because she did not have to juggle with complicated arrangements, but after a while she began to ease and slowly altered the tempo of her life. There were doctors to visit, a trip to Mombasa to consult a specialist, an operation to release the pressure in her eye. There were spectacles for short-sightedness, new diets, a medication regime, exercises, and life became pleasingly chaotic again if rather more subdued.

When Rashid reached his final year at school, he was still talking big, to his friends and his brother, and to his parents. He had grown more stubborn and difficult with the years, and liked to think of himself as a bit of a dissenter. In his last year at school he would not stop talking about leaving. This way of thinking had crept up on him unawares, and made itself evident in the way he was unable to restrain the irritation and scorn for so much around him. It was the things he had come to know and the books he had read that gave him an idea of the world that was ampler than anything he saw in the lives they lived. This place was stifling him, he said: the social obsequiousness, the medieval religiosity, the historical mendacities. He had a powerful vocabulary, and he was only seventeen. He'll go far, his friends said, if it isn't all hot air. Amin listened and smiled, teasing him and agreeing with him in turn. His mother was troubled as always about him, despite her own troubles, but she too could not help being swayed by his rage. What is going to happen to this mad boy? His father sat with him at length, encouraging and cautioning, don't be such a dreamer, be practical, what do you want to do? In the end, family and friends swung behind his big talk, and listened to his discontented account of their lives and urged him and advised him to work and aspire to his dream of the great world.

It was his teachers, in the end, who came up with the practicals. They marvelled at how he had grown from the ordinarily talented chatterbox student, to the confident and assured one who wrote the stern and mature pieces (in a bright schoolboyish way) that he did. They took the credit for this transformation. He was equally stern with Macauley, or Shakespeare, or Islam, and was precociously witty about it too. The wit was inclined to be supercilious but that was just high spirits, and time would see to that. Oxbridge material. His teachers were British, at least the ones with clout were, and perhaps they had taught Rashid to study their world so well that now they could not help but be impressed at what they had produced. They helped him apply to British universities, coached him to sit the scholarship examinations, imposed on him a regime familiar to them from their own far-away school days. It was as if they had entered into a conspiracy with him. The harder they made Rashid toil for knowledge of their world, the more Rashid wanted to succeed in it. It was more subtle than it appears, not only a desire to succeed and please, but something more seductive: the more complex his understanding became, the more it seemed that this world became his. The history and literature teachers, who were the ones who took him in hand, gave him texts to study that they never mentioned to the other students: Carlyle, J. S. Mill, Darwin, T. S. Eliot. Every Saturday he had to stay behind after classes for additional tuition with one of the teachers, who often offered him the passages he had read with some incomprehension in digestible form. Sometimes there was a surprise test, asking him in turn to bring up what he had digested.

So while Farida was launched on her dressmaking business at last, and Amin was a student at the teaching college at the age of nineteen, preparing for a career as a secondary school teacher, Rashid was in the final arduous stages of his flight from home.

6 Amin and Jamila

A MIN CAME HOME FROM the teachers' college one afternoon to find Farida had a client with her. That was not such a surprise. This was the time of day when women called on each other and conducted normal women business, which was to keep the fabric of life in good repair. There were exchanges of news, congratulations and condolences, of courtesies and kindnesses, and of whatever luscious or tart scandals had surfaced in recent times. The ground was prepared for the betrothal, years in the future, of recently born babies. Ailing bodies were commiserated over. Favours and loans were discussed and exchanged, and the shortcomings of husbands and sons, and the world they presided over, were enumerated and lamented. It was also a convenient time to discuss the design of a new dress, or to weigh the virtues of satin over muslin, or the high yoke over the gathered waist, and so this was also the time that Farida conducted business with her clients.

He knew her name was Jamila and had seen her before but had never seen her this close and had never spoken to her. He had always thought her beautiful. So close to her, he saw that her face was slim and subtly featured, something in it moving all the time. Her eyes were the colour of dark amber. They had light and movement, a kind of life, and a willingness to be amused. Her body was shaped like completeness. She had one of Farida's fashion catalogues open on her lap, and a length of material spread out on the mat where they sat, so he knew she had come to be measured for a dress. She smiled at him, a polite greeting, but it had something languid and knowing in it which Amin thought made her seem glamorous, someone who had travelled and who knew about the world. As he stood in front of her, frozen in admiration, he saw her smile broaden and her eyes glow for a second. Farida smiled too.

'My younger brother,' Farida said.

'Is this Amin?' Jamila asked, smiling, her voice thicker than he had expected of someone so slim and so subtly beautiful. 'Your mother was asking after you a moment ago.'

Amin put his bag of books down and sat in the nearest chair. If his mother had been there, he would have been bustled away. His mother did not like either Rashid or Amin to sit in the room when there were women visiting. They were expected to make their respectful greetings, and if the women concerned had known them since they were children, they were expected to listen smilingly to their affectionate banter and then disappear. They were too old now to hang around women, and would only inhibit conversation and earn themselves unsavoury reputations. She was especially vigilant with Farida's clients since they were usually *young* women, not because she thought anything dramatic would happen, but because she did not want any talk. She did not want to hear her sons accused of disrespect to one of her neighbours' marriageable daughters. But his mother was not there, so he sat down, staring. Farida made a small impatient noise, which made him turn towards her. Her eyebrows were raised, in enquiry, in warning.

'What is it?' she asked. Amin smiled at her and then got up to leave, but did not go. 'Is something the matter?'

'No no,' he said.

'He speaks,' Jamila said, her voice rounder now, teasing him.

'Karibu,' Amin said, turning towards her. You're welcome.

'Are you studying?' she asked, glancing at his bag. 'Where are you studying?'

'At the teachers' college,' he said, stopping in the doorway.

'Ma's looking for you,' Farida said, giving him one of her

mock-furious looks behind Jamila's back. He gave them a small wave and went through into the house.

'She was asking about you,' Farida told him later, after their parents had gone to bed. She often worked late into the night at her dressmaking, sitting in the front room with the radio turned down low. Amin sometimes sat with her for a while, to give Rashid more time at his revision in their bedroom. Rashid could not do his work if Amin was in the room, even if he was only lying on his bed reading quietly or even sleeping. And if he was not able to do his work, then crisis, self-doubt and silent sulks loomed. In any case, Amin liked sitting late into the night, reading while Farida chatted intermittently and the radio played listeners' requests from far and near. His work at the college did not make enormous demands on him, and much of the reading was for his own pleasure and interest, and did not frighten him with the sense that he would have to be clever about it later. So he did not always mind breaking from it to listen to Farida, for he could go back and read the page with the same pleasure when she finished. He found her company easy, and her chatting was not insistent. She talked, he listened, and sometimes talked back and she listened. Then he went back to his book or his notes, and she to her buttons and bodices. They were fortunate in this ease with each other. Most of her talk was of people and what they had done, and what she thought they were about to do. Their father called it gossip when Farida and their mother were in full flow, but to Amin it did not sound any different from what the men did when they talked among themselves, except that the men were a lot more malicious. Perhaps the women were like that too, when they were among themselves.

'The one who was here today,' Farida said. 'She was asking about you.'

'Asking what?'

'How old you were, what you were studying, when you were going to finish, you know,' Farida said, giving him a sly smile. 'She said she's seen you but she didn't know who you were. Do you know who she is?'

'Jamila. I've seen her,' Amin said. 'Tell me more. Tell me about her. What did she say?'

Farida grinned. He could see that she was enjoying this, and he knew she loved whispered confidences and tortured secrets. She had one of her own which she had told him, swearing him to secrecy. He thought at first that she told him so that she could have someone to share the tensions and terrors of her secret love affair, but he came to understand later that she was thrilled and proud to be in love. She met him in the year she spent as a schoolgirl in Mombasa. The older girls from her school walked home by a certain route, walking together as a group, and a group of boys from a nearby secondary school somehow always intersected with this route. They didn't even stop. They walked together for a while, laughing and teasing and making eyes. Later, among themselves, the girls selected which of the boys they wanted as their boyfriends, and through sisters and cousins sent word to the boys. Farida chose hers, tall and slim and serious, Abbas, and told her cousins who sent word to his sister, and he started to write to her. There were no meetings, no kissing or going to the cinema or anything like that. No furtiveness or scandal. It was as love should be, those daily encounters in the street, during which, perhaps, hands might brush against each other, and there were the anguished secret notes which passed from sister to cousin to Farida.

When she had to return to Zanzibar because she could not get through the entrance examination, it was a tragedy. The failing was sad. It made her feel stupid, when she could see silly girls passing just because they could do long division better than she could, and only because their parents paid for extra private tuition. So that was bad enough, but the real tragedy was leaving Abbas, who had told her in one of his letters that she was always in his tormented heart (and he was in hers, she told him). The cousins thought that their parting was a serious enough calamity for the lovers to be be allowed a tryst, nothing too irresponsible, perhaps left on their own for a few minutes on a walk on the beach. They began negotiations with Abbas's sisters, but Aunt

Saida found out and forbade the plan. Well, she didn't really find out anything in particular, she guessed that something daring was being planned and issued a blanket prohibition on pain of the direst punishment. Nobody wanted to upset her, or make trouble for the lovers. So they did not even get the chance to walk hand in hand on the beach or anything people in love like to do. Amin was sceptical about this last bit, thinking that Farida was trying to spare his brotherly honour and protect Abbas from fraternal outrage. Walking hand in hand was a marriagable offence in certain quarters.

Anyway, Farida returned to Zanzibar, a dubu without her boyfriend, and in those first few weeks she was heart-broken – she pressed a fist to her chest to show Amin where it hurt – from having lost Abbas and having lost her cousins in Mombasa. It was like having some part of her cut off. Had he ever felt like that? Then he had not known real heartache yet. Images and smells of Mombasa came to her in her dreams, and when she woke up in her own bed at home, she could not stop the tears.

When she first came back, she used to spend the morning with Aunt Halima, helping her with household chores as she used to before she left, and one day her aunt made her sit down and tell her everything. She could not take the long looks and the sudden sighs any more. As she confessed, Farida's agony was such that she wept for the whole hour that it took her to do so, speaking and wailing at the same time, and having to repeat herself before Aunt Halima understood her. Aunt Halima was distraught at first, then when all her efforts at consolation failed to have any effect, she sat there grinning at the magnitude of Farida's misery and in the end she offered to have Abbas write to her using their address. Her husband Ali would have to know, of course, since he collected the post, but he could be relied on to be discreet. Amin smiled to think of Uncle Ali's face when he was asked to be part of this conspiracy. He loved mischief and hoaxes and deliberately ambiguous signals. When someone was telling a story which turned on a misunderstanding, especially if it was one that was cynically engineered, Uncle Ali was always the first to see it coming and start chuckling. People saved up such stories for him, and laughed to see his glee. He would have chortled at the idea of a secret correspondence as if it were a kind of practical joke.

That was how it had been since. Abbas was still writing to her, and she was writing to him, and four years later they were more in love then ever. In his letters he always said he was dying of longing for her. Farida first told Amin the secret after he finished school, initiating him into adult intrigue and clandestine passion and the intricate ways of the world.

'Why is it a secret?' Amin asked, completely missing the point. 'You are twenty-something years old and he is probably older. Why can't you say to Ma and Ba that you love each other and you would like to get married?'

'Don't be so childish,' Farida told him, her mouth open in exaggerated horror at this reckless suggestion. 'Because we can't, not yet. You'll understand why later on. I can't tell you now.'

'Why not?' he asked.

'Because you're my brother,' she said, aghast at his naïvety.

That did not help him much, but Amin had to be content with being the recipient of tantalising whispered confidences hinting at other secrets for the time being, and occasionally to share in the torment of misunderstandings and doubts. The misunderstandings and doubts arose, quite rightly, from the writing, in interpretations of the letters and especially the poems they wrote to each other which, Amin could take Farida's word for it, expressed their innermost feelings and uncertainties. Was that sentence meant as a joke, or was it an inadvertent expression of irritation? Did the poem she sent him really capture what she had meant to say? Did his poem *mean* what it said or did it mean the opposite? 'You know what poems can be like,' Farida said. 'A poem can fill you with joy one day, and then on another reading can cast you into the very depths. I've told him I don't want any more poems, but he can't resist, and nor can I.'

'Resist what?' he asked.

'Writing them,' she said.

'Oh, he writes them. I thought he copied them from some-where.'

'From where?' she asked, giving him a quick, suspicious look.

'You can buy books full of them, you know.'

'No, he writes them,' she said after a moment's thought. 'And so do I.'

'You write poems too?' Amin said, incredulous. 'I don't believe you. Let me see them.'

'No,' she said sharply. 'They're not meant for you. And I don't see why you should be so surprised that I write poems. Or is it that you think me too stupid?'

Not too stupid, but he had not thought of Farida as interested in anything in particular, certainly not in writing poetry. She was always laughing and talking and sitting close together with other women in an affectionate group, and that was what he thought she did and all she wanted to do. Instead it turned out she had a lover in Mombasa to whom she wrote love letters and with whom she exchanged poems which they each wrote themselves. So that was what she did in all that time she spent alone, and that was the meaning of the smiles that hung on the ends of her words. The thought of Aunt Halima and Uncle Ali as the secret postmen made him smile too, to think of the sharp words that would be said in tensely hissed whispers when her mother found out. He looked at Farida differently after that, at someone who was capable of an intrigue of that magnitude and at someone who wrote poems that she refused to show to anyone else but Abbas, someone who had a life she kept safe from everything around her. The first time he saw Aunt Halima after Farida told him, he could not stop himself grinning. Aunt Halima gave him a long, suspicious look and frowned, commanding him not even to mention whatever it was that was making him grin like that.

Despite his misjudged surprise about the poems, Farida continued to offer him precious confidences, flashing an enve-lope at him sometimes, or talking to him unguardedly (so she made it seem) about her lover. Abbas was training to be an engi-neer with the Marine Authority in Mombasa, and had almost completed the first stage. The manager had told him that he was doing very well and he was putting his name forward for a further training course in England when the opportunity arose. The manager is a mzungu, she told him, in no doubt that Amin would understand that this gave the approbation greater weight. The praise of a mzungu was minted of the same true coin as his ingenious machinery and his infinite expertise. Amin was also the first to know that Abbas was planning to visit the following year, at the completion of his preliminary training. He had relatives who lived in the town, on the outskirts, but he couldn't remember for certain the name of the area. He was planning to stay with these relatives for a month or so. His mother was coming too. It would be the first time that Farida had seen him for four years and more, but in some ways it felt to her as if it was only yesterday.

'Is he coming to ask for you?' Amin asked. It was usually mothers or aunts who asked other mothers and aunts in such circumstances. 'Is that what the mother is coming for? You'd better tell Ma, you know.'

She hushed him urgently, and he was not sure if this was the wrong moment in her narrative for him to be given any further information on the matter, which of course was still secret, or whether she was hushing him from anticipating in case of bad luck. She grinned as she hushed him, asking him to be content with that.

'Will you live in Mombasa?' Amin asked, and Farida hushed him again, her grin even wider. 'Will you go to England with him when he goes for his training? Why can't I see the poems?'

'Because they belong to someone else,' she said, but he could see she liked being asked.

So when she told him about Jamila asking about him, her tone was lowered as it was when she spoke of her own secret love. This is what she told Amin about Jamila. 'You know that big house in Kiponda,' Farida said. 'You go past the old cemetery with the huge baobab in it on your right. Then you go past the bicycle mechanic on your left, and after the mechanic's shop, right opposite the big Indian school, there's a turn on your left as if you're going to the hamam. You know those lanes, and that big house there after the turning . . . that's where she lives. It's their house, the family house, that big house. She lives downstairs and the family live upstairs, her mother, her father and her two elder brothers with their families. She lives downstairs on her own. I couldn't do that, not in a big house like that. Have you seen it? Do you know the old house I mean? It must be dark inside, like a tomb or a cave. Like Bi Aziza's house. Although Jamila's house is not a haunted ruin like our neighbours'. Can you imagine living downstairs there, a woman on your own? It's asking for trouble. I would be too afraid . . . of both the shetani and the talk. When Jamila married, the family made a flat for her and her husband out of those downstairs rooms. They must've been stores or shops with a separate front door. People talk about her, you know. They talk about her a lot.'

'What do they say?' Amin asked, feeling sad for her.

'Well, she insisted on having the flat with its own front door, and people said she was secretive and arrogant or worse. Why couldn't she live like everyone else? Why did she have to be alone? What was she hiding? She had to have this done to the flat, and she had to have that wall knocked down and that window replaced. Her husband was wealthy, somebody she met on her travels, Nairobi or Dar es Salaam or something like that. Perhaps he paid for the renovations so they could be on their own. He did some kind of business. I don't know what kind of business. Just business, I'm not sure what exactly. After a year or two, he left her and then divorced her, and went back to wherever he had come from. It surprises you, doesn't it? Why does it surprise you?'

'She looks as if she knows things. She looks so worldly,' Amin said.

'And then she marries some swaggerer,' Farida finished for him, nodding. 'Well, perhaps she doesn't know as much as she looks. He toyed with her for a while and then he left her, like these dirty old men who take a new wife every year and then divorce her a few months later. It's surprising that Jamila should get caught like that, I suppose. Her family have no needs they can't meet, so I don't even know why she bothered with this man.'

'Perhaps she loved him,' Amin said, meaning to be sarcastic, but Farida looked at him with a foolish smile, as if he had said something charming.

'Anyway, everyone expected that Jamila would move back upstairs with her family after her husband left, and someone even sent word to enquire if the flat was available for rent, but she refused to move. So then people started to say she must be getting up to something, living there alone with her own front door. Then after that she started this travelling. People say it's business, but I don't know about that or about what kind of business she does. I know she has relations in Mombasa and even further up the coast. I'm surprised you don't know about her. People talk about her a lot.'

'People! They say such terrible things about everyone that sometimes I just don't listen,' Amin said.

'So you have heard something,' Farida said, grinning triumphantly. 'Come on, what did you hear?'

Amin hesitated. 'I've seen her pass by, and then heard people say who she was, what her name was. But I don't remember hearing anything bad about her, if that's what you mean. Only that her grandmother was a European man's woman, you know, his mistress,' he said.

Farida nodded portentously. 'She was. In Mombasa. I don't think she's still alive now. She can't be. But even when she was, no one went to visit her, and she didn't go out anywhere. We passed her old house once. Jamila's mother is their child, Bi Asmah. Look at her skin. It's like milk, so creamy, even though she's so old. She came here to marry, and probably to escape people's talk in Mombasa. I think she was brought up by relatives, but I expect everyone talked to her about her mother's scandalous life. People's talk can cut you to shreds.'

'Well, that's nothing to do with Jamila, what her grandmother did,' Amin said. 'It's useless malice and gossip. I don't know why people do that. There's much to be said for kindness. When is she coming again? What else did she ask about me?'

There is much to be said for kindness. That was so like Amin that Farida smiled when he said it. He would listen to his friends tell a story of thoughtlessness or cruelty, or a story of pettiness or neglect, or to another variant of unkindness, and after a moment of reflection he would say that. His friends laughed at him for it. Those not so friendly to him thought it a pretension of virtue, a genre of courtesy which was prevalent among those who affected gracious airs. His real friends did not see cynicism in him, and when they laughed at him it was not always unkindly, and not always to his face, but they laughed at him none the less, and took his lament as a kind of naïvety. They searched him out with tales of everyday brutality to hear him say his sorrowful words. Then when he did, they chortled convulsively and swallowed their laughter, or if they were good enough friends, they laughed openly and teased him for his impossible kindness. You're too good for this world, they said.

The night after he heard Jamila's story, he dreamed about her. He was sure it was her, although at the beginning of his memory of the dream she was only a presence sitting in a yard in the dark. She was silent at first but he knew she was there. He felt her there. Something vibrated in the air. She began to hum almost inaudibly, and slowly the sound strengthened and her voice rose in a modulation that hovered out of reach of his hearing. But he felt her there, and her humming voice burred against his skin. Her silhouette grew solid like a thickening of the night. In her song he heard the notes of primitive sorrow, notes of loneliness and of fear of pain. Later he saw her in a dimly lit room, perhaps underground or in a cave, lying on her back, fully dressed on a mat. A long-haired beast squatted on her belly, looking guilty but unmoving, paralysed by obsession. The desperation of the beast was so clear that Amin woke up, and feared that he had cried out, but Rashid was breathing easily a few feet away from him. He's probably dreaming of Oxbridge, Amin thought.

The next day he cycled past her house. Two or three times a week he went swimming with friends after college, and on this next day, on his way to call on them he took the road which led to the hamam. The street was narrow and deep in shadow at that time of the afternoon, and the house stood across the top of it, making a junction. Another street ran in front of the house in both directions, although that street too would be forced to twist and turn to avoid other houses and so on. That was how the old town was built, short narrow streets and deep humming silences. If you rode a bicycle down these streets, your thumb constantly worked the warning bell and your fingers stroked the bicycle brakes. The house was painted in a creamy whitewash, a little tarnished by the rains. The windows in the upper floors were painted an ashy green, with fanlights above them in the shape of arches mounted with stained glass. The windows on the first floor windows were shut, although some of the blinds were open to let in air. The second-floor windows were wide open, as were the huge carved front doors, allowing a good glimpse of a paved courtyard. He did not think the house looked like a ruin. He thought it looked roomy and airy and subdued. He saw a smaller, plainer door to the side of the house, which looked like an entrance to an office or a store. The downstairs window facing the street was the only one on the ground-floor level. It was shut, but all its shutter-slats were open. He gave a long intricate ring on his bicycle bell as he went past the window. No, it did not look like a ruin at all.

Their swimming arrangements were impromptu. Whoever felt like swimming called round on the others, and whoever felt like it came along. Sometimes it turned out to be a crowd of five or six of them, sometimes it was two. They never went swimming on their own, especially not at that time of the year when the seas were rough before the beginnings of the monsoons. Some people kept away from the sea altogether at that time, but it was so hot and dusty that Amin preferred to be tossed around in the water, even though it was exhausting swimming in it. But friend after friend was not at home, so he gave up after the third attempt and cycled slowly past the playing fields, along the avenue of casuarinas which was always cool at any time of the day, and headed for the beach by the golf-course. They were not there either.

He turned back along the hospital road, past the Victoria Gardens and then left after the courthouse to a secluded beach which they often came to for a swim. A lawn sloped down from the back of the courthouse to the beach, and on either side were two huge houses with walled-in gardens which looked out to sea. He had heard that from the upper floors of those houses, a person could see all the way across the channel to the mainland, although how that information was come by, he was not sure. At some time in the distant past, the houses belonged to merchants and Omani nobility, and they were built in the style they favoured, battlements and terraces, and huge blank walls to thwart the curious. At the time of Amin's visit that afternoon, British colonial officials lived in all the houses along this stretch by the waterside: perhaps the chief justice in one of them, or the medical officer or the attorney general in the other. There was no one in sight. Near him, a young palm tree twisted and turned its fronds improbably on their stalks, sinuous and snaky, seductively writhing in the wind, lifting its bedraggled hair with transparent intent. Amin sat under a huge casuarina tree, the ground beneath it littered with its dry kernels, and watched the sea churning. He loved the roaring silence of the sea at this distance from the shore.

It struck him that he had no idea who the British officials living in these houses were. Sometimes people came out on the terraces overlooking the beach and watched them swimming, sometimes they waved, and sometimes it felt as if they wished them away. Neither he nor his friends nor anyone he knew had any idea who the people who lived in these huge houses were, except that they were the rulers of the land and that they were relentless in keeping themselves separate. Someone knew who they were and what they did, of course: their servants, or their staff in the offices where they ruled. But Amin hardly ever caught sight of a European face in the streets, except perhaps that of one of his teachers or the unmistakable day tourists from the liners that stopped on their way to and from Europe. Yet there must be a whole crowd of them secreted away behind the walls of such houses, living quietly. Amin wondered what sense they made of the people they ruled. He imagined they would simply seem a babel of agitation and tetchiness, their cries and their gasps merely the whines of the subjected at any time.

He saw a door in the garden wall behind him was now open, and standing in the doorway was a man who looked as if he might be the gardener. He wore long brown shorts and a ragged white shirt. His feet were bare. Amin saw the cool shade of the garden through the doorway. Hands on hips, the gardener watched Amin for a few minutes, challenging his presence there. Amin waved to him and looked away, stretching himself out on the grass, refusing to be intimidated. They did that sometimes, the courthouse gardener and the ones from the other houses. They stared at them like that when they came here for a swim, as if they were invading their masters' privacy. But the gardener's presence there over his shoulder spoiled the feeling of tranquility he had begun to feel under the trees. He grew more aware of the casuarina kernels digging into his back, and so he mounted his bicycle and rode away. On his way home he rode past the house again, and this time saw a little girl come out of the huge carved doors, one of which was now shut. He gave a cheerful tinkle of his bicycle bell, and she smiled.

That night he had to go over a statistics homework with Rashid, who was driving himself to anxious distraction over his examinations for the certificate and the scholarship. He spent most evenings with Rashid, doing the same revision exercises to keep him company, testing him on what he knew, listening to his endless anxieties. The examinations were due in six weeks and Amin had already offered Rashid his opinion that he did not think he would survive until then if he did not calm himself.

'But you're clever,' Rashid told him. 'It's no good telling me not to worry. Some of us have to struggle for every slight thing we learn. This statistics is incomprehensible to me. Pointless witchcraft. But to you it's easy and probably useful in some way. How can I keep calm? I'm going to fail.'

'Your teachers love you. You won't fail.'

'What do you mean?' Rashid asked, looking pleased and glowering at the same time. 'Do you mean they'll fix the examination? I wish they could. Or are you saying I'm a creep?'

'Everybody says you're a creep,' Amin said. For a while the statistics had to be put aside while the two brothers sorted out a more urgent matter, bouncing each other off the walls and the beds, and making such a racket that their mother banged on their door and asked them if they had gone mad.

'No, Ma,' Rashid called out in a whining voice. 'Amin is bullying me again.'

'Stop that both of you,' their mother yelled. 'Open up, open this door at once.' She stood at the door and raged at them, although as always it was Amin who bore the brunt of it. Amin refused to cooperate after she left, but Rashid knew they would be back at it the next day.

The next day was Friday and a whole crowd of them went to a football match in the afternoon. Then there was a long cycle ride to the country on Sunday, as far as Bububu, and a picnic and a swim. Then back to college on Monday and the usual round of waiting for buses in the middle of the afternoon, homework, friends, revising. The rains came during this time, lowering the sky for days and then releasing torrents of clear crystal water that refreshed everyone. At first it was as if everything had been reborn: trees swayed more self-importantly than before, house-roofs gleamed through the rust, roads sparkled, but as the rains continued day after day, the gutters filled up with debris that the water had swept up in its rush, drains overflowed and pools and puddles formed everywhere. Roofs leaked and water found its way into the limestone mortar and loosened the fabric of the houses, some of which collapsed suddenly in the night. The ruin opposite their house lost some mortar and a shutter or two, revealing even more of its bones and molars, but it gave no further sign of surrender. There was no way of avoiding the mud and the muck in the streets, everyone had to pick their way through it as best they could. Leather sandals sprayed muddy water over clothes, and the leather itself soon rotted. In a few days the mosquitoes arrived in hordes, and the fevers started. Children playing in the rivulets of water picked up jiggers and infections in their feet. After classes, there was nothing to do but sit under cover and play cards or gossip. When the rains first arrived they were a release from the sun, the oppressor, whose appearance every day was the return of the tormentor. A month of dark skies and downpours made everyone smile whenever the sun burst through.

One afternoon during this season, several days or perhaps weeks after the first time, Amin came home to find Jamila sitting on the mat as before, a mail-order catalogue in her lap (for the fashions) and a piece of satiny material spread out on the mat between her and Farida as before. His mother was sitting in a chair under the window to catch the light, writing a letter. When he saw Jamila he felt an unexpected sensation of relief, as if he had feared that he would never see her again. He had thought about her often since that first time, but in a suppressed, guilty way, as if he had entertained improper fantasies. She held out her hand, smiling, and he leaned forward and took it, lightly, just touching her. He sat down in a chair nearby, smiling, a knot of pain in his chest. She was so beautiful it made him hurt to look at her. He had pictured her frequently, imagined her face as he lay in the dark, but that was something flat and still compared to the face before him. Her skin glowed and her features moved delicately, her eyes smiled with an uncomplicated ease.

'How are you?' she asked, speaking lightly in her deep voice, making conversation. 'They really keep you late in that college, don't they?'

'We have classes in the afternoon,' he said, and thought he heard his voice squeak slightly from excitement.

'Farida made my dress so beautifully I've come to have another one made,' Jamila said.

He wanted to ask if it was the dress she was wearing, but he feared that he would sound too bold. 'She is a very good dress-maker,' he said instead, and was certain he heard his voice tremble.

'What's wrong with you?' his mother asked behind him. 'Are you getting a cold? You didn't get caught in the rain, did you? No, well what do you want here? Go and put your books away and take your father's spectacles to him. He'll be at the café. He forgot them, and by now I expect he'll be convinced that he dropped them somewhere. Go on, what are you doing here? Oh, and could you buy me a 30-cent stamp? I'm writing to Aunt Saida, and I'll want you to go and post the letter for me later.'

When he glanced at Jamila he saw she was amused, almost laughing at the way his mother was pushing him out of the room. That is how mothers are, her eyes said, always hurrying you off somewhere. He went to his mother and kissed her hand in greeting, as he had done every day when he came home since he started school at the age of seven. And as she did every time he did so, she kissed his hand too. He saw that her eyes were luminous and watery from the strain of writing. 'Go,' she said. 'Go and get your father's spectacles. They're by the side of the bed.'

'I loved studying,' Jamila said suddenly.

'You were clever,' his mother said, relenting for a moment. 'Everyone said so. I didn't teach you, but everyone who did said so.'

'Which school did you go to?' Amin asked, relishing her, her face, her voice, her smile. This was new to him, the sensual depth in the pleasure he found in looking and listening.

'I went to Forodhani and then St Joseph,' she said. 'After St Joseph I went to a business college in Mombasa, and did short-hand and typing. Then after working there for a couple years, we came back to start a business services bureau here.'

'What's that?' Amin asked.

Jamila shrugged. 'Well, it didn't work anyway,' she said, smiling at him. He had heard the *we* and thought of her divorce, but she seemed untroubled. We always ask each other which schools we went to, Amin thought, and who we knew there. Sometimes it was like a way of claiming kinship.

'Amin, put your books away and take your father his spectacles,' his mother said, unable to take any more. 'And don't forget the stamp. See if Rashid needs anything, or take him out with you. He's been stuck in there since he came home from school. He'll injure himself with all this studying.' Her irritation and bullying were also a kind of boasting. Look how courteously my sons obey me even when I'm capricious. Look how hard they work.

That night he dreamed about her again, and dreamed about the beast squatting on her. He was that beast, he thought when he woke up. He had been the beast all along, but had refused to recognise himself, an ugly obsessive creature trembling with feelings and desires that he would do better to suppress and deny. But why should he trouble to deny? It was only a fantasy, a pleasurable play in which he imagined her face, and imagined her holding him and lying with him. Imagined her eyes smiling and glowing for him. She would laugh if she knew, and everyone else would be horrified. To her, and to everyone else, he was probably awkward and clumsy, a big child ignorant of the world. She was a woman, had travelled, had known love, for he was sure it was love that had made her marry the man she had brought back with her from Mombasa. She was a woman who knew she was beautiful, and would laugh disbelievingly if she knew what encounters he imagined with her. Well, there was no need for her to know that he lay in the dark with her, that he stroked her and spoke to her.

He often cycled past her house after that afternoon, perhaps every other day, sometimes every day. The huge carved doors were always open during the day, and sometimes he saw children playing in the courtyard. The smaller door to the side was always shut. He saw her coming out of the Municipal Offices one afternoon and wondered if she worked there. She was some distance from him, and he walked behind her without trying to catch up. She wore a buibui in the streets, as all women were expected to do, but her face was uncovered.

Once she walked past him into the cinema as he was standing outside with a group of friends waiting to go in. She was with two other women and a young girl dressed for an outing. He thought the young girl was the same one he had seen coming out of the house that first time, and had given her a cheerful tinkle on his bicycle bell. Jamila smiled at him, easily, and said his name. He waved to her. One of the other women looked back and smiled at him too. His friends teased him, calling him film-star names for attracting those smiles, and he played up to it, squaring his shoulders and strutting a bit, but he knew that, like him, they did not take those smiles to be anything more than friendly. Or at least they knew that none of them were up to doing anything about them. Those were grown women, and it needed worldly men to know how to make smiles lead to anything.

The examinations were soon upon them, and expelled all other thoughts from their minds. It was remarkable how examinations turned them all into troops of children again. Rashid was suddenly so sure of his chances that Amin began to fear that he really would confuse himself with over-confidence. Amin had to take examinations too at the end of his first year, but these were not given the global impact that Rashid's were. It was as if no one had taken a scholarship examination before. The school year ended with the examinations, and then groups of young people wandered the streets all day, or went cycling to the country, or slept until the middle of the day, or whatever else they liked. That was what holidays meant to most young people, lazing and aimlessly wandering the streets. There were a few unfortunates whose families ran businesses that required their services, but even they were able to escape without too heavy punishment, especially during the holidays after the examinations, when parents felt obliged to pamper their offspring for their efforts.

It was also the period of musim, and crowds of sailors and

traders thronged the streets and the open spaces, watched more vigilantly than in previous years, at least in recent times, by a battalion of the Coldstream Guards. In more distant days, the musim had been a boisterous and unruly time, when blood sometimes flowed in the streets from the high-spirited adventurers who came with the winds, and people locked up their children for fear of kidnapping. None of them knew that that was the last musim they would see. The Coldstream Guards were there that year because in addition to all the other momentous events of that month, there were rallies and campaign drives to the countryside to stir up the vote for the last elections before independence, which were to be held later in the new year. Amin sometimes caught sight of Jamila at the rallies he attended, and at the literacy classes. She was one of the activists, trying to persuade women to register for the vote. Literacy was a condition for registration, and Jamila was part of the group that ran classes for women at the main party branch, coaching them to write their names and dates of birth, which was all that was required to prove competence. Rashid volunteered to assist with the teaching at the local party branch, and their mother volunteered Amin as well.

There had been a failed election six months earlier, ruined by riots and a stalemate result. Political differences between the parties had become irreconcilable, as perhaps they do in small places with intimate histories and grievances that never fade, or at least that rarely need to be re-examined in the light of pressing events. There were few events pressing enough to make people think twice about their loyalties. Not yet. The riots were a shock to the young people, but perhaps not so shocking to the elderly who had seen street fighting and even the odd throat-cutting in the early years of the century. These new riots too would be put in perspective by later events, but in the innocence of the times, they seemed like an appalling lapse in manners, like family members abusing each other in public. There was still a great deal for us to learn about what harm we were capable of doing to each other, and how easy it would become once we had begun.

Anyway, a new election was due, and it was by then known that independence was due at the end of the year. The stampede had already started elsewhere: French West Africa and French Soudan suddenly brought forth a dozen new African nations. The British had launched Ghana and Nigeria on the long road to their glittering futures, and our own neighbour Tanganyika was suddenly and more modestly on the same road. The traffic between African airports and Lancaster House in London, where all the constitutional conferences (what a laugh!) took place, must have been thick and constant.

Ramadhan arrived at that time, so really, it was one thing after another in those months of that year. The coming elections charged the air, and people already had a taste of what was to come, with ministers of the caretaker government driving about in black Austins with special number plates and the sultan's flag on their bonnets. It made the approach of independence more real, that flag on the bonnet.

One long, hungry afternoon in the middle of Ramadhan, when schools and the college were closed for the duration of the fast, Amin was lying on the sofa in the living room reading while Farida was standing at her worktable, ironing a finished dress. Everyone had new clothes made for Idd at the end of Ramadhan, so this was Farida's busiest time in the year. Their parents were sleeping away the hungry afternoon hours in separate rooms, their mother in Farida's room and their father in his own bed. Husband and wife avoided each other during their afternoon siesta at Ramadhan, to be on the safe side. For even the feeling of desire, even for the lawfully wedded one, broke the fast. Lusting thoughts of any kind did that, and Amin suspected that his own feats of hunger amounted to nothing in the Almighty's ledger. One of the surprises of growing up, he had discovered, was that fasting did not inhibit sexual excitement, quite possibly the opposite.

There was a knock on the outside door, which they kept locked during these hungry afternoons because it opened directly into the front room and some neighbours could not resist an open door. It was Jamila, who had come to have dresses made for her niece. Amin stood up to shake hands, and then sat in a nearby chair, listening to Jamila explain that the dresses were a surprise for Idd, so could Farida make them using another dress as a model rather than measuring the girl herself. She gave her instructions and Farida noted everything down with the unfussy and unsmiling efficiency which always impressed Amin. Farida's face usually broke into a grin whenever you caught her eye, except when she was taking instructions from customers. Amin pretended to read but looked up every few seconds to watch her face, her hands, her lips and thought her every movement a vision. When Jamila finished her explanations, she turned in Amin's direction. He thought she knew he had been thinking of her in the way he had been. She asked him what he was reading and held out her hand for the book. He took it to her and then sat down again in a chair nearer to her. It was a paperback of *Dr Zhivago*, which a friend who had gone to visit relations in Dar es Salaam had brought back for him. She asked him about it and he spoke about the greatness of the writing and the compulsive narrative.

'I must borrow it from you when you've finished,' she said, holding it out to him.

He went back to the sofa with it and sat down, and soon after that she got up to leave. She looked his way for a second and waved to him without saying a word, and for some reason that felt more intimate than if she had spoken. Farida returned to her ironing without saying anything either, but looking thoughtful now. He thought she looked disapproving. She knows about my mania, he thought, and sat on the sofa in a tense silence, pretending to read, expecting words of mockery from her. But she said nothing for a while and then asked him to turn on the radio so that the noise would wake up the parents. Their mother liked to do the Ramadhan meals herself, although she was kind enough to allow Farida to help. And the sound of the radio was sure to get their father out of bed and out of the house. The voices of the sheikhs with their Ramadhan sermons grated on him. He thought they were hectoring and too holy to be true, and as soon as the tajwid which opened the afternoon programmes was over, he was on his way. He went to sit at the café with his friends until the siren went for sunset, when they all shared their first cup of coffee of the day before going to the mosque.

Ramadhan is during the day. In the evening people eat well, then they sit with friends or family and natter into the early hours, or stroll to the waterfront until late, or go to the late-night show at the cinema or play endless games of cards. Others go prowling the streets for different kinds of games which they prefer to keep secret from everyone else. Everyone stays up late, even children, who play out under the street lights until all hours. That night Amin saw her walking at the waterfront with her family. As he walked past, she gave him a bright smile but did not speak. He walked on towards the end of the waterfront promenade, away from the lights. The moon was past full, he remembered that later, hanging like a bright lost world above the sea. The next day, unable to stop thinking about her or think about anything else except food, he went walking around town, walking aimlessly, he said to himself, but he soon found he was heading towards her house. For once she was coming out of the smaller door as he walked past. She stopped at the door and looked at him with surprise, and after a moment she said: 'Amin, how are you?' He replied and hurried past, expecting that she would now begin to think him a nuisance.

That night he kept away from the waterfront, but the next night he could not. When he saw Jamila with her family, he kept his distance, watching her from afar, catching the flash of teeth and the sublime ordinariness of their gestures as they laughed and talked. Eventually he walked past them, but he pretended he had not seen them and went by without looking. There was no college now to distract him, no tedious bus journeys and undemanding assignments, only hot daylight hunger and a feeling of foreboding, a regular beat of terror that he could not suppress. He could not imagine saying anything to her, and could imagine only too well her horrified laughter if he were to do so. Yet he could not stop himself rehearsing what he would say to her, and there were times when he convinced himself that she wanted him to. It terrified him that he could be so obsessed. Sometimes he felt angry and capable of causing pain, and he did not understand why.

He would force himself to keep away from her. That was what he decided. That evening at sunset he put on a kanzu and went to the mosque, and later, after breaking fast, he sat outside the house and chatted with people in the neighbourhood. The next day he walked down to the sea, to the beach nearby where the fishermen kept their boats, away from the waterfront promenade. These were people he had grown up with, among them their neighbours who lived in the big ruined house opposite to them. Amin sat among them in comfort, even though his hands were soft while theirs were cracked from handling fishing lines and nets, and their faces were hardened by the sun and the sea. They were people rich in assurance, desparadoes, who bantered with merciless ferocity all day long, and then put off to sea in their tiny boats as the sun began to soften. He sat with them for some time and took more than his share of mockery to earn his welcome, then went to the mosque again in the afternoon and afterwards read until sunset. That was how he decided to forget her, by staying in the vicinity, going to the mosque, reading, playing cards, talking. It didn't work completely, because he thought of her when he was reading, and even when he was talking or listening, but he kept away from her.

Rashid said something about his unusual piety, teasing him in front of the parents, and got a lecture for his pains. 'You should be going to the mosque as well, you ungrateful boy,' his mother told him. 'Or do you think you are a mzungu already? You haven't even left and you are getting ready to forget everything. You should be ashamed of yourself, laughing at him when you have obligations to fulfil yourself.' His father had a few words to say too. The sermon, which was capable of many variations, went like this: 'Ramadhan is the holiest month of the year, when the angel Jibril first revealed the Koran to the prophet. We fast to practice restraint, and to return ourselves to our deeds before God. It is a time for us to repent and to make good the derelict habits we have fallen into in the preceding months. One of the derelict habits you have fallen into, young man, is not going to the mosque, and you would do well to follow your brother's example in this matter. And instead of playing cards all day, you should read a sura of the Koran every afternoon. Go and fetch your kanzu, and get yourself out of my sight.' Later, when they were in their beds a few feet from each other, Amin thought Rashid was lying in the dark, listening to his breathing.

Then Rashid asked: 'What is it?'

'Nothing,' Amin said, discouraging.

'All the praying. Have you done something bad?'

'I'm praying for your scholarship. I don't think you'll get it any other way. And to pass the time, and get some exercise, you know, up and down, kneel, touch the ground, good for the back,' Amin said. 'Come on, give your poor brain a rest and go to sleep.'

Late one evening, several days into this new regime, Farida said to him: 'Jamila came for the dresses this afternoon. They turned out well. She was very pleased. That's good, because she'll bring more work after Idd. She asked after you. She said she hadn't seen you for days.'

'What did you say to her?' he asked sharply.

She made a face of shocked surprise: 'All right, all right. I said you were fine. Should I have said something else?'

The following evening he took off his kanzu and went for a stroll to the waterfront to look for her. Crowds of people walked in small groups by the sea, in the light of the dying moon, some of them holding hands. Street lamps reflected off the water, and lit up the road, empty of all car traffic at that time of the night. It was only nine in the evening, but there was nothing to drive to at that hour. Women walked in their own groups, and men walked in theirs, and sometimes called out greetings and ribaldries to each other. Most of them were young. Some of the

Indian women were accompanied by a brother or an in-law, but otherwise no young man could bear to be seen walking with his sisters. Goan girls strolled unaccompanied, at ease with their glamour. They were Christian and had Portuguese names and worked in government posts, and so were almost European. Nobody dared to bother them, even with banter. Amin walked unhurriedly along the shadowy side of the road, away from the water. The lights in the sultan's palace were on and the trees in the park at the top end of the waterfront were lit with coloured lights. The spray from the fountain sparkled in the lamps. He saw her strolling out of the crowd in the park, heading in his direction. With her were the two women he had seen her with before, and whom he thought were her family. He crossed to the waterfront side of the road. As he approached he saw her face begin to break into a smile, and he felt his own grin spreading. He stopped a few feet from them, and they stopped too, everyone smiling.

'Amin, where have you been?' Jamila said, unmistakably pleased. 'I haven't seen you for days. And where are your friends? Why are you on your own?'

'Up there somewhere,' he lied, pointing towards the Old Fort. 'I'm just going to catch up with them.'

The two women with Jamila, who were about the same age as her but who looked as if they were already mothers, glanced at each other and began to walk on. 'You're looking well,' she said, and he felt her eyes browsing over his face. It felt like touching. 'Have you finished that book yet? I'd like to read it when you do, don't forget.'

'I won't forget,' he said, but somehow the words came out more portentously than he meant them to, as if he was making a more solemn promise. He looked at her in some confusion, and from her smile he saw that she was amused. But it was not cruel amusement, and there was something in the intricacy of her glance that made him ache a little. The two women had stopped a few feet away, looking out to sea. One of them laughed and Amin turned to look, assuming that they were laughing at him. Perhaps Jamila had said something about the way he stared at her, and how he turned up everywhere. 'Are they your sisters?' he asked.

'My sisters-in-law,' she glanced towards them and began to move on. 'I'll see you later. Don't hide yourself,' she said and gave him a small wave.

For the next two days he went back to his regime of the neighbourhood, the mosque and reading, but he was happy at the memory of the recent evening, pulling it out to look at it every few hours. Then on the third afternoon, on his way to the hospital to visit a friend who had been admitted for an emergency appendicectomy, he stopped in the Cathedral bookshop for a browse. He knew most of the books they had in there because they only sold schoolbooks, but he loved handling the new copies and reading a paragraph or two of familiar stories. The bookshop was run by the Society for the Propagation of Christian Knowledge, but it did not make a fuss about its proselytising, and was careful not to offend its mostly non-Christian customers. Amin came out after a few minutes and strolled unhurriedly towards the main road. Suddenly he saw her across the road from him. She slowed down when he waved and waited for him to cross the road.

'I'm going to the hospital to visit a friend,' he said after the greetings. 'He was rushed there for an operation yesterday. At least he doesn't have to fast now.' They stood under the shade of a neem tree for a few minutes and spoke about unmemorable things, but after he walked on, he was filled with a kind of heat at the way she looked at him. Her eyes were large with absorption, studying him as he spoke, lost in him, unguarded about what they revealed. He thought they revealed desire, for all that he knew about such things. He would have touched her if they were not standing by the main road in the middle of the afternoon.

Afterwards his mind raced with excitement and terror. He didn't know what to do now, or how to do it. The next day he went on a long cycle ride on his own, out into the country with a book, and on his way back sat on the beach near Sherif Musa, reading and marvelling and worrying about what he should do now. That evening, after they had broken fast and were drinking coffee – Rashid drinking on his feet, ready to rush off to that evening's boisterousness, their father fidgeting his feet, ready for the big talk at the café, and their mother settling in her chair for a quick snooze after her efforts in the kitchen – Farida called him out to the yard to help with the clearing up. He followed her with a feeling of relief. Something was going to be said. He guessed it.

'What's going on? I want talk to you,' she said in a fierce whisper. 'She came again today, and she asked about you. What's going on? You're not doing something stupid, are you? Later tonight. I want to hear everything.'

So later that night he told her how things were with him. It had been a hot, humid day, but now a strong cool breeze blew in from the sea. He had thought about what she might have said in the afternoon, and wondered about what had made Farida so fierce, but he decided he would not ask questions, would not hesitate. He would tell her about how he felt and wait to see what would happen. They sat on a mat in the yard, in the light of the moon now fast waning in the closing days of the month. It was a relief to talk and he did so at length, while she listened with few interruptions. Then when he was over the first flush of his outpouring, she told him that she had guessed, or at least had begun to fear about what he felt for her. 'You have to be careful,' she said softly, kindly, but also to keep her voice from being overheard. 'You don't know what she wants, you don't know what she has in mind. She is a woman who knows the ways of the world. I've heard a rumour that she's seeing someone, a politician. They're the heroes now, and soon they'll be the government. People like them want a woman like her for show.'

'What do you mean, for show?' Amin said, because Farida fell silent after that, waiting for him to prompt her.

'I mean a beautiful, glamorous woman like her with that bit of scandal about her family,' Farida said. 'They want a woman like her to play with. Maybe that's what you want too, to play. I hope not. I hope you don't mind me saying this, but it may not be a game you know how to play yet. Maybe it's what she wants too, a kind of love game. But she is older, she knows about things. You could lose your way with someone like that.'

'I thought you liked her,' Amin said softly, sadly, not wanting to think of Jamila like that. He was relieved that Farida did not laugh or rant at him with platitudes and warnings, but he did not enjoy this suggestion that he was too naïve for Jamila's worldly wiles.

'It's not that I don't like her,' Farida said, and then could not suppress a brief smile which glinted with a soft glow in the gloom. 'You have to remember that people like her live in a different world from ours. That's what Ma would say if she knew. They're not our kind of people, that's what she would say. They have a different idea about what is required of them and about what is . . . honourable. You have to be careful not to hurt yourself, and not to hurt *them*.' She gestured with her chin towards the house.

He said nothing to her, and after a moment she sighed and continued. 'When she came today and she asked about you, she was exposing herself to insult and rejection. She was inviting me to act between you. At first she only asked after you, how you were, but then she asked if you had said anything to me that I wished to pass on. I could have taken offence and shamed her. I think she wants you, but I don't know what she wants you for, so you have to be careful. The politician may be a rumour and nothing more. She was seen in his car, but he could have been giving her a lift, I suppose. There have been other stories, and she is older than you.'

He was sweating and aching from the uncertainty, and from a fear of making a fool of himself. These were feelings he had come to know well in the last few weeks. 'She can't be much older than you,' he said. 'And you're only two years older than me.'

'She must be five or six years older than you,' she said. Then still speaking gently, her voice down to the softest of whispers, she asked: 'Do you love her?' When he nodded, she burst into a huge, tired smile and touched his open hand. When she took her hand away there was a folded envelope on Amin's palm. 'She left that for you. After she asked after you, and I replied, she sat there in a terrible silence. I knew she was going to do something strange. She asked me if I would pass that on to you, and I said I would. I'm tired now, younger brother, and you have a lot to think about. Tell me about that tomorrow. Did I tell you I had one from Abbas today? It had a lovely poem for Idd.'

He sat quietly for a few minutes after Farida left, taking everything in, turning the envelope over in his hand. It was unaddressed and sealed. He went inside and opened it quickly, unfolded the thin blue paper and read the one line written there with disbelieving eyes: *I long for you, beloved.* It was like one of his fantasies. There were no salutations, no names, just that one line. He felt elated, he saw her, he imagined her. She smiled and reached to stroke his face. When she came into his arms, he felt a lightness in his body that was like panic.

What would she want from him? What was she asking him to do?

The first time they met alone was on the second night of Idd, after the end of Ramadhan. Farida passed the instructions to Amin. They met on the fringes of the Sikukuu fair, which was held for the four days of Idd on the playing-fields near the golf-course. In the afternoon, the fair belonged to the children. The stalls and kiosks and roundabouts were crowded with them in their new clothes and their precious pennies. They bought toys, and candy floss, and ice cream and took rides on the round-abouts, and some became rowdy and got slapped, and others were separated from their elder brothers and sisters and burst into tears of panic. Once it began to get dark, the children were required to get back home, as they are everywhere in the world. After dark, the adults began to arrive, although the pleasures on offer were, to all appearances, no different from those of the afternoon and hardly as exciting to them as they had been to the children: toy-stalls, candy floss and rides. The fair was lit with strings of fairy-lights and with powerful humming tilly lamps, but the lights were only around the kiosks and the rides and the cricket pavilion, which during Idd became an ice cream parlour. That left plenty of shadows a few casual steps from the melee, and pitch-dark beyond.

She called his name softly as he approached, to guide him towards her, and a moment later he touched her outstretched hands. She kissed the palm of his right hand and said, Habibi. Then she gently pulled him down so they sat on the grass, so they did not throw the faintest shadow on the ground. She reached a hand out and touched his face as he had always imagined, then she pulled his face towards her and kissed him, opening her lips to let him feel her moistness. You're beautiful, she whispered, her left arm around his back and pulling him down on the grass with her. He marvelled at the feel of her body under the touch of his hands. He had not anticipated its solidity and density, or the inexplicable sensation of stroking its shape. He had expected something lighter, he realised, because for him she had been someone abstract, a fantasy. They kissed and he breathed in her perfumed breath. They whispered each other's names and called each other beloved, their bodies pressed against each other. After a few moments, which seemed like seconds to him but also seemed like for ever, she said she would have to go back. She had only come to hold him and tell him how beautiful he was, but she had better go back before she was missed. She had told her group that she was going to find popcorn, to get rid of the cloying taste of the ice cream. She should go back before they began to think of looking for her. Would he come and see her at her flat? They would have more time.

When? he asked. Later tonight?

She liked his urgency and kissed him for it, then she rose to her feet. He rose too and groped for her. They walked like that towards the light, touching and holding each other. She told him her nieces were staying in the flat with her that night, a treat for Idd. Would he come on Monday night? At nine exactly. Then she would leave the door unlocked so he would not have to knock. If the door was locked, he was to go away and wait to hear from her. At nine exactly. Now she would have to go. She smiled and then kissed him quickly. Be careful, beloved, she said.

He stood in the shadows and watched her as she strolled casually, as if coming from nowhere in particular, towards the noise and the throngs. He felt no fear now, but a grinning confusion and incredulity. She thought him beautiful, when all the time he thought her beautiful beyond belief. She had kissed him with sobs of pleasure when he had expected her to be breathless with laughter. Her face was a multitude of details, the light in her eyes, the shape of her mouth, the smile that made him feel pain. Everything perishes, perhaps in an instant, a long moment and then gone, though only in procession into memory. He knew that those few moments would not perish from him while memory lasted: the taste of her mouth for the first time, her legs pressed against him, her hand on the back of his neck. In her embraces he had felt something like his own need, his own urgency. This must be what it feels like to love and to be loved in return, he thought, imagining, now that he knew, how terrible it would be to love and to be spurned, to crave to touch and to be denied.

He walked deeper into the darkness, away from the music and the lights, bearing gradually towards the road that ran along the edge of the playing fields. He wondered if they had been seen. He thought he heard a whisper in the darkness. There were always furtive movements and flurried courtships on the edges of the Idd fair, observed with sidelong glances and tolerant smiles (unless an elder brother was about), on the expectation that nothing really improper would take place. When he found the road he turned back on himself, as if he was returning from a stroll along the beach by the golf-course, or perhaps he was taking a sweetly solitary walk under the avenue of casuarinas. A soft wind blew through the feathery foliage, and every few steps a kernel exploded under his sandals.

He smiled to himself at these deceptions, at his pretence of being on an innocent walk away from the bustle of Idd, but at the back of his mind was a foreboding that this was how things were going to have to be. It was not a place which tolerated that such relations should take place openly, and an unblinking and unrelenting scrutiny made the furtive and anxious stratagems of lovers into a sordid comedy. There was someone always looking on and adding fragment to someone else's fragment, until sooner or later everything was found out. For Amin the ridicule and the shame of discovery were muted by exhilaration, but he none the less felt a slight tremor of aversion, a tiny swell of nausea for the deceptions that would be necessary.

He walked away from the fair, on the road past the white-painted Karimjee Jevanjee hospital, named after the Ismaili philanthropist who had given so generously towards its construction. The ward-lights were turned down low at that time of night, yet the gleaming squares of light illuminated the flame trees which made an avenue along the road. The hospital itself was like a softly lit ship moving silently under a lightless new moon. The road was empty and mute, lit by street lamps that were far apart and glowed yellow like oil lamps. On the right and opposite the hospital was the museum, built by John Sinclair, the colonial Master-builder in these parts, to commemorate the 1918 Armistice. It was called Beit-el-Amani, the House of Peace. Its cupolas, now only a white flush in the gloomy light, were modest models of the domed roofscape of the Hagya Sofya in Istanbul.

Amin walked past the disused cemetery opposite the hospital, silent now when during the day its shade would be crowded with traders selling fruit and snacks to the patients and their families. The Residency's iron gates were shut, and even at that hour of the night, a policeman stood in his guard-box inside. Behind those gates, and in a fantasy Moorish palace, also built by John Sinclair, resided the power of the land, the captain of the ship himself, the British Resident, Sir Henry Potter K.C.M.G., who on ceremonial occasions came gliding out in his black Humber, his white topee mounted with white plumes which rose through the open sun-roof like a feathery fountain. In times gone by, the topee would perhaps have been worn by a man on a horse, so the feathers would have swayed and nodded with the rider's movement as the horse ambled gracefully, but efficiency had replaced play-acting grandeur, and the sleek, silent Humber was a more appropriate symbol of the taciturn methods of the modern empire. Amin had once seen the Residency building from the sea when sailing with a friend, and he had felt like a naughty child stealing a look into a forbidden room.

Opposite the Residency were the Victoria Gardens, where in those days so close to independence, the new Legislative Assembly met. Sultan Barghash, another great nineteenth-century builder, who built roads and fountains and sewers and palaces, constructed the pavilion and the walled gardens so that the women of his household could stroll and take their discreet ease away from the gaze of the curious. He had his gardeners fill it with shrubs and sweet-smelling bushes and flowing water, and what he could not grow for them he left to their imagination. He grew plants and trees from different parts of the world, many of them gifts from the British consul of that time, a Victorian gentleman through and through who shared the Sultan's horti-cultural mania even though he mildly deplored the perverse luxury in the use the plants were put to. A later sultan, in a burst of gratitude to imperial agents who had expedited his ascen-dancy over a rival, named it after the immortal queen and gave it as a gift to the people. Amin walked past the courthouse, another Sinclair building with its replica oriental dome. Its clock was ticking loudly in that silent hour. On his right was another cemetery. The town was full of small cemeteries, at crossroads, in the lee of mosques, in walled yards, multitudes of the dead crowded up against their descendants.

Amin walked slowly towards the waterfront, relishing the silence of the dimly lit streets. He loved the town's silences, which were different in surprising ways. He loved to describe to himself the silent roar of the sea, or the humming silence of the narrow lanes. In some of the squares in the middle of the old town, he sometimes heard a silent echo of a woman's distant laughter. He met no one, although some cars drove past, perhaps on the way home from the fair or from visiting friends for Idd, yet despite the emptiness he felt in the midst of people. He heard murmurs and laughter through open windows, and some front doors were still open and unattended, as if their owners felt no fear of intruders. There were still people walking on the waterfront, and lights still on in the family quarters of the sultan's palace. The tide was going out gently, reluctantly, and the sea slapped on the waterfront wall with squelchy smacks. Out in the water were a crowd of lighters at anchor, and at the quayside, the ferry was tied up for the next day's crossing to Dar es Salaam or Mombasa. He walked past the Customs House where Uncle Habib worked, and where someone was sleeping on the steps, his face turned towards the sea. The Harbour-master's house had its upstairs jalousies open and its lights fully on, and from its veranda came the sound of laughing English voices and the smell of cigars. He took the road past the Ithnaasheri Dispensary and hurried past the site of the old demolished power station. He had a memory of its demolition, but some of the housings for the turbines and screws were still there, and during the rains filled with greasy soupy water that was iridescent in the sunlight. On such a moonless night (the merest sliver of a new moon had long since sunk below the curve of the sky), the pools looked pitch-black, like the black tern of the House of Usher. When he was younger, he used to think the pools were inhabited by oily, snaky creatures, and even though he knew better now than to think that anything could live in that poisonous soup, some dread still remained as he hurried past. The lights of the Sultana Cinema ticket office were switched off but the lobby lights were dimly on, a late show. He stopped to see what was on the late show on Monday night next, and then headed for home.

That was his explanation, a late show with friends. His mother did not like it. Why not the evening show? Because it's the going out late that makes it fun, he said. Why go out late on a Monday, when you have college the next day? she said. I've done all my work, and we're only going on a school visit the next day, he said. I'll be home by eleven. His father did not say anything, but Amin could see he did not like it either – a deepening frown and a spark in the eyes. Perhaps they guessed that he was meeting someone, but they could not hope to stop him doing that sooner or later, so *he* guessed that they grumbled and looked reluctant because they could not help it, but they could not think of a reason to forbid him going out.

On Monday night at nine, trembling and apprehensive as might be expected, Amin pushed gently at the door of Jamila's flat and felt it yield. She was standing just inside, and as soon as he entered she closed the door and latched it. The room was in darkness, a cave, but a dim light was on further inside, and in that light he saw her smile. She made a hushing noise, then took his hand and led him towards the light. It was the guest bedroom: a bed, an armchair, a drawer chest with a mirror in a gilt-edged frame. She led him to the bed and sat down beside him, and even in that dim night-light, he could see that the smile and glow in her face was happiness. He realised that he too was grinning at his limit.

'You came,' she said, her voice vulnerable and teasing.

He croaked something in return and then leaned forward for her. It was the first time that Amin was doing this, and he put himself in Jamila's hands without resistance at first. He could not believe the sensations of pleasure and pain and release, and after a while he was lost in the restrained frenzy of love-making, unanchored to anything except her touch and her voice.

Afterwards they lay talking, and Amin felt brave and happy, as if he had proved himself in some demanding act. She lay close to him, touching him and marvelling at his youth and perfection, while he stroked her and breathed the perfume of her body. The night-light was still on, and after all the time they had been in the room, he could see everything clearly. He saw now there was a heavily curtained window in one of the inside walls.

'It opens into the living room,' she whispered. 'There are no outside windows in this room. I thought we wouldn't be over-heard. I couldn't sleep in here, not alone. It feels like a tomb.'

'Why don't we use your bedroom?' he asked, wondering if that was asking for too much.

'It has a window which opens into the courtyard,' she said. 'Someone might hear us.'

Even in her own flat they had to be furtive. The thought brought a small spasm of nausea at the danger. 'That was like a miracle,' he said to clear his mind of the belittling thought, and he heard her laugh. 'Why are you laughing?'

'Because I feel happy, and because it's your first time, isn't it? I thought it was,' she said, and touched him. 'And because you're beautiful. When I saw you striding across the road to me that afternoon, I wanted you. I really wanted you. That's why I wrote you that note. I could not stop myself. I thought I would lose you. Will you come again?'

'Tomorrow,' he suggested, which made her laugh again so suddenly that she clapped her hand over her mouth to stifle the sound.

'No no, not tomorrow. We have to be careful, habibi, other-wise . . . Another day, later in the week maybe. Come on Friday. Will you?' she asked, stroking him.

He nodded. 'Yes, on Friday. Otherwise what?'

'Otherwise they will make us stop,' she said. 'They will say ugly things and they will make us stop. You're so young, still at school, and I am a divorced woman in my twenties.'

'I'm in college, and I'm nearly twenty,' Amin said. 'There can't be many years between us, and even if there were, you are the most beautiful woman I have ever met, and if I had been your husband I would never have divorced you.'

'My love, we have to be careful, otherwise they will make us stop,' she said, smiling and hushing him. 'Now you must go, so you're not late back from your late show.'

Amin slipped out without, he thought, even making a ripple in the air. He walked home like someone remade, beautiful and loved. That was how it began, in February of that year before independence, soon before the arrival of the long rains. Once a week, then more often, earlier and earlier in the evening, for months after that, Amin went to Jamila's flat. They whispered and made love and stifled their laughter, and when the time came for him to leave they clung to each other like desperate fools. She gave him a ring mounted with a ruby so that he would have something to remind him of her while they were apart, and sometimes she slipped a note in his shirt pocket, telling him how the thought of him, and how the smell and feel of him filled her life. He told her that his body was bruised and aching with love. When he was not with her he was afraid of losing her, afraid of words that would take her away. Then when he was with her he thought of nothing but her body and her breath and how his life was complete. He felt as if he could take on anything or anybody.

Some afternoon Jamila came to see Farida, to sit and talk or to have a new garment measured, because she felt she had to see her beloved even if she had only last seen him the night before. She did not say anything in front of Farida, but she could not always suppress her smiles. Farida pretended not to see anything, but the look of pleasure in her eyes gave her away. She loved their secret love. And sometimes Amin went into the Municipal Building, making an enquiry at one counter or another, wandering from office to office, chatting with anyone he knew that he saw in there, until he ended up in the employment office and caught sight of her.

It was a struggle to keep up with the college work, which now seemed even more arduously undemanding, because he could not always force his thoughts from her, and he always wanted to see her and be with her. He hid from people so he could think about her and plan how they could be together in years to come. She had told him stories of her life, and he knew now that he could not simply say to his parents that this is the woman I love and wish to live with. There was the mzungu grandfather and the years her grandmother lived in flagrant sin. Even if that ancestral lapse could be forgiven, which was not certain, there was her divorce, her age, and the rumours of affairs. Sometimes Amin thought she hinted at these, but he dared not ask. He did not want to know, not yet. He knew now what perhaps Farida had always known, that when it comes to love, parents always believe the worst, and enforce their authority with virulent righteousness and blackmail.

When he went to visit her, it was always after dark and always at a time they arranged. He walked there, took his time, varied his route as much as he could. He stopped to talk to an acquaintance or sit in a café for a while over a cup of tea, or lingered to listen to an argument about a football match, a young man indulging the undemanding pursuits of his town. He took care that her street was empty before he pushed the door which she left unlocked and very slightly ajar. If there was anyone in sight he walked past and came back at the same time the next day. When they were together they lay under the night-light in the guest bedroom, the furthest room from the street. When they spoke, they whispered, and stifled their laughter and made love with stealthy intensity. Yet for all that, they could not keep their affair secret. Someone might have seen through his elaborate subterfuges, or overheard a passionate sigh. Someone might have seen him from an upstairs window, or watched his unmistakable entrance from the darkness of an alleyway, but someone must have seen him and must have spoken about it to someone else. Then fragment was added to fragment to make discovery inevitable.

PART III

7 Rashid

I SHOULD HAVE KNOWN, but I didn't. He slept a heartbeat away from me, and I should have heard its altered tempo in all those months. I should have sensed that his sleep was broken by dreams and fantasies, and that on some nights his breathing was deeper from emotional exhaustion and satisfied passion. I should have smelled the difference in him. I should have seen that something was happening to him, something assured or even triumphant in his manner, but I didn't. What I saw I did not understand, and I heard and sensed and smelled nothing, or nothing that I recognised, or only did so later, long after their discovery, when fragments of memory rose to the surface like putrid matter.

By their discovery I do not mean that they were caught in the act of love. I don't think that happened. Our elders suppressed so much, kept so much hidden from us, some of them matters of such ordinariness and banality that at times I wonder why they needed to go to such lengths. Was it to save us from having to cope with the ugliness of the world? Was it habitual secretiveness which by then served no other purpose than to keep young people as ignorant as possible for as long as possible, so that they were obedient and tractable? Sometimes I am shocked to discover how much I did not understand of the events I lived through. I am sure that they couldn't have suppressed that they were caught in the act of love, though. I don't know exactly how they were discovered, but I don't think it was like that, otherwise there would have been public drama and gleeful stories and maybe some bruises. Perhaps they weren't even discovered, but exposed themselves with small acts of recklessness out of a feeling of invincibility, out of a sense that the cleanness of their feelings would keep them safe from the mean censure of the people around them. I would not have been capable of understanding something like that at that time, of understanding that feeling of the rightness of love. I was too full of my own triumph, my success at my examinations and my scholarship award to study at the University of London. This was towards the end of July in 1963, just a month before my departure, and there was no space in my mind for something as subtle as someone else's feelings, so consumed was it by egotistical fantasies. All I knew was that I had achieved what so many wished for me, and what I desired for myself. I thought I had given happiness to everybody by my success. I felt loved and heroic, and basked every day in the admiration of my family and my friends. I have no means to describe the deep poison that runs through the experience of flight and homelessness, but I didn't know that then either. How could I have known? How could I have had even an inkling?

On the evening of the exposure, I was lying on my bed reading. It was probably a detective novel or a historical romance if I remember rightly my tastes of that time. We read whatever came our way without self-consciousness or shame: girls' comics, *Anna Karenina*, Hemingway, encyclopaedias, like beasts of iron digestion, like Melville's ostrich, pecking at flint and grubs and succulent rare herbs without discrimination. It was close to supper, which we usually ate after the isha prayers, soon after eight, when our father came home. Every day, unless he was unwell (and he was almost never that unwell then), our father spent the late afternoon and early evening at the café, sipping coffee, talking with friends, browsing through the newspaper, listening to the radio, greeting passers-by, keeping an eye on the world. If he did not go, someone came to ask after him, in case he had been taken ill or there had been a mishap at home. When the muadhin called the isha, he went to the mosque, said the maghrib prayer on his own, because he would have missed it while chatting at the café, and then waited for the imam to lead the isha prayer.

Sometimes he came home between the café and the mosque, to get Amin and me to go to prayers. Perhaps the talk at the café was dull, or he had become irritated with someone's argument but did not want to make a fuss, or he had heard that there was to be a reading in the mosque for a neighbour who had died. For whatever reason, he sometimes thought to himself of his two growing sons lounging at home instead of going to prayers, and he came back especially to chase them out instead of going about his usual routine. So when I first heard his raised voice, and had not heard the muadhin calling the isha prayer, I thought he was shouting at me to go to the mosque. *Naam*, I called out with alacrity (I love that word *alacrity*), because I knew how it hurt him when he thought us disrespectful. *Naam* is the politest form of *yes*, and anything less counted as disrespect to my father. I went out to the living room and saw Amin standing inside the front door, his sandals still on, evidently having just arrived home. His face was still but his eyes were wide with panic. My father was facing him, his back to me, stiff and stooped, his angry posture. He must have shouted at Amin as soon as he stepped through the door. My mother was sitting in the corner by the window, where she usually sat, her head lowered, her right hand massaging her brow. Farida was standing next to her sewing-machine, her body pressed to the wall, watching our father. Her eyes turned towards me for a second and I saw that they were large with anxiety. She frowned, briefly and distractedly, as if my presence was a complication.

'Feisal, please don't shout,' my mother said, 'there's no need.' I heard from her voice that she had been crying. Amin heard it too and looked at her. My father turned to look at me, his face taut and frowning, his eyes sparking, perhaps wondering who I was and what I was doing there. He turned back to Amin, took two strides towards him and raised his arm with his palm open, and then stood there, arrested, unable to hit his beloved son, waiting to be reprieved. He had not hit us in years, and only a handful of times before that, an irritable slap or a smack in the arm to punctuate a stern lecture. My mother said his name again, and he lowered his arm and walked to sit on the sofa near her. I saw that his body was shaking, perhaps with rage, perhaps with hurt and fear.

'How could you do something like this?' my father said. 'You bring shame on us and on yourself. You have no thought except your pleasure. You ruin your life, as if you have no head to think with. As if no one has ever taught you anything or given you any idea of what is right and what is wrong. As if you're nothing more than a beast, without feeling, without respect for yourself or for anyone else. I don't even know what to say to you.'

What happened? I wanted to ask. What has he done? But the surprise and anxiety I felt at what I was witnessing deprived me of words, which was as well, because I think if I had said anything I would have been instantly expelled. My father had spoken quietly, but his face was scornful and the force of his words charged the air, he who only spoke gently even in sternness.

'Please explain this matter to us,' my mother said, looking up and taking her hand away from her brow. She lifted her agonised face at Amin, her eyes large and glistening, the fingers of both hands knitted together and clasped in her lap, tense but patient. The silence seemed to last some minutes.

'Who told you?' Amin asked, his voice deep and tragic.

'Amin,' his father said wearily, unable to suppress the merest smile, the merest wince of ironic amusement. 'It doesn't matter who told us. Your every act is an admission that what we've heard is true.'

'I don't know what you've heard,' Amin said quickly. Nor have I, I wanted to say. What happened? I want to know too.

'We want to understand,' my father said. 'What your mother asked you was to explain how this could have happened. How could you be so foolish?'

The muadhin's call drifted in among us, and we waited in silence until he finished, as custom required. It was a providential silence, because during it I saw my father sigh and unfrown his face. He closed his eyes for a moment and his lips moved as he silently accompanied the muadhin's words: *Allahu akbar Allahu akbar, Ashhadu an laillaha ila llah, Ashhadu ana Muhammad rasulu llah.* At the end of the muadhin's call, my father's lips twitched in a familiar gesture, whose meaning was something between a shrug and a shake of the head, between resignation and perplexity. I saw my mother glance towards him. I think I saw something pass across Amin's face too, as he glanced from one of them to the other. Perhaps that was the moment when he made his decision.

'I love her,' Amin said in the deep silence that followed the muadhin. That was all he said, that was his explanation, at least for the time being, and the way he looked after he said those words, lips pressed tightly together, made it seem as if he thought it was enough explanation.

My father rose to his feet, his face an unrevealing mask, his eyes lowered. He slipped on his sandals and left to go to the mosque, without saying a word, without requiring us to follow. He was good at exits. He would go away, after a long look, slip silently away without a word of rancour or blame, and leave you to stew in your sin, so that next time you saw him you were almost willing to be forced into admission and repentance. It was the teacher in him, perhaps, how to manoeuvre us into compliance without brutality.

'Love who? What's he done? What's going on?' I blurted, as soon as he was out of the door.

'You, go to prayers,' my mother said, but I ignored her as I would not have been able to ignore my father. He took such petty defiances so much to heart that I did not dare disobey him, but with her, orders came in a steady and relentless flow and so could at times be disregarded. She wiped her eyes briefly, and then beckoned Amin towards her. He sat down on the sofa where my father had sat a few minutes before, his eyes on the ground.

'Did she trick you? She did, didn't she? She must have done,' she said bluntly, certain and sure of Amin's gullibility. He said nothing, his eyes lowered, his face glowing with sweat. Her voice grew increasingly scornful as she spoke.

'Do you know who she is? Do you know her people? Do you know what kind of people they are? Her grandmother was a chotara, a child of sin by an Indian man, a bastard. When she grew into a woman, she was the mistress of an Englishman for many years, and before that another mzungu gave her a child of sin too, her own bastard. That was her life, living dirty with European men. Her mother, that same one in their big house there, the one who thinks she is someone with her silks and her perfumes and her gold jewellery, that is the child of that mzungu. She doesn't even know who her father is, except that he is some English drunk that her mother took home. When her husband brought her back from Mombasa, he knew all this, but they are a rich family, so they don't care what anybody thinks. They've always done as they wished. This woman that you say you love, she is like her grandmother, living a life of secrets and sin. She has been married and divorced already. No one knows where she comes and where she goes, or who she goes to see. They are not our kind of people. They are shameless, they don't think of anyone else but themselves. You say you love her, what do you know about love? You don't know people like her. We trusted you. Your father . . . You saw, you've broken his heart.'

A shudder went through Amin.

'You know what he's like,' she continued, her voice fraction-ally less scornful, slightly gentler, reeling him in. This was also her habitual role, to bludgeon and placate, to soften us up for submission. They were good at their work, but we must have been very easy to manipulate, schooled in obedience. 'He'll come home and he will say nothing, but you'll know that his heart is breaking. He is so proud of you. You must have nothing to do with her, and you must beg his pardon, otherwise you'll lose him. And he'll lose you. He's getting old now, I don't know how he'll take all this. And my sight is going every day, so soon I won't be much use to him. We trust you, don't forget that, despite everything. Promise me you'll stop going to her.'

Amin shook his head slightly and said nothing, like a stub-born, sullen child refusing to cooperate.

'Promise me,' she shouted and slapped him on the back of his head. 'Look at me when I'm talking to you. Do you want to kill him?'

Amin got to his feet and moved away, a look of rage on his face. He turned to look back at her as if he would say something, but whatever it was remained stuck in his throat. I expect it was to say that he would not promise, but he could not get the words out. I heard him go into our room and bolt the door behind him. I had understood during the exchanges that Jamila was the woman they were talking about, because everyone knew the story of her grandmother in Mombasa having an English lover. The idea filled me with wonder, that Amin loved her, that he could stand in front of his parents and say that. What did it mean? They wrote love letters to each other, and embraced and kissed, and gazed on each other's naked bodies and made love? It had never occurred to me to imagine Amin making love to anybody, let alone to a woman like Jamila. I thought her glamorous and part of the adult world, more than that, part of the sinning adult world of mistresses and scandals, and I suppose I didn't think of my brother as even an adult. I caught Farida's eye and realised that I was smiling at the thought of Amin's antics. She smiled back, at least with her eyes.

'That devil,' I said.

'It's no laughing matter,' my mother said angrily. 'I told you to go to prayers. Come on, get out of here, go, go now. And I don't want this getting told to anybody outside of this house. Do you understand that? You, blabbermouth.'

When I got to the mosque, the prayer was already into the second rakaa. I stood in line and joined the prayer. I couldn't see my father. The mosque was crowded and I was up against the back wall, when he was likely to be right up in the first line of worshippers. In any case, it was improper to look around you during prayers, for every word you said and every movement you made was addressed to God, and He did not like you to be desultory in your attention during your address, turning your head this way and that way and thinking about who knows what. You crossed your arms across your chest, lowered your eyes and submitted your whole self to Him. When the prayer was over, I had to make up the rakaa I had missed, and it was only when I had completed it that I was able to look around the mosque properly for my father. He was standing outside on the steps by now, a friendly, courteous smile on his face, talking with someone, waiting for him to find his sandals before they began walking down the steps together. Other people too were standing talking, or walking away in twos or threes, dispersing, going home for supper or to the café to listen to the news on the radio. It was a jolt to see him looking so effortlessly at his ease when he knew there was dirty work to be done at home, and I saw in that ease why it would be so vital to him to make Amin renounce his love.

Amin could not fight them off. They made them stop. That night they chased Farida and me away to our rooms (Farida protested, I went quietly) and sat with Amin until he promised to stop seeing her. I don't know what they said to him or exactly what promises he made, but I can guess. They would have kept him there forever until he promised to give her up, tangled him with their hurt and their fear for his disgrace, and Amin with his kindness and his dutifulness would not have been able to resist their love. Perhaps it was even simpler than that, and he knew what he would have to do the moment they appealed to his trust. He had been the reliable one all his life. That was how he knew himself, and how he had won the love and respect of his parents and beyond, and I think he would have found it impossible to say to hell with all that. So, in a way his affair was over by the time I found out about it, and afterwards Amin refused to talk about it to me.

I joked with him and tried to flatter his skills at seduction, but he would not talk about how he had done it and what had happened between him and Jamila. I even tried to hypnotise him by shining a torch on the ceiling while we lay in bed and telling him he was under my spell, but still he refused to speak. Then he made such a good job of seeming to have finished with the affair that there was no reason to disbelieve him. I had a terrible time keeping quiet about what had happened, especially when Amin seemed to have done with it all and no harm could come of speaking about it to friends. He went to college and came home and went out with his friends, like his old self, except perhaps that he was more silent than he used to be and read longer and longer into the night. In any case, by then I was close to my departure and I had concerns of my own, and when I thought of Amin and his affair it was as an adventure that almost ended up as trouble.

It was such a long time ago. I was in the throes of my own drama and my self-absorption, at the start of my great adventure which I know now I thought of as noble and deserved. I could not help thinking of what befell Amin as something slightly comic, an escapade. In my questions and promptings, I tried to get him to talk about Jamila like that: so what did you get up to, you merciless ram? He refused to talk and I was left to imagine their affair from the meagre resources of my own experience, which were extremely meagre. Even his silence seemed like a kind of worldly cunning, a sophisticated kind of subtlety. It was courteous to the lover without diminishing the triumph of the conquest, when boasting and explicitness would have made it sordid and clumsy.

I was young, and about love and sex I only had second-hand narratives of the place and the people I had grown up with, as anyone of my age and ignorance would have done. My elder brother had been making love to a beautiful, divorced woman and had been found out, the daring devil. I don't think I was envious. I was used to Amin getting there ahead of me in most things, and I never doubted that I would get there too in time. No, in truth I probably thought I was the one to be envied, the scholarship winner, justly rewarded for his talent and for his resourcefulness, whereas Amin was merely getting up to the dangerous mischief young men found irresistible.

When you were the age I was when I left, and brought up the way I was, you only heard about love and sex from the margins of conversations. You overheard things when your elders were talking dirty. Respectable older people did not talk about such matters anyway, at least not in the hearing of youngsters, and those who did, did so to provoke and mock, to express their worldliness and affirm their manliness. These latter, who were mostly younger men or men of reputation, did not mind having adolescent boys on the edges of their street conversations, listening and laughing at their manly cynicism. They turned love into a comedy, a farce, whose denouement was expected to be brutal. The lovers were spied on and their intimacies became the source of smirks and giggles. Another lover was beaten up by relatives, and humiliated in some slapstick fashion. Or another became notorious for the brutality with which he jilted his lover. Love was something transgressive and ridiculous, an antic, or at best an exploit. Amin's was an exploit, and his silence turned it into something more, turned it into a plan or a calculation, no doubt to be deftly executed on another subject in due course. It was in that way that it seemed merely a dangerous mischief, doing what daring young men do to amuse themselves.

Only I *was* there at the confrontation when they exposed his affair and made him end it. I saw his anguish then, his face glowing, his silence. I felt the tense significance of the late-night conversation from which Farida and I were excluded, and imagined the pleadings and the ultimatums. Yet I chose to misunderstand it all and make him into a seducer, chose to ignore his silence and vulnerability in favour of the comic narrative of love I was so familiar with. I don't think I could have done any different. As I said, I was young and overwhelmed with self-significance, and nobody's doings seemed more interesting than mine.

I don't remember leaving, not really. I remember the airport and who was there to see me off, and getting on the plane, but I don't remember the few days before or even the last night. At least I don't remember the feeling of it, the detail of it. I remember Amin saying on our last night together that I would miss the independence celebrations later in the year, and I remember him saying to me that I should send him anything good that I read. I promised that I would. I remember Farida crying at the airport, the embarrassment of it, and I remember my parents' smiles when I looked back for the last time. I remember them waving. Even if I strain I cannot hear a word they said. Such paltry mementoes.

London London! I have seen London London! In his great poem 'New York', Leopold Sedar Senghor exclaims like that at his first sight of Harlem:

> Harlem Harlem! I have seen Harlem Harlem! A breeze green with corn springing from the pavements ploughed by the bare feet of dancers

I didn't know the poem at that time, but when I did come to read it, it reminded me of my view of the city for the first time, there below as the plane circled before landing. It was like a miraculous rising out of emptiness, as if I had not known of its presence there over the horizon. Senghor's exclamation was not because he did not know that Harlem would be there, of course, but was a cry of fulfilment at a vision of something abstract and wished for, a mannered flourish at having reached that place at last, the scene of the Harlem Renaissance and of the diasporic African vitality which his poetry celebrated. London did not have that sense of identification for me, and I caught no sight of a bare foot ploughing the pavement into supple life. Neither did it have the spiritual and creative resonance Senghor sought and felt in Harlem ('Listen to the far beating of your nocturnal heart'), nor did it have the Mother Country delusions whose disappointment dispirited so many West Indians, but it was for me, as it was for many others in different ways, an abstraction of mythic proportions. It was an impossible destination now arrived at, a place of unexplained potency and mystery, rich in associations with our own endeavours. My own exclamation, if I had known to make one, would have been an egotistical one. There it is and I am now here. Aren't I the one!

I remember only fragments, not through wilfulness or denial, but because vision at such frenzied times is limited in inexplicable ways, and because new knowledge sometimes obscures what was known before, and I have been here now for a long time. I wish I could remember more. I know I did not feel afraid or intimidated, except in the ordinary way of a stranger arriving at an uknown destination, uncertain of directions, wary of misuse or mockery, self-conscious about getting things wrong. I thought of myself as someone who had travelled a long way to join an institution which would contain other people like me, conscientious, modest about their talents but secretly ambitious, novices to the intellectual vocation. In that institution I would do my best to dazzle and win praise and fulfil myself. So I was not afraid, and had no idea what I should be afraid of.

I arrived towards the end of August and was taken in hand by a slim, awkward man from the British Council. He seemed embarrassed by our encounter, and asked me trite leading questions between long silences. I remember he wore a college scarf and I envied him that, and promised myself one in due course. We took a coach to London, and then a red double-decker bus to Euston where I was to have temporary lodgings in a college hall until the beginning of term. The British Council man said he would check on me the next day, smiling wanly, but I never saw him again. There were long corridors of empty rooms, with a few other foreign students diffidently hugging the walls. Somewhere nearby (in a building across the road, it turned out) there was a dining room where I was to go for food, but I failed to absorb this information when the hall porter gave it to me, as I also failed to absorb most of what he said. I spent the first night without food. On the second day I went out for a walk, and with some of the sterling money my father had exchanged at the money-mart in the market for a farewell gift, I bought a big bar of chocolate from a newsagent. He was a small, elderly man in a green cardigan, whose tiny shop was filled with the sweet, strong smell of pipe tobacco. Even when I did locate the dining room, I was not at first able to persuade myself to enter it for a meal, unsure of what I would ask for and fearful of mismanaging the tools. So yes, I was a little bit afraid, after all. What I had seen of the city terrified me with its hugeness and rush, and I was not to lose the edge of that terror for several months, and perhaps not to lose it fully ever.

By the time the British Council induction seminars started, I was in some need of them. We sat there in our assortment of uncomfortable suits while a florid, balding man with an unabashed belly spoke to us with what I would later recognise as a kind of officer wit and badinage. He grinned and nodded to us, encouraging us to relish his wit as much as he did himself, inviting us to find more joy in life. His sentences were studded with words like palaver, badmash, hatari, inshaalah, establishing that he was an insider when it came to our cultures. He called us boys – we were all male – but I think he meant it affectionately, as if we were all in it together, members of the same team. He spoke to us about the etiquette of what to do and not to do when invited into an English home. When we first arrived at the house we were to wipe our feet thoroughly before entering, in case our shoes had picked up mud or worse. We were not to take off our shoes as this would give the impression of unwelcome informality. If invited to a meal, we were not to eat too much, or too fast, or to belch. We were not to ask for more, and most certainly not to serve ourselves unless we were invited to. We were always to leave something on the plate. We were not to get up from the table until we were invited to. It was some years before I could put any of this instruction to use, because it took time for the invitations to turn up. But our lecturer also showed us how to count the money, how to use the underground and where to get our student supplies, some of which information was of more immediate use.

In time, I moved to the hall where I was to be permanently accommodated, where I made friends with a group of other foreign students there. I had done all my dealings with the officials of the college, taking the bus as instructed, locating the academic offices, and registering for my classes, all done with trepidation that I might get something wrong, and then a brief feeling of triumph that I had not done so. It was in that mood of having managed that I sat down to write my first proper letter home. I had written on first arriving (and then carried the letter around with me for days before I found a post office that I dared enter) but this was my first settled-down letter. I can't remember the detail of what I wrote, but I can see the desk where I sat, with its smooth grey formica top that I thought so elegant and so clean. I imagine that I would have expressed in that letter my relief that I had been able to manage without mishap, playing up to my reputation as the incompetent dreamer. I would probably have written that I was unimaginably fortunate to be where I was, and how I would do my best. I would have said something about the hugeness of the city, and the multitudes that thronged its streets. Perhaps, despite my attempts at wit and self-mockery, I would have been unable to disguise my anxiety about what still remained to be done: the bank, the canteen, the doctor, the shops, all of them places where I could yet make a fool of myself.

I know I would not have told them how much I longed to be back with them, how homesick I was. Or how much I missed everything, my friends, the smells of the streets, the breeze off the sea. How chilling and belittling blue eyes can be. I would not have told them that, not yet, not at first. I would not have wanted them to think me childish and overwhelmed. And even when I did, it was only to Amin, after we started writing to each other properly in the months to come.

I made friends in the hall, a group of foreign students like me, all of whom were in their second or third years. They beckoned me over when hunger forced me to the dining room downstairs, and they welcomed me and made much of me because I was a new arrival. I remember them all, and because it is important not to make light of such gifts, I will name them here. First there was Andrew Kwaku from Ghana, who was quiet and watchful, but who smiled at the slightest eye contact. He spoke slowly, as if giving himself time to consider what he was saying. Then there was Saad from Egypt, plump and genial and wearing a thick moustache, like a joke policeman in the Egyptian movies we used to see at home. He was always talking and grinning, always slipping away. He was the eldest in the group, in his final year of a radiography course. Ramesh Rao was from India, and he was usually silent and deliberate in what he did, more than a bit dull from a certain way of seeing. His face always managed to look kindly but you could see his eyes counting and sorting, pricing everything that went past him. He was the butt of many of Saad's sexual innuendoes, because he assumed that Ramesh did not get the joke, which made the joke even funnier. Then there was Sundeep, also Indian, but suave and dashing where Ramesh was cautious and watchful. Saad called him cosmopolitan and Sundeep liked that. He had a head of thick glossy hair which he handled lovingly, and an expensive wardrobe which he displayed at least once a week when rich friends came to collect him in a car. He sneered a lot, though not at us, and under the circumstances, his arrogance made me feel a lot better about some of the slights we had to endure. Then there was Amur Baadawi, who was from Sudan, and who with Andrew became the friends I got to know best in that first year.

It was not easy to get near the English students, even ones in the same class. The feeling of resistance was there from the beginning, a feeling I sensed but was not sure of. I had not known what to expect, but I sensed it in the slightness of the smiles I was given in return to my beaming ones. I saw it in the way the eyes slid away, and in the frowns when I followed the other students out of the class, trying to join in whatever they were doing next. I saw that I was not included in the rendezvous outside the library or in the coffee bar or wherever else. I saw this in the quick looks of mischief they exchanged, and in their suppressed smiles. Sometimes I saw embarrassment, especially in the women students, although I thought the men intimidated the women in some way. And one day soon I was allowed to overhear one of the students as I hovered on the edges of the group at the end of a class. *What is he doing here?* a well-spoken, round-cheeked young man of medium height with a fringe of dark hair who was called Charles asked in a loud, exasperated hissing whisper. Only he didn't say *he*, and I can't be bothered to remember exactly what he did say. So at first I sensed this feeling of resistance, and then I heard the embarrassed sniggers and saw the looks of surprise and irritation in anonymous faces in the corridors and in the streets, and in time I came to hear their vexation and dislike. It was all a bit of a surprise. It took a long time to learn not to care, years, a lifetime.

It was not all I learned in those first few weeks, but the feeling of those encounters has stayed when other lessons were revised by repetition and new knowledge. I saw and heard many other things, and learned to live, or at least learned to make a way through life, as everyone does in all circumstances, but the earliest lesson I received in London was how to live with disregard. It was the same lesson many of us had to learn in our different ways. Like many people in similar circumstances, I began to look at myself with increasing dislike and dissatisfaction, to look at myself through their eyes. To think of myself as someone who deserved to be disliked. So at first I thought it was the way I spoke, that I was inept and clumsy, ignorant and tongue-tied, perhaps even transparently scheming, wanting too much to be liked. Those beaming, ingratiating smiles must have embarrassed everyone I talked to, because they had to struggle not to laugh. Then I thought it was the clothes I wore, which were cheap and ill-fitting and not as clean as they could be, and which perhaps made me look clownish and unbalanced. But despite the explanations I gave myself, I could not help hearing the slighting words or the irritable tone at petty everyday encounters or the suppressed hostility in casual glances.

I realised that I did not know very much about England, that all the books I had studied and the maps I had pored over had taught me nothing of how England thought of the world and of people like me. Perhaps I should not say England, as if it was not differentiated and various, although I think in this matter of how the non-European world and its denizens were perceived there was largely a common cause. So I might have made my observation about suppressed hostility in reference to Britain or Europe and its dispersals and still felt that there was some truth in it. Living in our small island, deep in the uproar of our complicated dramas and our self-regarding stories, I had not grasped the significance of those English teachers talking to us about Shakespeare and Keats and the golden mean, had not understood the global magnitude of what seemed only a local phenomenon. There were English teachers everywhere in the subjected world, speaking about Shakespeare and Keats and the golden mean, and what mattered was not what the subjects thought about these writings, but that they were being told about them. The teachers too were not all English, but how could we tell and what difference would it have made if we could?

So I had to learn about that, and about imperialism and how deeply the narratives of our inferiority and the aptness of European overlordship had bedded down in what passed for knowledge of the world. I had to learn something about that before I could have an inkling of the meaning of the dislike and embarrassment I encountered and could not at first withstand. One of the teachers spoke to me about this. He must have seen me cringing, or perhaps was familiar with the phenomenon I was experiencing. British people like to think of themselves as cold and unfriendly, he said. It makes them feel tough and hard to fool. If you tell them they are welcoming, they'll start whimpering with self-pity, assuming you mean they are credulous. Be cold and unfriendly and you'll soon make friends.

We talked about these things among ourselves, of course, but the way we talked was not how it felt to experience them. I think when we talked we simplified the complex sense of hurt and diminishing that we felt, or at least that I felt, the sense of injustice and incomprehension at being both misused and despised. What were they so upset about, when it was they who went overbearing over the world and filled our heads with our unworthiness? That sense of shock was truer to how I felt than the way we talked about these things, at which times we came up with our own summary defences and were abusive and condescending in return. At such times, we piled story after story, our own and other people's, petty ones and global ones, suitably salted and dressed as the moment required, to describe the small-minded meanness of the people we found ourselves among. We did not understand that our squeals of protest were already anticipated and explained as petulance and a deficiency of character. I learned to evade the questions that seemed to invite you to speak about such matters because they were accompanied by that sceptical look, so that even before you opened your mouth or marshalled your petty grumbles into line, you understood what the eyes or the tilt of the head, or the tight smile were saying. Go on then, let's hear your trite moans about colour prejudice, after everything we've done for you.

If Sundeep was around, he would take charge of our grumbling conversations about the English. His eyes would glow and glitter, the man of bitter experience. He had lived longest in England and obviously knew his way around, and it was predictable that he was the most irregular of our group of foreign students. He had complicated arrangements, engagements and phone calls, about which he was discreet and slightly mysterious, pursing his lips with courteous reluctance if anyone asked him too directly. He would wrap up our discussions with an invective of such cruelty and scorn that it made me thrill with guilt: 'Listen, they're scum. I know them better than any of you. I've been to school here, remember. They bathe once a week, if that, the whole family in the same scummy water. They clean their arses with paper. Every time you shake hands with one of them, be sure to go and wash your hands immediately afterwards, and certainly don't touch food without doing so. Their women are whores. They eat blood and hooves and fur, and they have sex with animals. When you listen to them talk, you'd think they invented the world. Poetry, science, philosophy, all their doing, and yet everything they know, they learned from us.' He was gracious enough to include Andrew and I in his *us*, nodding firmly in our directions. We were from darkest Africa, and I suppose Sundeep did not want us to feel left out, even though he probably did not think that much had been learned from us. I certainly could not imagine what anyone could have learned from me and mine that they would not have arrived at themselves in good time, but Sundeep's arrogant flourishes made us laugh and feel good enough to cast our own contemptuous looks. Later he was to become a writer famed for his mockery of the intolerances of Africans and Muslims, but at that time we were all happy to share in these blustering summaries of the English.

Back in my room, I wrote letters, three, maybe four, a week. I studied for a while in the evenings, then when I tired I wrote a letter for an hour or so, the Sony transistor I had inherited from Saad tuned to the BBC World Service, and then read until midnight. The letters just flowed, dutiful, lonely, homesick, excited and supercilious, I expect, depending on who they were for. I was probably not that guarded about what I wrote, because I don't think I felt I had anything very much to hide. I wrote to Amin once a week, and distributed the rest of the letters between my parents and friends. In the early days, there was a letter for me every day in the students' pigeon-holes. It only took three days for the post to arrive, so I could send a letter and get a reply in the same week, although this did not happen frequently enough for my liking. In quite a short time I exhausted my other correspondents, but not Amin. My mother pleaded lack of time and aching eyes, and took to sending regards and messages of exhortation via Amin, who sometimes added a jeering twist of his own. My father wrote once in those early days, a serious and stern letter of advice which was composed with obvious care but whose contents have completely evaporated over time. I don't think it was very long, and there was a quality of ritual about it. It was a letter from father to son, a bestowal of blessing, which made me feel adult and slightly abandoned, although I knew that was not its intention.

I wrote freely to Amin, unburdening and complaining, lamenting my loneliness, describing the indescribable cold of that winter, the blizzards and the frozen lakes. He wrote back with news and encouragement. *Homesickness is inevitable. You've made friends*, he said, *that is so important. Soon you'll have made so many friends you'll forget about us. Seriously, don't feel lonely and low, don't allow it, don't tolerate it. Make the best of it, because what matters is that you fulfil your talent and your gift, that most of all. Tell me more about these friends, they sound a good bunch of people. Tell me about snow. How does it feel to touch it? Describe it to me.* So I did, and described the arguments and conversations with my friends and the places we visited. He even suggested places I might go and see, and things I could do. *I envy you, being able to see so much of the world. Have you visited the British Museum? Have you been to the theatre? You must go and see a Shakespeare play, and see how they do it properly there in London. Have you seen Bush House?* I had walked past Bush House, the great shrine from where the BBC World Service broadcast its programmes, and which for some people had greater potency as an abstraction of London than Downing Street or Trafalgar Square. I stood across the road from the great building, shaped like a battleship from one angle and like a cave-village sprawling down a mountainside from another, and watched people striding in and out of its revolving doors, and felt a small hiatus of disappointment. I think I expected to see a crackling traffic of sparking sound waves in the air around the building. I told Amin about these visits, and about my classes, and my petty triumphs. I boasted about my essay marks, something to show for all those hours alone in my room, and what the teachers said, and Amin asked me to send him copies of the essays so he could read them. I sent him some books instead, after I had read them myself.

I remember, these were the first ones I sent him: *The Mystic Masseur, Go Tell It on the Mountain, A Passage to India*. I bought them from a second-hand bookshop in Charing Cross Road. I stood outside for an age, looking at the display in the shop window, unable to pluck up the courage to go inside. In the end the shopkeeper, who was an Indian man of mature middle age, came out and called me in. He asked me if I had been in London long, unsmiling, even a small thrust of the chin as he asked, speak up, you trembling insect. I felt no hostility towards him. I recognised these scowling gestures as the privilege of age, but I also felt a kind of care behind them, an extension of intimacy, and could imagine my father or my mother speaking to me in the same way. I told him that I had been in London for a few weeks, and he nodded, but I saw that he also suppressed a smile. He asked if I was looking for anything in particular. I said I was looking for some interesting books to send to my brother, and he suggested those. I wonder now about that shopkeeper, how he ended up on that street selling books, and whether his smile had something sardonic in it. Here is another blundering one to put through the anguishing mill, I imagine him thinking. I wonder whether he knew that when he suggested those books to me, it was as if he had lit a torch to illuminate a darkened path.

I went back some long while later, about a year or so after the first time, and found someone else in the shop. From the way he greeted me when I entered the shop, I guessed he was German or Dutch. My ear was not well enough tuned to recognise the difference at that time, hearing only a slight thickening of the voice. I was probably making my guess from appearance as much as from anything else. He smiled and went on with his work, and after a few moments of irresolute browsing, I wandered away.

Amin wrote me a letter on the night before the independence ceremony. I still have it, a beautifully written letter whose tone is subdued and reflective, hoping for the best at a time of grandiose optimism. I haven't looked at that letter for years, and I don't think I ever will, but I remember the tone, the shapeliness and restraint. He always wrote so well, with such wit and self-possession that I often found myself smiling as I read, not because what he had written was funny but because it was so pleasing.

There was an item on the television news about our independence ceremony. We were on TV. The pictures were black and white in those days, and the ceremony took place at midnight as such ceremonies did, to add a touch of mystic symbolism to the ritual, to make it into sacred play, a literal handing over of the burden of rule. From the brief clips of film, shot at night in insufficient light, it was impossible to recognise the terrain, to see the casuarinas that lined the beach or to hear the sound of the sea a few feet away. All it was possible to see was the lowering of the flag and the soldiers marching past, and Prince Philip standing to attention. On his right stood the sultan in his black robes, and on his left the British Resident in his white uniform and feathered topee. The straining voice of the reporter made the scenes into an episode from the landscape of Empire so familiar from newsreels, with everyone behaving honourably according to their degree. It was over in a moment or two, and the pictures moved on to something else. Almost exactly one month later I was tuned to the BBC World Service evening news, and heard a report describing the overthrow of the new government. The report was sent by an amateur radio operator who was the wife of one of the colonial officials who had stayed on as part of the hand-over administration. Or perhaps she was not an amateur radio operator, but someone trained and armed to do exactly what she did in the event that what happened should happen. At the moment of speaking, her voice anxious and loud, her words hurried, she was hiding under a bed in her bungalow. She was hiding there because bullets were flying overhead. The announcer gave her name, and I recognised it as that of the games and swimming instructor at the women's teachers' college. She cut a dashing figure at Inter-Schools sports events, blowing whistles, handing out winners' tickets, bustling about with ambitious strides. It was she, in any case, who announced our most recent ugliness to the world.

In the days that followed there was news of more violence, and of mass slaughter, and brief, knowing analyses by journalists and expert commentators, but there was no word, no letter, and it was only weeks later, when what had happened was no longer arguable, that disbelief and fear and shame began to turn to an understanding of the terror that had overwhelmed our home. When the first letter came from Amin weeks later, it was brief and cautious, and had obviously been opened. It was to say they had received a letter from me that day, but had not received any of the others I mentioned sending. That they were all well, and I should take care. I understood from that letter that he could not write freely, and that I was not to do so either. I told my friends that I had received news at last, and that none of my family were killed or hurt, as we had all feared. They shared my relief as they had shared in my anxiety and lamentation in the preceding weeks, and after that I rarely raised the subject with them. Sooner or later we would all have our turns at lamenting distant tragedies, and would have to learn to grieve with restraint.

Some time later, I received a letter from my father, battered and folded and posted in Mombasa, telling me that terrible things had happened, that there was danger and that I must not think of returning. I did not know what to write, afraid of causing them difficulties, and when Amin's letters came, at long intervals, they were brief and businesslike. Ba has lost his job, as have a lot of other people. Many things have changed. Ma has not been able to get medicine for her eyes and her sight is troubling her. She grumbles about it, as you would expect. But all is well and everyone sends regards.

In the months that followed, I began to think of myself as expelled, an exile. I make it seem a gradual process, and indeed it took months for me to find the words for the condition I was in, but I felt the sense of it a lot earlier. My father's letter about not returning stunned me, paralysed me with quiet panic. Where was I to go if not return? What did he mean I was not to think of returning? Where else could I go? It was after this surge of fear subsided, and the days passed and there was no reprieve, no further letter cancelling the instruction of the previous one, that I looked for words to explain what had happened, words that I whispered to myself in shame and self-mockery. For the first time since arriving in England, I began to think of myself as an alien. I realised I had been thinking of myself as someone in the middle part of a journey, between coming and going, fulfilling an undertaking before returning home, but I began to fear that my journey was over, that I would live all my life in England, a stranger in the middle of nowhere.

In time I drifted into a tolerable alienness. Living day to day, this alienness became a kind of emblem, indeterminate about its origins. Soon I began to say black people and white people, like everyone else, uttering the lie with increasing ease, conceding the sameness of our difference, deferring to a deadening vision of a racialised world. For by agreeing to be black and white, we also agree to limit the complexity of possibility, we agree to mendacities that for centuries served and will continue to serve crude hungers for power and pathological self-affirmations. No matter, I uttered my lies and thought them a greater truth, and found a kind of self-affirmation in raucous songs of grievance and rebellion (of which I partook in spirit more than in voice). I had my eyes opened to the even bigger lies that had us all tangled and bound beyond relief. In the midst of the uproar about wars, and civil rights and apartheid, with a sense of being present while the pressing issues of our world were being argued over and fought for, I was drawn away from the complicated cruelties that were happening at home. They could not be inserted into this conversation, with its pared-down polarities and uncluttered certainties, and I was only able to suffer them in silence and guilt when I was on my own.

I studied, I drifted away from my foreign student friends or we went our own inevitable ways. Andrew lasted the longest. We went on a hilarious holiday to the Lake District on his last vacation before he returned to Ghana. It was still possible in those days to turn a corner in the streets of a small town or follow a bend on a country road, and come face to face with someone who was astonished, flabbergasted, struck dumb, by the sight of a dark-complexioned person. We had plenty of that in the Lake District, and not all of it was funny really, but we played up to it, pretending to be anything but who we were. We were Brazilians, two princes from Madagascar, novice priests from Panama, and when I told Andrew about the Italian phase of my childhood, we even tried out being Italian for a while. It seemed that people were prepared to believe anything about us, although it is possible that they were humouring us because they thought us unstable and childish. We thought it was hilarious, anyway, when perhaps we were only young people who thought our jokes funnier than anyone else's, and who pretended to look on everything as if it was a bland form of the absurd.

He is now in the United States, teaching sociology in a college in Montana. Ghana did not work out, it turned into a cesspit like everywhere else. He calls me once a year or so, or perhaps less frequently than that, but somehow or the other we have not manged to meet again, even on the times when he has travelled through London. I don't suppose now we ever will. How will I ever find my way to Montana and what would be the point of it? Each call seems more strained, our conversation forced in brightness. The questions we ask each other are gestures towards a friendship that neither can fully return. I wonder sometimes what makes him call me, at what seem to me such strange hours. I never call him, although I feel I should. I don't know what to say, where to begin. I wonder if he calls me because memories have made him sad, or if his life is lonely, or whether he feels a desire to speak to me out of a mood of generosity and well-being, or if he had just had a recollection of something we had done that made him smile. Now as I think this, I feel sad at the way our affections and friendships are so steadily and thought-lessly depleted by apathy.

While I am on the subject, I will describe what I know of the other good friends I met when I first came to England. Amur was offered a temporary post with the Arabic service of the BBC World Service. He was to work in radio when he returned to Sudan, and this temporary position was a form of training. So at last I was able to enter Bush House, pass through the monster doors of the building and strut up its sweeping staircase and through its warren of offices and studios. I remember Amur got me into the building by making up a schedule in which he needed to interview me. Perhaps security was more casual at that time, because I don't remember anyone checking or asking any questions. Bush House was disappointing, naturally, when you are used to imagining it as a voice crackling through the sky over thousands of miles, conveying news of the world with an impartial solemnity. The hall and the stairs lived up to these expectations, but the studios and offices were low and cramped and stuffy and crowded. Everywhere hummed with industry and purpose, though, and I confess I was envious of Amur. He was only there for a few months and then returned to Sudan, after which I lost track of him completely. Sometimes, in those purposeless nostalgic moods when you make plans to track down all your long-lost friends but which never even last until the break of day, I have thought I would find the frequency for Radio Sudan and catch him describing the waters of the Nile or the arid plains of Dofar, and at least confirm to myself that he is of good voice. But before morning, I would have told myself that his words would be meaningless to me and I would not even know if it was the same Amur, and that more likely than not he was now working in a school in Dubai or Sharjah rather than waxing lyrical on Radio Sudan.

Sundeep, as I mentioned, has become a writer of some fame. He spent a year living in Malawi and wrote a stylish and satirical novel about that country, an irreverent comedy about post-imperial absurdities, mocking the colonial bwanas who effortlessly became expatriates without budging from their carefully tended government bungalows. I don't suppose the bwanas minded or cared that much about the novel. They knew who had built those bungalows and much else besides, and who had the moral right to occupy them and stroll in the intricately planted gardens. But President Banda did not like it and had the sale of the book banned in Malawi. Sundeep was well out of harm's way by then, and having his book banned by a President-for-Life who was just reaching the peak of his authoritarian career did not do his reputation any harm. Since then, Sundeep has written other stylish and provocative books and has found many admirers. I've read most of his books but I no longer look forward to them. I think that despite their zest and fluency, they have grown increasingly certain of their judgements, and to be too certain of anything is the beginning of bigotry. It is a liberal dogma, a paradox in itself, which if taken too far leads us to the idea that frivolity is the only authentic seriousness. I don't mean to go that far. Sundeep has found a subject in Africa, and in his books he returns there again and again, but what he writes about the people there is intolerant and needlessly scornful, something of an exhibition, something like his youthful self. I haven't seen him either in all these years, although I wrote him a note of congratulation when his first novel came out.

Ramesh is now an economist of international renown, an advocate of moral limits to economic development. He is quoted in solemn editorials and consulted by governments and UN agencies, and holds a Chair in Economics at Grandiose University in the United States (I can't remember which one). I went to listen to one of his talks when he did a visiting series at the LSE, and he was cautious and deliberate as ever, but there was no mistaking the poise and conviction with which he spoke. I got close enough to greet him, and he gave me a restrained smile which did not reach his eyes, and I guessed from the look in them that he did not recognise me at first. When he did, he nodded solemnly while I grinned in anticipation of something friendlier, and then he asked me if all was well. I said all was not bad and that I hoped all was well with him. He hesitated for a moment and then looked away. I would have felt bad if I had not spoken to him. Even at that moment I thought of Saad, and how he used to torment Ramesh, and the thought made me smile. I don't know what happened to Saad after he left.

Anyway, this was later. At that time, after the dispersal of my friends, I was swept along by the logic of my circumstances, living day to day, studying, set on an ambition I did not know would be there waiting for me. To do what was required for that unacknowledged ambition meant that I had to surpass the standards they had set for themselves, even as I found much of what they represented hateful. So I hated what I had to do, and hated that I had to do it, and felt a sense of triumph when I succeeded in doing it. To anyone who knew me, it would probably have seemed I worried more about the appropriate critical language in which to conduct the argument of my dissertation than about the affairs of the far-away place I left years before, when alone in the rooms I lived in my student squalor, I wept with grief and guilt for those I had lost. When Amin's taciturn letters came, I dreaded them as if they were accusations, although their tone was always mild and even eased as their lives became less terrifying. I wrote back steadily, not frequently, minding my words. Often I felt that what I had to say was bland or even feigned, and then I tried harder to send news, something with substance and detail: where I had been, what I had done, the railway strike, the weather. The primroses are in bloom and I wish I could describe to you the delicacy of their creamy colour, as subtle in its way as the fragrance of jasmine on a cool night. It is suddenly sunny and beautiful, and the landscape is transformed. Gardens are full of flowers and the trees in the parks are big with leaves. You can't imagine what England is like when it turns green. Once in late spring I saw marigolds in snow that had fallen unexpectedly in the night.

I pictured Amin reading those words to my parents and Farida, and saw their looks of disappointment and bewilderment. Why is he telling us these things? Does he not understand that we live in fear and confusion and scarcity? Why does he not send us *something* instead of this blather? I sent them a calendar with photographs of the countryside once. I could not make the strivings and the anxieties that I lived with seem important enough to convey to them. I could not even make them important enough to myself, not as words.

Then at last, after years of what now seems incomprehensible labour, I was able to write one day and say that my studies were over, that I had successfully completed my Ph.D. and had miraculously found a job in a university. The university was out of

London, in the south, which suited me very well. I was glad to leave the huge old city with its multitudes and its grime, and live in a small town. That would suit me very well. I would live in a quiet street on the edge of the town, grow a little garden and work at my profession. For relaxation, I would take peaceful walks in the quicksilver dusk or go to the cinema. I had a reply in the same week, like in the old days.

Beloved, you have made us very proud. Many, many congratulations. When I read Ma and Ba your letter, earlier this afternoon, they both started to weep. First him, tears running down his face, snuffling and trying to control himself, then her, joining in and sobbing, then the rest of us, weeping as if we had lost our senses. I think we were crying because we were proud of you. Despite being so far-away, on your own, and with all the worries and the difficulties that must be with you every day, despite all that, you were brave and persevered until you achieved what you had gone so far to achieve. I think we were also crying because life had robbed us of you, because now we would have been thinking of welcoming you back. Well done, my little Italian. When I finished reading, Ba took the letter and read it through himself, although he had already read it once. He is not well now, Allah preserve him, and he does not go out very far any more. These have been difficult times, hard for everyone, but harder for some than for others. After reading the letter, he put it in his shirt pocket and went off for a walk, and everywhere he went, as I discovered when I went out later, he told people your news. If it was up to him, he'd have put it on the radio this evening. I think he has over-extended himself, and is now fast asleep on the sofa. Farida is still here with us, and she too sends many congratulations. She is married to Abbas now, at last. They had to wait for the papers. The wedding was a few weeks ago, and she will be leaving in a few days to join him in Mombasa. She tells me to tell you she will write to you when she gets there. Don't hold your breath. Send news about your little house in the country when you move, but for now Ma and Ba send their blessing, and love from all of us. Amin.

As is only to be imagined, I cried too as I read this letter, especially the part where they were all weeping like lunatics. I joined them. Then I cried again when I got to that part about how brave it was to persevere. When I thought of their circumstances, I thought of myself as pampered and lucky, and expected that that was what they thought as well. I also thought I was brave to persevere, that there wasn't really very much choice but to do so, and how nice it was to find out that that is what they thought too. When Grace came home from work, I passed her the letter and waited for her to start snivelling, and sure enough, when she got to the weeping in unison part she started too, and I had no choice but to join in again. Oh, it was such a joyful letter!

I hadn't told Amin anything about Grace, although I had told her everything about them.

It has taken me longer to get to Grace than I had anticipated. I had not meant to go on at such length about those early days in England. After all, what was there to say that has not been said by so many others who had come before me. I had meant to explain how it was that I started writing the story of Amin and Jamila. And why it was that when I started thinking about it, I found myself forced to imagine how Jamila's grandmother Rehana and the Englishman Pearce might have met, how they might have come together at a time when their worlds were so divided, so far apart. But once I began writing about arriving here, it seemed I could not stop myself saying many other things. I could not stop myself living that time again, and tasting the bitterness and disappointment of it even after all these years. It is my egotism – when I start talking about myself I ramble on endlessly, silencing everyone else and demanding attention. That was what Grace used to say, and she said it was one of the things that drove her away. That and many other things, but that is one story I plan to leave well alone.

It took many years for Grace to leave, and for most of that time our lives together were more than tolerable. At times we were happy and fulfilled, and we helped each other mature and find reprieve from our memories and inadequacies. But in the end the antagonisms became absurd and venomous, and she said she would go while she still had a desire for life and the possibility of finding love again. I tried to dissuade her, of course, but once she began talking like this she could not stop, and the more she said, the easier it became to say more. One day she loaded up the car and drove away to her new life (and came back later for the things she could not take away all at once). I lived on in the quiet street on the edge of town, within walking distance of the university, and did not need a car.

I was exhausted by the time she left, and thought I would feel nothing but relief at her going, finally. But instead I felt more lonely and heart-broken than I ever had in my life. After she left, I realised that I had tuned into her way of doing things, her way of thinking things, that I had fitted something of my mental life to hers. Suddenly, in her absence, I could not keep pace with my own life. I wrote to Amin in my wretchedness. We still wrote to each other, but infrequently by then. Usually I had nothing dramatic to say, and the details of my life were too banal and too complicated to know where to begin talking about them to someone who did not share it. He wrote when he had news, but his news was often sad, and I think it made him sad to write it. When I told him about Grace, he wrote back at once, and in his commiseration he mentioned his own pain at the loss of Jamila all those twenty years before. It was then that I began to think about writing the story of Amin and Jamila. I had come to understand over the years that Amin's affair with Jamila could not have been as I thought of it when I first heard about it. I had thought then that he was the dashing young man who had carried out a daring seduction, but I did so because I could only imagine love as a cliché. When I understood more, in my years with Grace, I began to have a sense of the tragedy of Amin's life, and perhaps Jamila's too, although I hardly knew anything about her. But I knew Amin, and remembered the night of his discovery and the silence of those last days before my departure, and his silence about her since then. In time, the absence of her name and of any lamentation of his separation from her seemed uncanny, increasingly present in their absence. In letter after letter I teased him about getting married, and he made jokes about enjoying being a bachelor. So when he mentioned Jamila after Grace left, for the first time after all the years since I had left home, comparing my wretchedness to his, it made me understand something more of what he had given up. I had time then to reflect on so many things I had neglected, so I thought I would try and write about what had happened between them.

One day, in the midst of writing about them, I had a telegram from Amin to say our mother had died. They did not have a telephone in the house, but I rang the local party branch and left a message, which was our way of communicating urgently. I called again later and they told me that they had passed the message on and Amin was thankful that I had received the news. I sat quietly alone in my house in the quiet street on the edge of town, and mourned my mother whom I had not seen for the last twenty-two years. When I contemplate myself and what I have become, I think of those battles my mother and my father fought to live and love as they wished. I think of their plans and anxieties for our futures, of my own labours with uncongenial material, of all that planning and striving to arrive at this life of small apathy that I could have arrived at with no effort. Irony is the unforgiving register which gives everything back to us.

A few weeks after the telegram I had another letter from Amin (I was beginning to fear his letters), telling me about his blindness for the first time. He was completely blind in one eye, and the sight in the other was beginning to go. It was the same infection that had blinded Ma, but there was no medicine or hospital there to cure him as there hadn't been to cure her. I wrote and said come over here. I'll take a loan on the house and we'll get you seen to privately. They can do anything here. Why didn't you tell me before? Come, don't be stupid. Don't waste what is left of your life. But he said it was too late, the infection could not be cut out any more. That's what the doctor he went to see in Dar es Salaam said. And he could not leave Ba on his own. *To tell you the truth*, he said, *I don't think I care about being able to see, not any more. Over these last few years I have found that in the country of the blind, one eye is more than enough trouble. More important than these old men's grumbles about declining bodies is Farida's news. Last year she published a collection of her poems in Mombasa. She brought a copy over when she came for Ma's funeral. Who'd have thought Farida would end up a poet? She's been writing for years, you know, only she smiles and jokes so much that people think she's a fool. But she isn't, I found that out a long time ago. Anyway, the book has won a lot of praise, and she has even read some of the poems on the radio. She has been invited to a cultural event in Rome, and she'll post you a copy from there. I don't know why she wants to post it from there rather than from Mombasa, but she does. It's her first time in Europe and perhaps posting it from there will make her feel closer to you. I have something small to send you which I will also give to her. For now I send you my love and good wishes.*

A few weeks later a parcel came from Rome, with a copy of Farida's book of poems, *Kijulikano*. That Which is Known. There was a packet in the parcel, wrapped in rough brown paper and tied with string. My name was written on it in Amin's hand. There was no note with Farida's parcel, and no inscription in the book, only the book itself. Farida was not much of a letter writer, and never replied to a single one of my letters over the years, despite repeated promises conveyed to me through Amin, to say that she would write as soon as she had completed this chore or that task. There was a photograph of her on the back cover. It looked like a passport photograph, a picture of someone who had just walked in off the streets and asked the photographer to please not make a fuss and hurry and take the photo. She was on her way to the hospital to see an ailing aunt, perhaps, and did not want to miss too much of the visiting time. She still had her buibui on, the veil pulled back off her face for the purposes of the photograph, but ready to be pulled back in place when she stepped out into the street again. She wore spectacles now, dark plastic above and metal-rimmed below. She also wore a large smile, as if she had been caught unawares by something the photographer had said, or perhaps she was smiling at her husband Abbas who had accompanied her, and who was standing there out of the picture. As I looked at the photograph of the smiling middle-aged woman, I realised that this was an image of someone I hardly knew anymore.

Her book had this dedication:

To my father and my mother who taught me to care. To Amin who is good and to Rashid who never left us. To Abbas with all my love.

Never left us. Trust a poet to come up with a sentimental lie. He left us, all right, but I appreciated the kindness behind the words. When I read the poems I was surprised, of course. They were exceptionally moving, thoughtful and intimate in ways I had not expected, and so intelligent and unforgiving in their observation. Many of them were about the small lives I was so familiar with. They were witty and ironic about the life of a woman, and I guessed that the title itself was an intertextual reference to one of Shaaban Roberts' collections. One of the poems was about Amin and Jamila, although it did not name any names. It brought tears to my eyes. Yes, I was surprised. I imagine it would always be surprising to read something written by a brother or a sister, someone you had known so closely from childhood. But Amin was right, I had always thought of Farida as a bit silly – there were all those failed exams and those unrelenting smiles – and if not unintelligent, then at least as someone made silly by her goodwill. It had been years since I had had any need to reassess my thought of her, but those poems made me realise how mistaken I was. I wrote to her with my most sincere congratulations, and kept quiet about my surprise.

I read the poems several times, the one about Amin and Jamila most often of all. It made me wish I had the courage and skill to write with such truthfulness and humility. I also read the poems repeatedly to delay opening Amin's packet. I could tell from the feel of it that it contained a book, and felt a slight dread that it was a book he had written in. It made me unexpectedly nervous to imagine what Amin would have written in his own account.

8 Amin

AM I ONE? I am the pool in which she mingles with me. I have never known a time of such lack and such longing, as if I would die of thirst or lunacy if I did not hold her and lie with her. Yet I don't die and I don't hold her. But I have never known very much, and perhaps all love is like this sooner or later. Something blind and immovable is lodged in me, its teeth sunk in some tender part I cannot locate or reach. I can feel its malice. This desperate misery passes, is passing, when at first I did not even have the strength to lift my voice or use words to explain it to myself. I have loved unwisely, but it has not been an oppression on me. I have been fortunate in my foolishness. I will never abandon her. I will see her every day for as long as I can, for as long as the years allow me a memory of her. Praise the beauty of the day in the night that follows it, and my night will be long and her beauty endless.

She frightens them. They fear that she will make me into a comedy, and people will laugh at all of us. People laugh at everything, I told them. Think of her reputation, Ma said. Think of your good name, he said. You're nothing without a name.

They didn't think like that when they were fighting their own battles together those years ago. Now they have some eminence and respect from neighbours and sundry, and I was carelessly about to turn myself and them into figures of fun. People will laugh at us. They will laugh hardest at her, I said.

Those people don't care about being laughed at, Ma said. They are hardened to it. Her grandmother was a dirty woman who lived a life of sin with an Englishman. Her mother and that family in their big house are so high and mighty because of their wealth. We regard everyone as equal except in their piety, as al-Biruni has said. That was him. He can always turn a weighty quotation from a long-ago century if there is need. Then he quivers there with the assurance his morbid words fill him with. She lives on her own in a flat with its own front door. She has been seen in a politician's car. She has no sense of shame. For all I know, letting me into her flat is the most shameful thing she has ever done.

It's weeks now. When I come home every day my mother studies my face, to see if I have seen her, to see if I mind not having seen her. Neither of them speak about her, out of embarrassment maybe. Out of fear of another encounter like that night. The threats, the bullying, the tears. The tears were mine, and when they saw them they must have known that they had won. Let us not speak of this matter again, he said, as he always did when he felt the moment had come to show his superior form of mercy. I know how they found out. Uncle Ali brought home a rumour. There are always rumours, and he probably brought this morsel home like that, something to chortle over. That dog, do you know what people are saying he's up to? Aunt Halima probably frowned, and then sent word for Farida to come and visit. It was Farida who told me. Aunt Halima pressed, using her full, rich range of expletives, and threatened to tell Ma anyway. So Farida told her that if she did, it would be like killing me, because Ma would tell Ba and they would make me stop or make me disobey them. Farida thought that because Aunt Halima had kept her secret about Abbas, she would keep my secret too. But Aunt Halima thought Jamila so hateful, a whore she called her, that she hurried to tell Ma straight away, with Farida hurrying beside her begging and pleading until the last moment. Farida blamed herself.

I could not see her. I was too ashamed. Farida went to to see her, to explain and to beg forgiveness. I could not see her. She would think I did not love her enough, but I do. Or that I was too faint-hearted to fight for her, and perhaps that is true. I could not disobey them, not after all these years.

I crave to touch her. I did not know what that word meant until I craved her touch. I ponder craving in the dark, and dream of wastelands littered with bits of bone and rocks and dead insects. The ground is hard as metal and I wake with aching feet even though I have been on my back all night. I dream of a bed littered with dead cicadas and I hear a sound like the sighing of the wind through casuarina trees. It is the saddest sound I have ever heard, apart from the words I imagine her using to describe her disappointment with me. A cry wakes me in the middle of the night. The sheets are moist with sweat, and my body feels to my touch as if it had been lying under a pool of red pulsing light. I list these symptoms like a patient or like a mad science student. What science would that be? The science of how to obey.

I expect him to wake because of my sleeplessness. I expect him to stir, at least, from my involuntary groans and sighs as I fidget to rest a sore hip or shoulder. I cannot get up. They would hear me and think that I am going out to see her. When I wake from a nightmare I lie for a while and listen, in case I had disturbed him. I wait to see if I had said anything that he would repeat to me. But nothing disturbs him, it seems. He breathes lightly and sleeps like a guiltless boy, a smile on his face, dreaming of England. He is already far away from here. Even when his eyes are open, you can see that they are looking at something far away. I almost wish he would wake and force me to speak about her. He watches me. He wants to know but he won't understand yet. When he speaks of her, he makes admiring jokes and I leave it at that. If he repeats something I said in my sleep, I'll tell him that a person cannot be held responsible for what he says at night because he might have been asleep when he said it, and was not himself speaking. Or something in the dark might have captured it and twisted it, and made it into something else. I praise her in the night. How did they all come to hate her so much? I am so hateful.

*

236

She told me her story. She had only a slight memory of her grandmother. She saw her once when she was four years old, a corpulent lady with piercing eyes who smiled and said little. Her brothers remembered more and talked about her often when they were younger. She was the story in their family, the one who had caused all the trouble. For a long time the stories were mixed up, one layer on top of another, some layers missing, so later, when she wanted to know the story in full, she could not get to where it all started and where it finished.

His name was Pearce, and one day he stumbled out of the wilderness and into the arms of her grandmother Rehana. No, not like that, she said, she was only joking when she said into the arms of her grandmother. He had been lost in the interior for a few days, robbed and abandoned by his Somali guides. When they brought him to the house, it was her grandmother Rehana who had given the Englishman his first sip of a drink for days. She must have put something in it, because he was besotted with her from the moment he opened his eyes. It was her grandmother, Malika herself, who told her this. She was the wife of her grandfather Hassanali. She outlasted the others, and was still alive until *she* was fifteen or sixteen, old enough to ask questions about such things. She never met her grandfather Hassanali. Her grandmother Malika's voice *always* caught when she spoke his name. He must have died before she was born. I am reluctant to use her name. It feels like an audacity.

Her grandmother Rehana had been married to an Indian merchant who went away and never came back. She had several proposals after that (kaposwa na watu wengi) but she refused every one of them. She was difficult. By the time the Englishman came she was no longer young, and there were scandals about her already. No one could say anything to her. When the Englishman came and loved her, she went to him. She did not say anything, but every afternoon she put on her buibui and went off on her own, and no one could say anything to her. If you said anything to her, it would be to accuse her of zinah. Nobody dared to do that. It was a terrible crime with unspeakable punishment.

Stoning. The only person who could say anything to her was her brother, Hassanali. He was, in addition, Rehana's guardian in the long absence of her husband, even though the brother was younger than the sister. A woman always had to have a guardian: her father, her husband, and in the absence of both, the eldest of her brothers. In the absence of all of these, the nearest male relative will do. I didn't know that. When she told me that, I couldn't believe it at first, that any male relative could turn himself into a guardian and command a woman. Hassanali refused to say anything about the afternoon absences. What was he to do if she confessed to zinah? Have her stoned to death?

Until in the end someone shouted something from the darkness of a lane as she walked past one evening. In her rage she blurted out something to Malika when she got home, but she could not repeat the word that had been shouted at her. I won't soil my mind with their filth, she said. Someone complained to the DO about Pearce. It probably came from the noble Omanis (watukufu wamanga), who like to display their holy, small-minded scruples. They would not have complained directly. That was below their nobility. A word in the wakil's ear perhaps, to be whispered to the DO later. The Omanis had strong views on scruples and propriety. Even the sight of a naked navel was offensive to them (makruh), and a fart released in their vicinity could lead to injury. Imagine what torture the rumours of Rehana and Pearce must have been to them.

So the lovers moved to Mombasa, first Pearce and then Rehana after him. They lived in an apartment for some weeks or some months. It was the same apartment that Rehana lived in all her life, and the one in which she died. That was where her mother Asmah was born. The one without sin: that was how Rehana named her. In hope. By then Pearce was gone. He left once and then returned, but left again.

It's something that he returned, that he was torn about leaving her, she said. It makes you think he must have loved her, even though he still left. At some point, he must have come to his senses and made his way home. There would have been any number of reasons why he would have left her. It must have been impossible for both of them. She was a brave, battling person to go as far as she did. That's what I think now as I try to picture her. Someone who can sit still and return a stare. A woman who can sit still and return a stare.

What did Pearce look like? I asked her.

She smiled and said that she liked that I used that name. He was her grandfather, and sometimes she secretly used that name to call herself. She said that her grandmother Malika told her that he was thin and tall, and that his eyes glittered. She didn't think grandmother Malika liked the way he looked, or even liked him. Her mother Asmah told her that Rehana used to say that he was always gay.

She told me these things as we lay on the bed under the night-light. Sometimes I could not see her face because I lay in her arms while her voice brushed my temples. Or she leaned against the wall while I lay in her lap, the tangle of her hair brushing my cheek, looking up at her as she spoke, and stroked her thighs and her breasts. Or sometimes we lay beside each other as we spoke, touching, always touching. When she was feeling strong and happy, she liked to plan. How long would we have to wait before I completed my training? Once I had a job, I could tell my parents and then I could move into the flat with her. She filled my life with happiness, always gay. When I was away from her I could not always withstand anxieties and terror. One night we lay sweating after love and heard someone walking on the road, sandals slapping as he strode by, whistling. She lay tight against me, silently holding on and shuddering. What is it? What is it? I asked her. *I'm afraid*, she said. I tried to make a joke. Of the whistling? I asked. The spirits who roamed the world after dark used it as a signal to summon each other. *Of them. Of that man and his whistling. Can you not hear how sure he is? I'm afraid of you leaving me.* I'll never leave you, I said.

*

She did not tell me about the other man for a while. I think she did not want me to rush to judgement of her grandmother. She wanted me to like her first. Pearce had made some arrangement with money, but Rehana knew it was not going to be enough for long. He had arranged to pay the rent on the apartment for six months, so she could have the baby in a decent place. He also deposited a small amount of money in a bank account in her name. Perhaps he thought that after the money was finished she would return to live with her brother behind the shop. He left her an address in England in case of an emergency. Pearce did not explain how she could get the money out. When Rehana went to withdraw some money from the account after Pearce's departure, the bank refused to allow it. She did not understand why. She had never been to a bank before and she did not even know for sure that they had refused. In her confusion and shame she thought it was because they disapproved of what she had done. She did not write to Pearce. She asked her brother Hassanali and his wife Malika to take Asmah for a while, until she had organised her life better. It was only to be for a short while, but Asmah stayed with them all her young life. She was the only child they had.

While he lived in Mombasa, Pearce made friends with a Scottish man called Andrew Mills. He was a water engineer who had a room at the Mombasa Club (Members Only), which really meant Europeans Only. European visitors stayed there when they travelled or went to meet friends. Andrew Mills stayed there all the time. He liked to drink. He visited them in the apartment while Pearce was there, and he went on visiting after he left. After a while he moved in and took over the rent.

What is a water engineer? I asked her.

She shrugged, and then ran her wet finger over my lips. So discreet, she said. You ask what is a water engineer when you could have asked what kind of friend he was, moving in like that. Or what kind of woman Rehana had become.

A courtesan, I said, practising the English word. It's not a word you often get the chance to use.

That is what everyone thought, she said.

What else could they think? I asked.

She shrugged again, meaning she did not care what they thought. He was an elderly man, she said. He moved into the apartment and helped her set up a small cloth business. She opened a shop and employed a tailor, making and selling curtains and bed-covers and other such items.

How did she think of such a scheme? Would you have thought of something like that?

It must have been the old shopkeeper blood in her, she said. This was her dream, this was how she thought she could look after herself. When the business was flourishing, she would collect Asmah from her brother and look after her herself. I think this was when she started to drink.

I knew then that this was going to be a tragic story. How could a woman who was abandoned by her husband, who had a child in sin with a European man who also abandoned her, who lived with another elderly European man and who drank herself, find her way back to content? She watched my silence with a sad smile and I felt my eyes watering with love for her. I didn't know what the sadness meant at the time but it made my heart fill with sorrow.

Nobody knows the life they lived together, she said. She still visited relatives, but she never talked about her life with the water engineer. I don't know what relatives she visited. There are always relatives. The servant was never a native of Mombasa and so could not be pumped for information. But there were empty bottles to dispose of. The man who collected the refuse every day sold the empties to shopkeepers. He explained where the bottles came from and how many he could bring in a week from all his various calls. No one visited their house, and Rehana rarely went out in the evening. All those things made everyone understand now that Rehana too was a drinker, but no one knew what else went on in the house, whether she was really a courtesan. When Malika and Hassanali and Asmah visited Mombasa, they stayed with relatives and called to greet Rehana during daytime. The water engineer did not come home until after they left, so they never met him once.

They lived like this for many years, fourteen years, until the beginning of the war in 1914. He was angry about the war, the water engineer. Then one evening, while Rehana was stitching the hem of a skirt or something ordinary like that, Andrew Mills collapsed in a drunken daze in his own room. She heard him fall, and when she reached his room she found him dead. Wait, wait. He left her money in his will, so she could live in their apartment and carry on her business.

The little Italian left today. He looked dazed, a bit tearful in the end. That started Ma and Farida crying, and Ba's face went into a tortured pucker as he tried not to snivel. I had to stop myself smiling. It was as if he was going away for ever. It's what he wants to do, I want to tell them. He's been dreaming about it for years. Sometimes he wakes up out of a deep sleep and starts to talk in English. What does that mean? He dreams in English. He'll go there and he'll do well. I'm sure he will. He's ready for it. He'll keep going on over-confidence and frenzy, and when the time comes to be tested he'll succeed without difficulty.

It's a relief to see him go. Life will be less exhausting without him, and there'll be more space in the room. I need more space. That sounds mean and I don't intend it like that. I feel more need to be alone now. Life will be less for all of us, less for his absence, but he'll be back soon enough. For the last week, he's been saying goodbye to his friends, visiting them at home. One at a time, each one a drama. They're as bad as each other, making promises to meet in Cairo or Budapest next summer. Then last night there was a long debate about whether he should wear his suit to travel or something more casual. Ba thought he should wear a clean shirt and trousers, preferably of a pale colour because pale colours always look elegant. What he didn't say, and probably did not realise he *was* saying, was that was how he thought he looked best. Ma preferred the suit. He didn't know who might be meeting him at the other end. Oh, it might be the

Queen of England, Ba said, with uncharacteristic sarcasm, but Ma ignored him. Anyway, you don't want people to think you don't have a suit, she said. That is how English people dress there, even though they wear baggy shorts when they come here, and it is a nice suit. Farida nodded, I shrugged, leaving it to the aged ones to battle it out. He wore a suit.

I would have been terrified. I think he was. Neither he nor I have ever travelled anywhere before. Do I feel envious of him? Yes, it would be a relief to get away from the things of everyday. Perhaps it's because of her that I feel like this, although I don't want to get away from her. I don't think I feel a deep envy. Perhaps a stab of regret that I have not been invited to the picnic. I don't expect life to deliver challenges and excitement, and I am not discontent. I would like to go fishing more often, and learn to handle an outrigger with more skill. I would like to know about plants and trees, their names and seasons, and what uses they are put to. It thrills me to hear the names of different woods, and to see people smell the wood to confirm their judgements. I would like to know what they're smelling. I would like to teach in the country, to get to know that life more. I like to read slowly. I asked him to send me anything good that he reads. Perhaps he will, or if not he'll bring some back with him.

I fear the things he wants. You can't just go there and see what there is to see and return. What you see makes you different. I fear that when he returns he will have the unassailable way of others who have been there. Someone will ask him a question, and he will listen with a tolerant smile. Then he will speak slowly, not wanting his listeners to miss a word he is saying. He will try to keep his answer uncomplicated, so as not to confuse his listeners with his sophistication, but he will expect to be heard with respect. He will think he has done something important.

When the time came for him to go, he stumbled his way up the plane. We waved to him but he was too preoccupied to look back. He paused for a moment in the doorway and then plunged into the darkness. A moment later he was back in the doorway, looking for us, waving. Then as the plane took off, Ma really wept, saying that idiot will get lost somewhere. Ba said, you can't get lost on a plane. He will, she said, or he'll let someone steal his sterling money. She went on in that style, without tears by then, all the way back to town in the taxi. By the time we arrived home, she was silent and so was he. There were smiling lights in both their eyes, and I think they were proud of our little Italian, and probably already planning his homecoming.

I thought of the water engineer when I saw her in the minister's car. He is the politician about whom there were rumours before. He has children and a wife already, but he does not mind everyone knowing that he is courting. Will she become his courtesan? That is what everyone thinks. In three weeks we will be independent and the minister will then become powerful enough to take no notice of rumours. Perhaps powerful men need courtesans.

I have seen her every day in all these months. I imagine myself with her every night. We talk softly in the half-dark as we used to, and then we make love. We discuss the precautions we have to take to avoid discovery. I have never gone back to the flat, and I have never tried to see her. She has not come to our house. Farida did all the talking for me. She sent word with Farida to ask if we could meet and talk about what had happened. I said I could not. I promised them that I would never see her again. I have been too ashamed to face her. I know how ashamed she will be of me, how she will think that I too think her dirty. She will be angry with me, who deserves worse.

I caught glimpses of her twice, and both times something leaped in me but I looked away before I saw her properly. I see her every day. We meet secretly, late at night, behind closed doors. My name is Msiri Amin, the one who is trusted with a secret.

Today I saw her in the minister's car and I did not look away. I got off my bicycle and looked. He is not a full minister yet, so his car did not have a flag, but soon, in three weeks' time, it will. I cycled to the sea at the back of the courthouse, and sat on the lawn for hours, thinking about things I already knew. There was no sign of the gardeners or the courthouse policemen.

It was so calm and hushed that I became aware of my breathing. Even the sea slipped in softly. It made me think our rulers had already quietly slipped away and we were so used to obedience that we still went about our slavish duties unsupervised.

Today I sat there for hours and knew again that I had made a horrible mistake. I had had no choice. I should have gone to see her, and lived the secret life I pretend to. The talk would have turned us into something furtive and ridiculous. Our lives would have become intolerable, but perhaps we need not have felt as filthy as the talk. I was stung by the sight of her in the minister's car.

When I came in, I saw Ma sitting by the window. She looks tragic sitting there but I cannot get her to move. She says she needs the light. She was reading one of the little Italian's letters again. He keeps a steady supply, but there are three or four that she is fond of, and she keeps these in her sewing basket. It was evening, and the radio was playing a request programme. Farida was out or in her room. It was when she looked up as I entered that I thought how tragic she looked. She searched my face but I knew she could not see very well in that light. She was trying to tell from my face whether I had seen her. Even though it was now months since I had abandoned her, she still did that every time I came home. I composed myself and went to sit beside her on the sofa, so she could get a good look at me and feel reassured. She is slowly losing her sight, and the terror of it looms over her life. Sometimes I realise suddenly that she has been sitting nearby, weeping silently.

I wrote to Rashid today. I wanted to write to him because tomorrow is a special day. It's independence day. I felt I should write to him, I don't know why. So I wrote to him seriously, like one grown-up person to another, which probably means I was solemn and sagacious. I wanted him not to miss the day, and to have a way of remembering it even though he is not here. That was when he wrote me that pompous missive full of solemn ponderings, to mock me probably. It would have been fun if he had been here, so I suppose I miss him sometimes although I am never going to tell him that. His friends are always asking after him. He must miss all that. They were always in a crowd.

He would have written a poem about independence if he had been here. He would have organised a poetry competition to write the best poem on independence in a language of your choice. Then he would have whipped up a frenzy among friends and neighbours to get them to contribute one. He would have got himself all the gadgets of the moment, the mementoes of the celebrations: the badge with the new flag on it, a record of the new national anthem, the bunting to put above the doorway, and perhaps a large flag on a pole if Ba let him. The new flag does not look that different from the old, the same Busaid banner except for a clove cluster in a green circle in the middle. It could have been worse. It could have been a parrot on a twig or a barracuda over a background of blue with black ripples to represent the waves. They seem such fragile tokens of a state. The new national anthem was played on the radio this evening, to give us a taster so that we would not look at each other in confusion when the moment comes tomorrow. I could not catch hold of it. We will get used to it, as we will get used to the flag.

Everything has changed at once. There was not enough time to get used to anything. We have to find a new way of speaking about how we live now. They don't like to hear people say certain things, or sing certain songs. We must not mention the names of the sultan or the old government. It only lasted a month and then everything changed at once. The new flag no longer exists. It's against the law to possess one, even out of curiosity. I'm already beginning to forget it. I can't remember the colour of the clove cluster, if it was brown or golden. The national anthem is already forgotten. I don't think anyone could hum a line of it. If they did, they would certainly get a beating or worse. People have been killed. I cannot write these things. They have frightened us too much, and it would be stupid to be found scribbling what we are required not to know about.

She was attacked. It happened on the night of the uprising. They were looking for the minister, who was not at home, so they went to look for him at her flat. She opened the door to them. We all did. No one knew how to resist or what to do when the gun butts and the boots started hammering on the doors. They attacked her after that. When I heard, in the talk in the street days afterwards, I tried not to hurry away but I went to her flat. It was morning, but there was a curfew on gathering in the streets. There were gunmen everywhere, and some walls were pocked with bullet holes. A few houses had been burned down. When I got to her flat, I knocked on her door for several minutes but it did not open. I said who I was but there was no reply. I felt a movement above me and looked up. Someone was at the window above me, and I stepped back into the road to see who it was, but the person who was there retreated further into the room. I thought it was one of her brothers. I stood in the road for a minute or two, looking up, waiting, but no one came back. I didn't dare shout, and I didn't know if the attackers found their way into the house. The house might be full of injured women, and they would not want a stranger asking after such shameful wounds.

Perhaps it was because of the minister that they attacked her. Or perhaps it was because she is beautiful and talked about in that dirty way. One day, I heard that she had left. The whole household has left and that huge old house is locked up and empty. Hundreds are leaving, thousands are expelled, some are forbidden to leave. They want us to forget everything that was here before, except the things that aroused their rage and made them act with such cruelty. I forget myself and write these things that will cause me trouble if they are found. I don't know how she left or where she went. Sometimes I wonder whether those who leave know what they're doing. There may not be a way back.

I don't know why I started writing this. I think it was because I had so much time and I felt that something momentous had happened to me. I started to write to replay the anguish for myself. I think in some way I still felt that there was a way back to her. In some way, if I felt tragic enough, someone was bound to take pity and say: go back to her, you deserve her, you have suffered enough. Since those weeks ago when I saw her in the minister's car . . . Poor minister, they captured him and humiliated him as they did all the other ministers. They're all in jail on the mainland now, guests of President Julius Nyerere of Tanganyika, who glows with pleasure at what has befallen us. Since those weeks ago when I saw her, this writing has become a burden. Now, after the killings and the expulsion, it has also become dangerous. Today I began to think that I had found a reason to go on writing these bits and pieces. She has gone, Rashid has gone, so many others have gone. Those of us who remain are almost too frightened to live. Writing these scraps will be to tell myself that I live. It will be a way of not forgetting.

It is late. Ba is fidgeting next door, and soon he will knock on the door and tell me to switch off the light. He worries if any of the lights are on late. He thinks that will attract the gunmen, who will take us for plotters or who will find it hard to resist the opportunity to intimidate us. Farida is not allowed to sew late at night as she used to and I am not allowed to read into the early hours. Ba closes the windows and bolts the door at nine in the evening. The streets are empty. No one goes out at night.

It was nine months ago when I promised myself to write in here so that I would know I am alive. I have not written anything and yet I am still alive. How foolish. I am now a qualified teacher and have been posted to a country school. Ba has lost his job. Dozens of teachers have lost their jobs, and been replaced by people like me and by school-leavers. It is just meanness. He is crushed. When we were younger and Rashid was still here, I used to think that nothing bad could happen to us. Ma and Ba were so hard-working, so unassuming, such good people. What could happen? Then I lost her, and Rashid left and everything changed. Now Ma and Ba are dispirited and frightened. She does not want me to take the posting to the country school. I tell her that it is safe in the country now, unless the soldiers wish to make it unsafe, and they can do that anywhere. She shouts at me, calling me naïve and a fool. I promise to try and have the posting changed, but I won't. I would like to work in a country school. I'm good at breaking promises. I would like to know the names of trees, and learn to tell wood from its smell.

Ba does not say much. His stoop is more pronounced and his frown is permanent. He stutters unexpectedly. He still observes his café ritual but most of the people he used to sit with have gone or are in jail. Most of the day, he sits at home and reads and then goes to the mosque. When Farida told them about her lover Abbas in Mombasa and how she wanted to go and join him, he cried. Not howls and sobs, just quiet tears running down his face. Poor Ba, there is no reason for anyone to know of his existence, but in some way he makes me believe in virtue, in the possibility of it.

We are all becoming increasingly addicted to the mosque. The government delivers its socialist lies and we all rush for the mosques. The days are getting darker in every way. Food is becoming more scarce. There are power cuts and water shortages. So it's inevitable that mosques will get fuller and prayers last longer. I find an unexpected pleasure in this communion.

Very quickly we have learned the limits of our expectations, and somehow the terror has slightly diminished as a result. We sit at home or in our chosen corners in the streets, and talk about the latest rumours and upheavals. We have lost our fastidiousness, many of us. We say that things are getting better every day. Those who said they would have nothing to do with the evil people who now run our affairs, have had to learn to do so. No one mocks them. People work if they have work. They marry and have children. Old enmities bring their venom to the surface. Young people grow up and leave if they can.

The streets are so empty. So many people locked their houses and left: for Dar es Salaam, Mombasa, Nairobi, Dubai, India. They probably still have their keys in a safe place for their return. Their houses did not stay empty for long, though. The government took them over and distributed them among themselves, but their occupation is forlorn, dark and unloved. Many of the houses have crumbled into the streets from lack of care. One day in the last rains, our neighbours' house collapsed at last. The upstairs wall went first, so there was time to get everyone out of the house before everything collapsed in a heap of perished mortar and stone and rotten beams and scattering chickens. No one was hurt, and there was even some laughter and hilarity that the old ruin had gone at last, although our neighbours were not that amused. But it also felt as if something else had changed, something big had gone out of our vision. Everything looked different when you glanced out of the window.

Today we had news of Rashid. He has completed his studies after all these years. It seems incredible, and as incredible that he is anything to do with us. Ba waited until I came home from work, and then pulled the letter out of his shirt pocket. He goes to the post office himself these days, every day, he has so much time. Usually there is nothing to collect. So as soon as I came in, I saw the airmail letter in his pocket even before he pulled it out. He gave it to me and told me to read it to Ma, who cannot read any more because of her eyes. The letter was open, so Ba must have already read it himself. Farida was somewhere inside, and he called out for her to come. I read Rashid's letter to a full house. His tears began after the first few lines, after I had read the main item, which fortunately Rashid got to very quickly, because I could see the alarm on my mother's face as she waited to hear what the letter was to announce. She thanked God softly when I read that he had finished his studies, and his silent weeping turned into sobs. She said Ba's name, straining to see him as he sat on his own on the sofa, but he said *Read*, commanding me. I read on, how grateful he was for the way they had brought him up to care about studying and excelling, how sad he was to be so far away, how fortunate to find a university position in England, and the description of the house in a quiet street where he would grow a garden. By the time I finished the letter we were all weeping. I don't know why for sure: relief that he had not stumbled, sad that he was not with us, crying for our own sorrows that we could not share with him, and that everything has turned out as it has.

I felt at that moment . . . No, I knew then that we had lost him. It was not a new thought, but the description of that quiet street on the edge of town made me certain that we will not be seeing him again. It makes me long for that street myself. In one of his letters he had sent me a picture he had cut out of a calendar, of a small lake and green hilly countryside. He said it was where he had been with one of his friends for a holiday, and how beautiful it was. What would make him return here? To do what?

Ba took the letter from me and left to announce the news to the world. I sat with Ma and Farida and reminisced about the little Italian, and missed him. Then I started a reply which I finished this morning. It feels like the end of something. Farida leaves in a few days to join Abbas. I'll have them all to myself soon.

Some days everything seems so close, and the events of years seem like yesterday, everything squeezed up and crammed to bursting. I think about her every day. No one ever mentions her name and I dare not ask what has happened to her. I asked Farida once and she looked pained, and annoyed with me. I meant to ask if she knew an address so that I could write to her, but I didn't and perhaps I would not have dared to write. I did not ask again, and Farida did not mention her. I think her look of pain was to tell me to forget her. I can't forget her. I imagine myself with her. For hours on end sometimes. I relive the times I was with her, and I am astonished at how much I can still remember even after all these years, and how real it feels. Today I lay on the bed beside her while she talked about that first time on the evening of Idd when I first held her in the dark and called her beloved. She loved telling that story and laughing at my eagerness for her. My hands stroked her as she spoke, stroked the firmness of her thighs and the cusp of her hips. There was a thud of a door shut too vigorously upstairs, and she stopped speaking. I looked at her to see if she was frightened or startled but she had gone and I was lying alone in the dark. The memory of that door thuds through my body as if it has just happened.

I remember walking home after meeting her for the first time, and the terror I felt for what lay ahead. That terror never left me, but it was made small by the exhilaration I felt when I was with her, or even when I was not. Sometimes when I walked home after being with her, I could not stop myself grinning with joy every step home. Then I listened again to all the tender words and the promises we made, and was incredulous. I still hear those words and promises, but now they don't make me incredulous. Sometimes they fill me with shame and a strange and irresistible disgust. I cover my ears and cringe but I cannot stop myself hearing them. I cannot imagine how she looked or how she felt or what she thought of me when she heard about what I had done. I cannot imagine the terror she would have felt when those men attacked her.

I could not abandon them. I could not disobey them. Here they are. She is now blind and fearful. She sits at home all day and all night. Sometimes I forget that she is in the room because she is so silent. She likes to look at the photograph album. We only have one. She runs her hand over the photographs and describes them while I turn over the pages. That's the one of Farida in Mombasa with her cousins on the beach near Tiwi, that day we took the ferry at Likoni. This is Rashid in the school play. He's wearing that huge false beard and pretending to be the wazir Barmaki. She only speaks of Rashid as a child. When he wrote to say that he was married to Grace she only asked if it was an English woman and then fell into one of her silences. Days later she told me to get an airmail form for her. Write this down, she said, exactly as I say it. Then she dictated ugly words and threats which I pretended to write down. The blind talking to the one-eyed. I did not post the letter although I told her I did. They never mention her, Grace. I don't know why they are so surprised or so distraught. What did they think he would do? That he would live alone all his life? How is it that even the best of people are also unkind?

She laughs and comes to life as she runs her fingers over the photographs she can't see any more. She does not grieve over these photographs. But often she grieves, and she sits silently until you speak to her. Then she only tells me to get on with my work, with marking or reading, and not to take any notice of her. I remind myself to speak to her about what I'm doing, to speak without inflection, as if I were making a casual conversation. Sometimes this makes her laugh because my intention is too transparent, and she tells me to stop prattling at her. She can't hear herself think. The silences can be deadly, and we sit there paralysed by them.

When Ba is at home, he often puts the radio on, and then she spars with the announcers, challenging their news and catching them out on the lies. In the country of the blind, who needs eyes, she tells the announcers.

Ba goes out for long walks in the mornings. He goes to the waterfront and strolls among the fishing boats. Then he goes through the lanes until he reaches the market. He buys some fruit and vegetables and walks home via the post office. He cooks the vegetables when he gets home, slices the fruit and puts my share aside for when I get home from my school in the country. Aunt Halima sends over a basket of food for our lunch, because Ma has burned herself too often trying to cook on the charcoal seredani. Farida has sent an electric hotplate but often there is no electricity, and even with a hotplate Ma is not safe any more. She has given up, I think. She is overwhelmed by what has happened, and the loneliness.

He trembles. He never goes out after lunch. Sometimes he sits outside and reads, and if there is a reading at the mosque for a neighbour who has died he goes to that. Otherwise he sits at home and he trembles at raised voices and the raucous, hateful speeches of government ministers on the radio. He won't allow me to go out at night, not as if I am a child he fears for, or because he thinks I'll get up to something evil. I don't think so. It's because he is afraid something will happen to me and they will be left alone. It makes me happy to think that one day soon they will die. I don't say that because I hate them or blame them, but because it will bring the loneliness and emptiness to an end. I think it makes them happy too, to know that they will soon die. It makes me happy to think I will die.

I have become something of a minor actor in ceremonies of death. It began with my frequent attendance at the mosque. I found the communion strangely comforting, although I could not always believe the things I was saying. I became familiar with a variety of prayers and ceremonies. I could not help taking them in. After a time people directed their questions at me as if I was a scholar, or asked me to recite a prayer as a gesture towards what they took to be my piety. That is how I found myself assisting at funerals and readings. Now it is expected of me. When someone in the neighbourhood dies, I am one of those who is summoned to assist with the arrangements. So many people have left, and now there are only the children and the elderly, who like to think that neighbourly voices will mourn their passing. It does not feel like handling the dead.

I say almost nothing about the dead. I go through the motions of what is required. I plead for their lives in the hereafter. It's like a trick. There is nothing out there, but if it will make you feel better, lying there without voice or breath, I will plead that your life hereafter be attended with mercy. The living find meaning in that, in imagining where the dead live and in praying for their equanimity and rest.

Today it rained. It poured with rain from dawn until early afternoon. It brought the aged ones to their feet, laughing and exclaiming, Ma leaning on Ba and shaking his arm with something like the old mischief. It brought children out in the streets, running and splashing in the floods of rainwater and overflowing roof gutters, racing hastily made rafts of matchboxes and coconut husks.

A letter arrived from Rashid. I did not hurry to read it. He writes brief, desultory letters now and then, and he always sends regards from Grace to Ma and Ba. I pass them on to no effect, and send their regards to her when I write. I feel his weariness in the letters he writes, and I suspect that my laboured replies are just as revealing. When I came to read his letter tonight, it said that Grace has left him. It was anguished and I felt sore and distressed for him. I could only imagine him as my younger brother who was so full of talk and a vulnerable bravado, and I ached to think of his loneliness in that strange place. I began a reply which I'll finish tomorrow, but I found that to imagine how he feels I was thinking about Jamila, so I've told him something about that in the letter. I haven't written or mentioned her name in all these years. That's why I want to wait until tomorrow, to read the letter in broad daylight and see how it feels.

I don't think I'll mention Grace to them, especially not Ma. She is ailing, breathing heavily and painfully. The nurse at the hospital told us it's her lungs and nothing can be done about it. There's no doctor to examine her at the moment, not for a few days, for some reason we could not find out. The pharmacist refused to sell me anything without knowing what is wrong with her. So now she is heaving for breath and lies sleepless in their bed, and he lies fussing beside her. I can hear them as I write this.

It was a release to mention Jamila to Rashid. I don't know what use these scraps can be put to, but writing to him about her will let him see how stupid people can be, how stupid I am. Maybe I'll send these bits to him. I don't know how long I'll be able to write or work, and I don't know what will happen after that or how we will all live. One eye is almost gone now.

I am beginning to think that the dark and the silence are a kind of bliss. If our rulers forbade us music and banished the radio and the television, I don't think I would mourn. It sounds bad to forbid music, like the sternest of Wahabbis, as if life and gaiety were banned, but I would have that in return for silence.

Sorrow has its gifts. Ma went four days ago and brought an end to her suffering. Ba seems to have found some energy from her going, and he has started going through their things and talking about her and their life together. Farida is here for the mourning, and she has brought her book with her. So at last I get to read her poems. She read one to him last night, and he listened and commended her when I thought he would cry. It was a poem about Ma when we were young. He listened and smiled and said yes, that was how she was. He wants Farida to help him go through Ma's things. I think he just wants her to be with him for company. I don't know how long he'll last. He seems strangely energetic. It saddens me that he will not see Rashid before he goes. It saddens me that I may not see the little Italian before my sight goes, or hear him breathing nearby, and chattering his gibberish.

The radio has broken down and we can get no news. The water has been cut off for most of the day because something has broken down in the pumping station. We no longer know how to make anything work. We don't know how to make anything for ourselves, not anything we use or desire, not even a bar of soap or a packet of razor blades. How did we allow ourselves to get into this state?

A Continuation

SOME SHORT WHILE BEFORE I read Amin's notebooks, I attended a conference in Cardiff, organised by someone I had known as a graduate student and with whom I had recently renewed contact. When we were students, we were writing our dissertations at the same time, attending the same research seminars, playing squash twice a week. We were friends, in the way of these things. Then we got our jobs and headed in different directions, and completely lost touch. I never heard anyone mention his name and never came across anything he had written. I am quite certain he would be able to say the same about me. I thought about him now and then, perhaps because a name reminded me of him or something equally accidental like that. Then he wrote me an email, having got my address on the university website where all our names and addresses are listed out of absurd vanity. He wrote because he said he remembered a conversation years ago when we discussed *Othello*, and that at the time he was so impressed with my argument that he tried to persuade me to write something about the play. He said in his email that he hoped I had. In any case, he was now organising a conference on the treatment of mixed-race sexuality in English writing, and he wondered whether I was interested in contributing a paper. It would be lovely to meet again and catch up on the interim, he said. I thought so too, and agreed to go.

Instead of offering a paper on *Othello*, which I never did write despite his flattering suggestion, I did one on race and sexuality in settler writing in Kenya. I made some low-key observations on the fiction as well as on some memoirs, remarking on the absence of sexual encounters in this writing or their sublimation into gestures of pained patronage or rumours of tragic excess. In the discussion phase of my presentation I mentioned the story of Rehana, or what I knew of it, as an example of the kind of story which failed to appear in this writing. I mentioned which town it had taken place in, approximately which period, and its unexpected consequences for her granddaughter Jamila. I did not at that point know Pearce's name. Well, it wasn't much of a paper, nothing challenging or ambitious, more like a brief chat about issues that interested me in this writing.

There were only six participants in the session, most of the others having chosen to attend a parallel one on William Faulkner. I probably would have done too if I hadn't had to give my paper. After the presentation, one of the participants came to speak to me. She told me how interesting she had found the paper (these are the necessary courtesies of such moments), and wondered whether she could talk to me about the story of Rehana and her affair with an Englishman. I waited to hear more, already shrivelling from contact. She was an attractive woman, in her late thirties perhaps, some years younger than me. I waited because I wanted to know how we should proceed. I was weary, and wary of encounters. After Grace I had made no effort to start anything with someone else, and my life was painful and lonely as a result, but it was calm and manageable. I am not usually vain in this way, and do not assume that every encounter is an attempted seduction, more likely the opposite, but sometimes there are complications which do not amount to seduction, misunderstandings, wounds, embarrassment. So I waited.

She told me her grandfather was briefly a DO in a small town on the Kenya coast at the turn of the century, the same town I had named as the location of Rehana's story. He had written a memoir of his colonial service, which did not last very long, and in this brief memoir, which was never finished, he mentioned an affair between a native woman and an English traveller, although he named no names. She wondered if this might be the same story I had referred to, because the point of her grandfather mentioning this affair was that the English traveller lived openly with his native lover for a while, and that was unusual. The point was also to say, as I had argued in my paper, that such affairs were doomed. The English lover went home and the native woman took up with another man.

That was how I met Barbara Turner.

We spent the evening together, and she told me a great deal more than I could have expected. Her grandfather was Frederick Turner, who came back home on leave in 1903 and never went back into the colonial service. His wife hated the empire, and he missed her too much to carry on. So he became a teacher of literature at the University of Nottingham where Christabel, his wife and now a published poet, had admirers and influence. It was during this period that Frederick Turner began the memoir. He put dates in the margin of each installment of the work. The last installment was dated June 1905. Their first son John, Barbara's father, was born in June 1905. That may have been why Frederick abandoned the memoir, overwhelmed by the arrival of a perfect little progeny. I don't know how serious an undertaking the memoir was, whether it was to fill empty days, or was a burst of nostalgia for the other life which spent itself soon enough when baby John arrived. By this date he had probably also renewed contact with Martin Pearce, who lived nearby in Newark. That too could have been the reason for abandoning the writing. He would not have wanted to offend a friend. In fact, Martin and Frederick became firm friends, and even though Martin moved to London to take up a post as a researcher at the British Museum, the families visited and kept in touch.

All this might have been expected. I had a name now for Rehana's English lover and for the colonial officer who looked after him. That Martin Pearce turned out to be an orientalist is not that surprising, although Frederick Turner ending up as a teacher of literature was. He could do no worse than many others in that pursuit. That both Martin and Frederick survived the war was their good fortune. Martin was sent to Mesopotamia as an antiquities expert and Frederick stayed safely at home. What was unexpected was that Pearce's daughter Elizabeth was Barbara's mother. She told me the story of these connections briefly on this first meeting, but later she told me more. For my purposes here it is enough to say that Barbara's mother Elizabeth was Martin Pearce's only daughter (although we know she was not), and that she married Frederick Turner's eldest son John. It was Elizabeth who told Barbara about the identity of the Englishman who had an open affair with a native woman. After Frederick's death (1940), Elizabeth read the memoir and asked her mother-in-law Christie Turner if she knew who the Englishman lover was. Your dad, she said. By then Martin Pearce was also dead (1939) and secrecy was pointless. Death was all around them.

I explained my interest in the story. I told Barbara about Jamila and Amin, but at first all she seemed able to take in was that there had been a child, that her grandfather had had a daughter with his native lover.

Her name was Rehana, I told her. Rehana Zakariya, not native lover. She named her daughter Asmah, the one without sin. And Asmah named her daughter Jamila, which means beautiful.

Jamila is my cousin, Barbara said. There were two elder brothers too, I told her. I have two elder brothers as well, she said.

A few days later Barbara's mother Elizabeth wrote me a note, inviting me to lunch. I had asked to look at the memoir, and she in turn had asked me to meet her. Barbara was not invited. She did not want me to think ill of her father, she said. She was in her late seventies, but still well and alert, almost matronly in her appearance rather than feeble or worn-out. She cooked a light but elaborate lunch: corn soup, baked salmon and spinach, and a spiced apple tart. Barbara had reported the story I had told her. She wanted to know about Jamila and about her mother. I told her what I could. She had had no idea that there had been a child. Not even Frederick could have known that, but her father must have done. At least he must have known she was pregnant when he left her to return home. She asked me if I knew if her father had ever written to Rehana and the child, or visited them. I said I didn't know. I have a sister, Elizabeth said. Her husband John would have loved that. He died two years ago, she said, and then after a brief pause she added: I still can't believe that he's gone. She asked if her sister was still alive and if I knew her name. I said her name was Asmah but I didn't know if she was still alive. She asked me to write the name down for her, and asked if there was a way of getting in touch with Jamila, or her mother if she was still alive. I said I would ask.

Soon afterwards I received and read Amin's notebooks, and I understood that despite my real desire to do so, I would not have been able to imagine the anguish of their lives. After that I knew what I would do. It was time to go home, in a manner of speaking, to visit and to put my fears to rest and to beg pardon for my neglect. It would give them pleasure, and give me pleasure, and would bring to life nerves and fibres that had lain unrefreshed for too long. Barbara asked if she could come with me. What for? I asked her, surprised. It won't be that easy for you in that place, different customs, discomforts. I said this but I wanted her to insist. I wanted her to say that she was coming whatever I said, because she wanted to be with me as well as everything else. I wanted her to say that she would miss me if I was away for so long, as I knew I would miss her. She probably knew me well enough now to know what a timid creature I really was, that I wanted her to come but was reluctant to cause a stir.

'Perhaps we'll be able to find Jamila,' she said. I don't know, I said. Everything is scattered, dispersed to the farthest corners of the world. No one can find anyone. Someone will know, she said. She had read what I had written. I was done with it, I told her, done with the writing, another abandoned memoir. It had got me to the point where I feel like trying again, where I feel like starting again. Even if that were no more than an illusion, it is one that gives me a sense of well-being, and that is quite enough.

'I'll have to write and explain about your coming, in case it upsets Ba. You'll have to sleep in a separate room, you know,' I told her, and the comedy of that at our ages made us both smile.